Praise for Claiming T-Mo

"Bacon explores a four-generation alien family saga in this gleeful, wacky debut."

—*Publishers Weekly*

"[Bacon's] eloquent, elegant and lyrical prose gripped me from the very first sentence of this immensely passionate, moving and thought-provoking story . . . [an] amazing, magical book."

—Linda Hepworth, *NB Magazine* (5 stars)

"Bacon enthralls readers with an innovative narrative that extols the potency of using poetic language in fiction . . . the true substance of *Claiming T-Mo* is in each woman's process of understanding T-Mo."

—Megan Kelly, *Aurealis Magazine*

"*Claiming T-Mo* silkily links reality with the surreal, and grounded with the unearthly. "

—Angela Wauchop, *Other Terrain Journal*

"Nothing is off limits in *Claiming T-Mo,* with a literary eloquence and decadence, which transports the mundane into the magical, suspending time and place into a kaleidoscopic universe."

—*Weekend Notes*

"Lush, hypnotic and absorbing. Bacon speaks in a language all her own, transporting us to an original, surreal, very real invented world."

—Kaaron Warren, award-winning author of *Tide of Stone* and *The Grief Hole*

"Bacon's sentences are endlessly full of these nimble, assured, madly inventive leaps. Her work is striking; I've never read anything like it."

—Keith Rosson, award-winning author of *The Mercy of the Tide* and *Smoke City*

"*Claiming T-Mo* is more than a novel—it is a life force, a beautiful and heartfelt sentience that speaks to you in equal parts charm, thrill, and wonder. Eugen Bacon is an emerging force in literary and genre circles alike, and quite simply her work is highly recommended."

—Eric J. Guignard, award-winning author and editor,
That Which Grows Wild and *A World of Horror*

"Bacon scrambles and codifies and defamiliarizes with a deft hand, bringing characters to vivid life and evoking worlds within worlds. Singing plants and sons severed from their best selves by bad intent; blue-haired aliens, murderous laws, and mothers who hide in the shadows—lyrical and mesmerizing."

—J.S. Breukelaar, author of *Collision: Stories* and *Aletheia*

"With *Claiming T-Mo*, Eugen Bacon has written an unforgettable saga of power, curse and hope, as lived by three generations of exceptional women. Magical, violent, enthralling, it is a book that shines with its own specific aura, a somber and beautiful unique object, designed by a truly splendid writer. A must."

—Seb Doubinsky, author of The City-States Cycle series

"Prose with a rhythm that sets it apart. Come for the music, stay for the story."

—Michael Pryor, author of *Gap Year in Ghost Town*
and the Laws of Magic series

"*Claiming T-Mo* is a story of generations of women striving for fulfillment, but caught in webs of passion, magic and stardust. Eugen Bacon embraces the strange and estranged in this unanticipated contemporary trickster myth."

—Emmet O'Cuana, author of *Faraway*

"The use of language—the breadth of vocabulary and the attention to detail are absolutely engrossing."

—Dominique Hecq, award-winning poet, novelist,
short fiction writer and playwright

"*Claiming T-Mo* takes the reader on a breathless journey through kaleidoscopic worlds which, on looking closer, resemble the mythic veins and sinews of our own, pulsing with unalloyed vitality . . . As playful as it is thought-provoking, this is a work of dizzying originality and profound humanity."

—Prof. Oz Hardwick, award-winning poet and
author of *Learning to Have Lost* and *The Lithium Codex*

"A highly imaginative and well written novel with some highly evocative scenes and well realized characters, it uses the conventions of its genre to explore sophisticated themes."

—Julian Novitz, award-winning author of *Holocaust Tours*
and *My Real Life and Other Stories*

"The voice is particular and energetic . . . the sentences have a bridling, writhing energy . . . The style is reminiscent of Toni Morrison, particularly in works like *The Bluest Eye*, where she experiments with non-standard English, but is far more playful. The combination of voice infused with the playful energy of a form of Standard Black English, combined with a story of quests and magic produces a unique work."

—Nike Sulway, award-winning author of
Dying in the First Person and *Rupetta*

"Eugen Bacon's novel is ambitious and skillful . . . a novel with several types of magic in it, the magic of beautiful prose, the magic we expect of these characters, and a magically large heart within the telling."

—Prof. Kevin Brophy, award-winning poet, novelist,
short fiction writer and essayist

"Worlds are described, like those from Calvino's *Imaginary Cities*, held up for the reader to admire, and then disappear to invite extrapolation . . . strange and yet familiar; more importantly, the worlds are fully imagined and fully realized. We are placed into them confidently and with assurance, and allowed to make our own way."

—George Green, author of *Hound*

CLAIMING T-MO

EUGEN BACON

Meerkat Press

Atlanta

Cover Art by Micaela Dawn

ISBN-13 978-1-946154-13-2 (Paperback)
ISBN-13 978-1-946154-14-9 (eBook)

Library of Congress Control Number: 2019904850

Printed in the United States of America

Published in the United States of America by
Meerkat Press, LLC, Atlanta, Georgia
www.meerkatpress.com

To Nicholas

C**O**NTENTS

My deepest passion was reading. At some point—not early, I was thirty-five or thirty-six—I realized there was a book that I wanted very much to read that really hadn't been written, and so I sort of played around with it in trying to construct the kind of book I wanted to read.

—Toni Morrison, *Time Magazine*, May 2008

SALEM

· 1 ·

T-Mo happened exactly one week after the puzzle-piece woman with fifty-cent eyes.

One night, black as misery, Salem Drew stood, arms wrapped about herself, at the bus depot three streets from the IGA where she worked late shifts. A bunch of commuters had just clambered onto a number 146 for Carnegie, and Salem found herself alone at the depot.

She waited for a night express bus to take her back to a cheerless home that housed equally cheerless parents. An easy wind around her was just as dreary, foggy as lunacy. There, just then, the shadow of a woman's face jumped into her vision.

Salem blinked. Was the woman real or a figment of thought? Singular parts of her were easy to file, were possibly real: maroon hair, rugged skin the color of coffee beans. And the scar . . . But all put together, cohesion was lost.

The puzzle-piece woman stood head lowered, quiet in the mist. When she raised her face, silver shimmered from one good eye, petite and round as a fifty-cent coin. The other eye was broken, feasibly some bygone injury. Even though it was as smooth and flawlessly round as the right eye, it held no sight. The coin perfection of its shape was embedded in scar tissue, a disfigurement that needed nothing but a single glance to seal the hideousness of it.

If Salem thought to speak, to ask, "Who are you? How long have you been standing there, watching me, and why?" the mighty keenness of the woman's good telescopic eye, the one that filtered, turned inward, then came back at her without translation, threw it right out of Salem's mind.

Thunder like the hammering of a thousand hooves did it. Salem ran without a scream, all the way through all that night, never minding the night bus when it whooshed past. All she minded was the gobbling eye, and the unwarned sound of deep belly laughter that chased behind.

· 2 ·

Freedom and beyond. That was where T-Mo took Salem. He foisted himself into her life, waltzed her straight to liberty.

There is a magical quality about a man who steps through locked doors, unbroken walls. One minute he stood outside her window, next he was beside her in front of a projector show on the wall, one calm hand stretched along the back of her seat.

They were watching Part I of *A Moment with God*, Salem's parents' idea of an unchaperoned date, inside a cul-de-sac chalet that held no sink or toilet, not even a tacky kitchen. It stood three meters from the back door of the main building, close enough for a parent to sniff out trouble. That was the little servant room the pastor had sublet to his daughter.

Even though they had been going out some time now, Salem's temple fluttered, as did the veins in her neck. Her gaze wavered each time it met his, all through Part II of the monologue on the wall. She shifted on the couch to create distance from his reckless hand. So disoriented was she, it took awhile before she noticed the tape reel still rolled but showed nothing except snow lines on the darkened wall. Somehow T-Mo had managed to maneuver himself within inches of her skin.

"Life-forms," he said.

She jumped. "What?"

"Do you not wonder what else exists in the universe?"

She stuttered. "W-what sort of existence?"

"Complex. Minds beyond human. Do you not wonder?"

"N-no."

"But I do." He held her gaze. "And I am."

"W-what?"she said, part in trepidation of never being able to understand him, the rest in misery that at this point she really didn't.

"Complex." He reclined. "Do you not wonder," his voice drawled, "how molecular composition tolerates teleporting?"

"Teleporting?"

"See me walk through that door?"

"N-no."

"Well, then."

She blinked, studied him anew. The man whose eyes were full of space when they were not holding something wild. They were chameleon, shifting appearance with light, as did the color of his skin.

Sometimes he seemed quite tanned, sometimes tan lifted to gray. The first time she saw him, she was sure it was an ailment. How creased, so youthful a face: it had to be a disorder. The disorder soon became art under her study. The more she analyzed its pattern, the weaves and crossings of the cells on it, the more it confounded her.

Salem wasn't sure at first what it was that drew her to him, because he wore the same fossil skin then. She was nineteen, he looked forty. But the jazz in his eyes made her whimsical. She wondered about this man of darkness and light who yet felt more natural than wind. How did he measure up to her father's barometer?

She knew that choices needed to be made. She could never go back to *Milk is Available Here*. Not the IGA again. Never.

· 3 ·

Salem was a little turtle locked up in its shell, before T-Mo. Her parents conversed with her on a need-to-know basis. Her mother had stormed out of Nana Modesty's womb the very night of a Christmas pageant to earn the name Pageant. Her father . . . she could think of no other name that suited him better. No one set eyes upon his righteous face and felt no need to go: Ike! He was a militant man, raised her so.

Both parents were immigrants, second or third cousins to each other but singly raised in spartan households by Salem's equally migrant grandparents, Modesty and Roam. Ike and Pageant found themselves tossed together in a flight to freedom, thousands of miles on foot as refugees, an army of them, sometimes fearful, often cold, always hungry. Fleeing war from a troubled country. Soon as they found peaceable settlement in a place called East Point, Ike clasped a hat in his fist and told, not asked, Pageant to be the mother of his babies. "Marry you?" she said. "Yes," he said.

Growing up, Salem nurtured dreams of abandoning her parents. Walk, trot, run—anything to take her to a place far enough that her parents could never find her. In her dreams she did trains, streets, park benches, dumpsters. In real life her ventures outside the house were the dentist, the library, the church.

The only moments she found recreation were when Pastor Ike shared his congregation with a visitor reverend. Like Bennetts Brooke. Reverend Brooke was a wired little fellow with mouth and bounce. His voice thundered, his feet danced. He bobbed at the pulpit, tossed knees and elbows, and boomed his voice at the faithful through a wireless microphone: "Who, Lord?"

"Us!" the brethren cried.

"Who, Lord!"

"Us, Lord!"

"Who did Bless His Holy Name choose?"

"Us!"

"He loves you," pointing at a woman in the front row.

"Yes, Lord."

"And you, and you, and you."

"Oh yes. Lord, oh Lord."

His eyes went intimate or wild to hush or animate the brethren. "This," he cried, holding the crucified savior on his timber cross, raising the wretched savior to face the faithful. "This"—a whisper now—"is the completeness of His Love."

"Mercy."

"Hear us, Lord."

"Amen."

The pastor's eye fell upon her. "Amen," he whispered. "Amen," he shouted.

"Amen," she whispered.

Beside Salem, Pageant shook. Her eyes were closed in fervor, quite unusual for a most unemotional woman. "Yes Lord," she whispered, over and over, moments before she fell convulsing from the pew. Reverend Brooke held his cross on her convulsing self, held and held it, even as the choir burst into song:

Come Thou Holy Spirit,
Holy, Holy, Infinite,
Come Thou Power and Peace,
Oh Ye Seraphim
Oh Ye Blessed Light
Come Thou Holy Spirit.
Come.

"Amen," said the reverend. "Amen," repeatedly. Held and held the cross as, around the church, people spread their hands and began to speak in tongues:

Ahmm-bralla-gaither-malu-theologa-umber-trivo!
Pla-ci-te-reciter-spiriniu-printa-go!

Salem, thrilled and curious, watched as the reverend held and held that cross on her mother's chest until Pageant came to and, meek as a person hypnotized, took the reverend's hand that steered her back to the pew. The choir chimed a lustful chorus from page 37 (b) of the hymnbook:

Sing to the mountains.
Lift your hearts!

Pageant's palm was sweaty when Salem slipped her hand into it. Somewhere in the back of the church, commotion as another of the brethren had the shakes. Somewhere to her right, a little child was asking his mother why she was "crying in God's garden."

To Salem, it was the best day ever, an occasion. Marked the turning point from lack of adventure to escapades in the church. Outside church, Salem watched people come and go. Often there was tea and people brought things: lavender sandwiches, salad buns, face fingers, frost-cream scones, honeydew puffs, poppy seed muffins . . . and much tea and lemonade. Slowly she learnt people, understood those whose sincerity flowed easy as water, those whose charitable words reeked with malice, those who came to observe and collect gossip, those who shook hands and genuinely cared, those who collected around each other and showed brand new bags, veils, hats, gloves, jackets, neckties, anything that glittered. Some gowns had lace, others didn't. Some were ankle length, others above the knee. Some ballooned before the knee or hugged thighs or ran down tiered or straight. It was a parade which, in her modest tunic and level heels, Salem found delight in watching. She understood all kinds of folk, filtered them like a sieve.

When she grew up enough to earn the chalet at the back of the house, her distractions were mainly visitor reverends, church fetes and family bees. Her life was empty, she knew. But how to change it? There were harmless tea parties where she swallowed lemonade that looked and tasted like cough medicine, nibbled finger food that was scrumptious but meager; you put it in your mouth and it melted. There were tongue-tied girls and polished boys who never wore bad socks or a single hair out of place. But these boys knew enough of Pastor Ike Drew not to muck about with his daughter, or the daughters of his parishioners.

Secretly, Salem continued her fantasies, dreaming not just of escape but of white gold and blonde bracelets and dark knee-hugger boots, everything Pastor Ike would never tolerate his daughter wearing. But for all her fancies, she was still wrapped like a nun at the local IGA shop, nurturing runaway thoughts in a stifling hot room. No wonder her mood was not right when T-Mo happened.

• • •

She processed a pack of cigarettes at the cash register and looked up to announce the cost, and her heart went soft. He stood before her, looked at her with a careless smile that cracked something inside. A sense of imminence grabbed her in so ruthless a fashion it rendered her immobile.

"Your curls," his gaze touched her hair. "Soft as the feathers of a baby bird." That tied her tongue too. He might have touched it, her hair, or perhaps only his words touched it. He at once captured her with his impetuous nature and pulverized any restraint she might have shown, so much that the beat of her heart sped to insanity.

He glanced at the barcode reader and slipped a note from his pocket. So hypnotized was she when he moved away from the queue, she rose from her stool to follow him with her eyes. Follow him where? Away from it all, the IGA, her parents, to a place filled with radiance.

How much for a dozen? A female voice severed her entrancement and Salem turned to face her, eyes astonished still. *A dozen,* the woman said. *How much?* Salem lifted the bar of soap. "Was the price not on the shelf?" she said. She sat back on the stool, looked one more time for her man but he was gone. She turned the bar of soap until she found a barcode. Beep! the reader. "Three dollars twenty for a dozen," she said. Her hands were shaking.

Two hours later she signed off the till. She was in desolation still at not having spoken a word, not a single croak, to the man whose gaze touched. He was waiting for her at the car park opposite the IGA entrance. His gaze more than touched; it fondled.

At once she brightened. "Y-you?" The longer she looked at him the more perfect he grew.

He pointed at a crimson sign on a snowy background at the top of the IGA door. It read: *Milk is Available Here.*

"That true?" he said. She nodded, held helpless in his gaze. "That's true anywhere. They have to proclaim it?"

She liked him. She liked him very much.

He spread his hand, gave her that winning smile that coursed rapture through her veins. He held a careless jacket across his shoulder. His eyes indicated a soft-top parked in a slot. Its bare metal gleam dazzled her eyes. "Care for a spin?"

"Holy moly," she said in wonderment. He felt right. She didn't need to be someone else.

"First girl I ever heard say holy moly like that," he said. "You say jeepers creepers too?"

Her mother was a preacher's wife, she blurted, the first thing that came to her head. Her father was, well, a preacher! She giggled nervously.

"Is he, now? How about that? A preacher's daughter. Get in the car." She paused. He shifted his foot. "Would you care for a spin with me?" he said.

"Okay."

His smile was musical as a lark. It penetrated. His palm lightly brushed her waist. When he tightened her seat belt, his hands lingered. A flood of warmth climbed to her cheeks and Salem yielded to a longing to fill the space between them with words.

She lived in a custom-built house of basic detail, on the generosity of the faithful. Pastor Ike could never spend on tiles for a new bathroom. No music no radio no TV: just Bible hour after dinner, she babbled. He never swore, either; the only time he did was when a visiting preacher from a nearby parish floated to him the idea of a Jazz Society for the youth of East Point to keep their hands from bedevilment. Even then (she glanced at her hands) Pastor Ike's swearing fell short of "f" or "s" words and he said "drummer" in place of "bugger." She spoke and spoke until he pulled the car to the side of a road and silenced her with his lips.

The kiss was as delicious as it was troubling. It filled her with a cavalcade of emotions, bands and bands of them. And she felt something new. Freedom. This man who made the sky resemble a crystal ceiling, who turned the ground at her feet to a fairy tale, he brought her freedom.

But that was no surprise, she later thought after their unchaperoned date. There was something magical about a man who walked through doors . . . who traveled between worlds. One minute he was there, the next he was gone. So on a whim, the first daring whim in her life, she presented a man to her father with intention and announced her plan.

"Father, you have met T-Mo," she said. "I am going to marry him."

They stood in the space between the back door of the main house and Salem's servant house. Pastor Ike eyed the male beside his daughter, took in the ripe plum color of his sleeveless t-shirt that carried bold white words on its breast, words that said: Hearts & Beds. Where was the mystery in those words? The intrigue? T-Mo had done bugger all, drummer drummer, to try and impress a possible father-in-law. Pastor Ike looked at Salem without indifference. Then he looked at the way the brazen boy or man stood, reckless, how he held his head, how a strange curiosity spread in his eyes. How the dazzle in his rainbow smile made his looks fetching despite dinosaur skin.

Might have been the hearts or beds, not the sleevelessness of his t-shirt, or was it T-Mo's unabashed smile? Whatever it was, it immediately squandered any goodwill Pastor Ike might have had. Gator skin or not, that alien buffoon standing with hair as yet uncombed beside his daughter . . . Pastor Ike had one question.

"This T-Mo," he said, speaking to his daughter. "Does he have a second name?"

Salem stood with tumultuous heart, looking at her father who directed words at her without removing his gaze from T-Mo.

"I am sure he does, Father . . ."

In the deadly silence that followed, Pastor Ike unmasked his hitherto somber countenance to disclose a vulnerability to fury. He purpled and a furious pulse pumped on his neck. It calmed, the pulse, and ceased being noticeable, as did the florid hue on Pastor Ike's face. Pageant fled into the house. She had looked and felt desperate at the boldness of her daughter; now perhaps she would hide her joyless face under the kitchen sink and clasp dismay in her trembling hands.

"And you are going to marry him?" There was no rebuke in Ike's voice.

"Yes, Father."

Ike's preacher face acquired calm, not sag, and with no more erosion of control than that which he had already displayed, with no dislike or hatred in it, he said, "You are both strangers to me. Get out of my house."

• 4 •

Calm words, but they knocked two people out of the house. Not a grand or gracious house, just a sturdy two-bed custom-built that was no longer home to Salem.

That night, that same one of the homelessness, the soft-top shot through the road. Headed for a place where power lines dissolved and there were just shrubs and space. Headed past trees that hugged their leaves tight and stood tall like closed umbrellas. Sometimes shorter ones took their space and spread wide like amethyst curtains in the horizon below a blackening sky.

T-Mo drove and drove, floored the car's accelerator as if they were going to the end of the world. He gazed at Salem sat beside him in the car, and she cast him eyes so full of personal appeal he could restrain himself no longer. The car slid to a halt beside a road sign that said *No Left Turn*. Or was it *No Through Road*? Salem couldn't tell, half blinded by tears. This felt like the most tragic turning point in her life, not the liberty she had so yearned for—for which she had almost been ready to fight or die.

"Why are you crying?" he asked.

She shook her head, knuckled a tear away.

"Don't know why you are crying?"

She nodded, knuckled another tear. But more came. Endless tears that splashed down her face and she did not have enough knuckles for them all. Hadn't she herself accepted the risk, and the goodness it offered?

"Look at me."

She looked, turned her mind over and over, questioning. It came back at her with every reason why this man—who possessed her thoughts, whose touch on her body brought starlight to her skin, made it look as if sprinkled with diamond dust—was better than home.

She remembered how the dinosaur on his skin smiled to put butter in her knees. How when he vanished, gone from her view, a distant voice in feral wind, she felt lost. Then a swift darkness and he would be there. Right there facing her. Not content to travel through time, he was time itself. She felt found.

She remembered how despite the ghosts that haunted his face, when she timidly smiled he completed the laughter for them both with something deep, wholesome. How husk filled his voice when he said something plain, words as simple as "Care for a spin?" How her heart rattled so loud at the sound of that husk she thought the whole world would dance from the composition of it.

She trembled at his approach round the car. But his musical-as-a-lark smile when he opened her door tossed away her unease, and she melted into his arms. His fingers were tender as mist when he drew her away from her seat, from the car, from . . . anything that kept her from him.

Together, they moved as far as they could from the road, any road. Fifty yards or five thousand, didn't matter. When at last they stopped, her head felt light but he guided her swoon to the ground. There, on a carpet of ivory hydrangea, he peeled every layer of clothing from her and her shiver was not from chill or a deep, terrible fear but from an overwhelming need to be complete, to be free. She found, in his arms, that she was both: his and free.

It snowed. Snowdrops like blooms gliding from the sky. Moon collapsed into a veil of mist. Darkness, black as octopus ink, rose above the fog, stooped low to spray and swallow it. Salem quavered but T-Mo calmed her unreasoning fear.

Lanterns in his eyes guided her, fingers nudged gently. Hands like wings cradled her, lifted her from the ground, carried her to a place of awakening inside the feet of frost. The wings laid her gently on a dais. Breath soft as summer rain not just raised the temperature of Salem's skin: it spread her feet, arched her back and took her to the pinnacle of a nameless place. *Sing to the mountains. Lift your hearts!* Swallowed in a church hymn.

Somewhere outside her sleep, as her head rested on T-Mo's chest beneath a sky full of murmuring, a sword of lightning across the night sky chased a blast of thunder that rolled like belly laughter. Just then, right there, in the instant lighting of the firmament, Salem saw a clear silhouette a few meters from her feet. It was the puzzle-piece woman with fifty-cent eyes. Head lowered, her feet apart, the woman's broken eye was smooth and round as when Salem first saw it. As for the gobbling eye—the good one—it keenly filtered, turned inward and wondered.

SILHOUETTE

· 5 ·

I was betrothed between chants when a Sayneth priest, immortal, came to bless the new birth in a home at the edge of Bruthen. Unlike the other ten children, I was different, not just for being a girl. Unable to lift my own head in a cot, a baby, eleventh baby, eleventh blessing, I was betrothed. It was an honor. Ma Space in her own quiet way, without doggedness, reminded me when I was older and older. I was betrothed to be the first wife in a plural marriage to a Sayneth priest.

By the time I was old enough to understand, I liked the sound of his name. Novic. *N*. The sound was nasal. Teeth, lips apart, tongue pushing. The sound vibrated my throat. And he was a Sayneth priest. *S*, like for snake.

What-am-a-say? Makes a sing-song sound when I say this. What-am-a-say. I liked him. There was not a mutinous streak in my bones, any bone that shaped me, when I found myself a wife at eleven.

Ma Space, she took me from my room, my dear room with its pale moon-shine through the window. When the door handle turned and she entered, something about her face told me it was time. I wanted to step on my bed, lift the hand-painted frame of rainbows from the wall behind, lift it and take it with me. The frame was a gift from a midwife the day I was born, Ma Space said, years ago. I had no memory of the midwife, but the story of her gift was a memory, something told. The frame was real. It was the one thing I owned, *one* thing. Eleventh child—what do you expect? Maybe *two* things: the room felt like mine. My brothers did not share it. They slept in bunks in a dormitory down in the basement. My room was in the attic and the in-between belonged to Ma Space. But she said no to the rainbows. Ma Space, she said: "We go light, my chile. Everything you need is there." She took my hand and we stole into dusk like thieves. It didn't occur to me to wish the boys goodbye. Farewell was unlikely to impress them, and I could not wait to get away from the kings. They liked to think they were monarchs in their grand dormitory with its high walls and bright lights and locked cupboards. Bring me, give me, fetch me, said the kings. Sod off, said the kings. Dash, Kit and Hedge were the worst, such swagger they had. Blaze was the angry one, but he never hit me or showed rage on his face. I remember the day, without provocation or deep resentment, he put an elbow around Tiny's neck, throat punched him, pressed the boy's head in the toilet bowl. Gave him a *royal* flush.

Footloose was always outdoors. He was so big, horses would run away if he wanted to ride them. But he didn't need horses. He was always doing donuts on the ground with a cart he had built, horn helmet on his head.

"He'll put holes in the lawn, Ma Space," I said.

"If he put hole in it," she said, "it not end of the world to fix it."

"But Ma—"

"Where him? Happy."

What-am-a-say? I gave up, could not be bothered to protect what Ma Space didn't need protecting from her boys.

Bluey—mouth like a shriveled apricot—was sometimes kind, until the younger troublemakers Boxer and Donzo came along. One moment, Bluey was a complete stranger at the dinner table beside me. The next, as Ma Space asked the boys, "What dessert you want?" in her absent-minded way, he had scribbled something, pushed the paper toward me, and the scrawl said: "I have lost the will to live." Another time he glanced at Ma Space's platter of oat pancakes, said: "This doesn't look safe." But he gobbled his whole lot, rolled his tongue around the bowl and then wrote: "Three visits to the toilet, I think I know where this is going." That is how I knew he too wanted to get away, that Ma Space failed him entirely. But it was Rusty—I liked to think of him as a terrible hollow—who surprised us all when he swung a coat on his shoulder and left to take work in the mines in Lockwood down south. Then he married a girl in Mount Bright up north.

The day she took me, Ma Space, we walked swiftly, furtively, as if toward a secret. We strode into a mist where tussocks of weed caught my toe, but Ma Space urged me forth until we found a waterfront. The span of her silence was a canvas, as was the water surface with its sparkle of moonshine. On occasion, I tugged Ma Space's elbow but she said nothing, just walked. She was never one for fluffy feather talk. She who had tried to learn me a few things, like how to scrub my brothers' dorm until it shone like a lantern, and

I learnt those things well, she had no last words as she tugged me to the one to whom I was betrothed. I went along without rebellion.

The wind was gasping when we arrived. Perhaps I was exhausted from the walk. We reached a sweep of lawns, curving pathways. Novic was waiting. His lips on my forehead were cold as a mother-in-law's kiss. Inside his house, a mansion built like a cathedral, its embellishments scaling and branching across three main towers and a rear expanse, I did not regret that lack of rebellion. I gazed at the oval face of the mansion's front, the gilded tips and pediments at the end of the roofs. The doors and doors, some shut, some ajar, others thrown wide open. There were doors everywhere, walls sparkling like mirrors. Room after room there was exuberance of light and shade, form and intensity. Everything about Novic's mansion spoke of rhetoric, of theater. I looked at the opulence, at Novic's achievement, and understood it was mine to own with him, shape with him, first wife in a plural marriage. An honor.

The coupling did not happen straight after we wed. Novic waited.

Every third week in her inobtrusive way Ma Space slipped into the mansion, come to visit. But her intention was distinct. Each time she found moment to put a finger just below my collarbone.

"Stop it, Ma Space."

"It don' hurt, my chile."

In her absent way, she brought random botanicals from home during those visits. One minute she was in the back garden patting soil around baby herbs unstitched from a petticoat where she had sewn them, sprinkling crushed potato water over them and gently massaging their sprouting leaves; next she was poking my collarbone. Resisting was no use.

"Why a petticoat for the herblings?" I sought to distract her.

"Chase away bad luck. No homesick."

Truly, I never missed home as I knew it. I did not miss my brothers; just my room with its yellow moonshine and my frame of rainbows.

I put to use everything Ma Space had learnt me, like how to put a knotted bag of sand and willow seeds at the bottom of a wooden chest to keep laundered clothes from getting damp in winter. Like how to fade burn taste in stew with a dollop and stir of black bee honey. Like how to fill a hole in the wall with soap and unclog a blocked drain with the right mix of scalding water and vinegar concentrate. But I refused to stoop to her strange ways, like how she never let a black lizard cross her path. If one did, Ma Space recrossed its path three times and spat in the direction its tail had vanished, all to chase away bad luck.

One day inside the year of my marriage Ma Space found what she was looking for: the budding node of fertility.

I stood tiny in that opulent kitchen, hands dipped in scorching water, plucking feathers off a fowl, when, with a scoop of arms, strong arms, he claimed me. In the bed, despite my unknowing body, a whole body tingling without discernment to his fondling, I stayed fascinated with the bedhead. My fingers ran along the contours of its face as he took me. I missed my room with its pale moonlight, my hand-painted frame of rainbows. But I did not miss the cold in the old house—layers and layers on my chest and feet to keep warm, but still the cold in the old house. Novic's house was warm, I thought, as my head bump bump bumped against the bedhead over and over until his eagerness finished.

Then Ma Space's visits altogether stopped.

It was not the bumping that stayed with me, the things Novic did when he took me; it was the things he didn't do. He didn't run his fingers on my skin or whisper tender words as I thought a curious husband might. There was just a sense of rush . . . and release. That became his pattern: stalking me in the throes of domesticity. Then an abrupt scoop into arms, naked lust, hungry fingers stealing into folds of my loose dress. Noiseless stalking, noiseless thrill—that was Novic.

I too had a pattern: discussion with the bed chamber all during the taking. I would notice as if for the first time objects. Like the velvet coating the buttons on the bedhead. Like the handcrafted leather shelling our chest of drawers. Like the thread pattern in Duchess curtains covering the tall window, or the Duke carpeting on the floor. Like the sovereign tallboy, the v-shaped pillow, the studded sofa, the beaded lamp with its legs angled like an elegant woman posing. Like the seamlessness of pure satin in soft gold in the quilt we had just soiled.

My examining the bed, the chamber, outlasted his terrible desire. I lay still long after Novic was gone, my fingers still racing along the artisan bedhead that had mutely witnessed my sacrifice to whatever Novic's desire prescribed.

I never really came into my own.

A look. That was all it took. Not the full weight of his shoulder behind the slap, because lovemaking always followed that. The coupling, what do you expect? Novic, he . . . loved me. Mad, but he loved me—past tense.

I remember those emery hands, stroking the soft in my hair until it shimmered like his mane. Those leathery lips so strong, they buttered mine. Shadows dancing in those eyes old as Jacob, in that contained look that drew secrets from my longing. His skin furrowed into itself with age, clinging to bone, but there was nothing old in his taking.

When he pulled back my head and, like a grown beast, bit my neck in mating, his face looked like death. But his hair! It was a magical mane that fell to his waist. Pitch-black, polished like metal. So soft, even now the tresses of it bounce in my words. Pitch . . . Peach. Same, different. My hair was always peach, a spiral curtain that twirled down my shoulders to my bottom. Kept it long so Novic could touch it. How he loved to touch it. After the look, I shore it, then it grew back all maroon.

· b ·

My mother's easing me into the marriage did not prepare me for that gut wrench. Novic bedded me soon as Ma Space confirmed my coming of age. So she was integral to this partnership. It was only natural then that she was at the birthing, in her own preoccupied way.

Present by my bedside were a bunch of Grovean midwives. Best of them. There was Nene, eyes full of sand; Corio, dimples on her pensive face; Anakie, pep in her step; Blanket, leaned toward me in an intimate way, hushed tone like she was sharing a secret; Norlane, like a low-priced engine: low gear, high talk; and Ma Space, the youngest of them, with her dark liquid eyes, long face and tight curls. Hers was a distracted kind of beauty you sometimes forgot, sometimes remembered.

A woman without means was fortunate to get one midwife at her birthing. Sometimes, if her husband was not near, she would snip her own baby's umbilical cord to disconnect it from her body. But I . . . I had six midwives. I was, after all, the first wife of a Sayneth priest. An honor.

Birthing T-Mo was . . . like someone grabbed my gut, wrenched it out of my stomach and it came out with a baby. Not sure what I expected . . . What does a girl-bride who has never seen birth expect? A baby crawling out of a hole or something, its crown glistering with body sweat? Or something.

It was Nene that shoved a fist inside to grab and turn the head, that yanked him out. *Tssk*, the sound that pushed out from between my legs, or was it *p-pop*? Sometimes I remember it like *shfffff*. But my birthing hips were still in formation and the pain was too loud, I don't recollect too well that yank-out sound.

Anakie snipped the umbilical cord. Baby's arms and legs were all bent up close to his body, fingers clenched. He was a scream, literally. Opened that mouth and shook the room. I remember the birthing chamber: cathedral walls, mustard color. Or was it custard?

By the time he unfolded from his fetal position to tug at my tit, my gut felt already whole. They say babies come out face all squished, looking a mess. Not mine. He came out face all beautiful: big brows, full lips, smooth skin—softest ever; looking at it made you feel at home.

Blanket leaned toward me, intimate, baby in her arms all swaddled already, and said, "What's his name?"

"His poppy decides," said Nene.

"Novic? Why he got to decide?" said Corio.

"Take all my souls if a woman don' name her own chile," said Anakie.

"Yes, we matriarchal."

"But Novic, he a Sayneth priest."

"Jus' cos he a priest don' mean he take our rights."

"No he don'. We matriarchal."

"What mother she be if she don' name her own chile?"

"Baby look like a Jules or a Wally," said Ma Space, absently.

"An Avon or a Brooke to me," Anakie.

Names ping-ponged back and forth like balls in a game but all I was thinking was not how the child didn't crawl out like I thought he might, or how he pulled out *tssk*, *p-pop* or *shfffff*. Didn't even think about the pain. I just thought what a dream, most gorgeous baby ever.

"What's his name?" Blanket in my face.

I looked at the midwives, scouring their faces one by one for a muse. What-am-a-call-him? Staggered myself with the choice I came up with: "T-Mo."

"T-what?"

"His name is T-Mo." I smiled. *T*, I liked the sound it made, quiet-like, no pull on the voice. I wanted to put my hand on the throat and say *T, T, T*, but instead reached and took him from Blanket, who was so stunned at my naming of the child, she nearly dropped him.

Looking at him, I said it over and over in my head: *T*, my throat does not move. Not always a soft or a light sound, depends on how you say it. You trap air with your tongue against the roof of your mouth, release the tongue downward. *M*, I press my lips together and make a circle to start the rest. *Mo*, air comes out to finish the sound.

The midwives looked at me as if I had tied empty tins to my ankles. "His name is T-Mo," I said firmly.

"Say who?"

"Name her son a syllable."

"Two syllable, not one."

"If *T* is what you want name him Transfix."

"Or Trap."

"Or Tell."

"Pops out baby one time and her brain goes all over."

"A muscle-head like her da," said Corio, her face all flat, her scorn close enough to touch. Even her dimples vanished.

"Dropped eleven babies and my head not muscle," said Ma Space. But she was random as always. "T-Mo" defied them all. "I think I like it."

The look in the rest of the midwives' eyes confirmed she was crazy too. Crazy, foolish, or both.

Novic. He took one look at the baby, stood straight as a board and contradicted us all. "His name is Odysseus. The traveling one."

The hush that fell . . . everyone knew it was a curse. Sayneth priest meant nothing—only a mother could name her chile.

·7·

Same one—two people. That is what Novic created. Was it tunnel vision, or insight? What caused Novic to do the deed that brought this chaos?

My stomach took his contradiction very seriously—in a matriarchal society, a mother names her child. My belly took such offense, it curled up. And although I still ran fingers along the bedhead, discovered anew my bedroom, Novic saw no more babies. Not from me, he didn't.

What he created was an enigma that was weird, electrifying and heartbreaking. T-Mo. Odysseus. It mattered which side of him you saw. It was T-Mo that closed his baby eyes as he fed, closed them like there was heavenly flavor in my milk, angels pissing nectar on his tongue. When I touched his palms, fat fingers clasped me back. He sucked and sucked, grew like a magic bean. He sneezed, he hiccuped, he kicked—like when I carried him in my belly—but he also sucked sucked sucked like it was life and death. Dropped his guts often, no wonder.

When I strapped him to my breast in his carry sack, I never for one moment felt the cling, the soft lean of baby hair against my neck, the quest for comfort. T-Mo was always an independent baby, but so was Odysseus.

The main difference is how Odysseus hated touch, shrugged to get loose from my clutch way before he could crawl. He frothed like he was being strangled when I tried to pick him up, but showed little range of emotions most times. He didn't respond if someone cooed or clucked at him. He did not stretch out fat arms and say "ah-ah" or "ooh-ooh." He ignored people or looked at them with flat eyes, unless he wanted something. Even then, when he wanted something, he reached and snatched the object (a ball, a fruit, a pebble . . .) without babbling, but with a flash of triumph in his eyes.

At first, I thought he was deaf and could not hear sounds to echo them. But he responded to sound, like the slam of door—not with startle, just a glance in the direction. And he did make a sound early on, it was a giggle, almost a belly laugh, the sound he made when he rolled onto a moth down the hallway and crushed it. The only times I heard him giggle again like that were when he was with Novic.

It was T-Mo that grunted and squeaked, baby-talk-like. He wasn't a fussy baby, not a whisper of colic. His smile, when he learnt it, was wide as a rainbow, poems in his eyes. Loved the sun—soon as he could toddle, raced out the house at daybreak to find soil or a rock, sprawled himself tongue out, lapped up heat like a reptile.

But it was Odysseus that Novic knew, reared. The boy picked his father's powers, walked through doors. T-Mo I could hold close and cuddle; Odysseus I couldn't draw near. He was cunning, greedy. Nothing like the child that lay in a cot following objects with his eyes, stretching, kicking on his back, exploring with his hands and mouth, rolling both ways, gleeful, when for the first time he raised his chest from a stomach position. With Novic, the child was grown and strong and dark, even as an infant.

Toddler T-Mo and I walked hand-in-hand, marveling at Grovea. His eyes mirrored the city: diamond stars in the jeweled sky before the moon turned bloodred. Charcoal pebbles along Turtle Cove. Amethyst sand from waves on the great reef at Rocky Point. I watched as down the esplanade of the inner city, Bruthen, he chased fireflies that glowed crimson, yellow or lime.

"Tell me about Nana Space," he asked when he was breathless, a Vulcan eagle—gold breasted—on his arm.

"What about her? She was a midwife."

He would give me a look. She had ten brothers named Hook, True, Bone, Fever, Pretty, Cute, Lantern, Comet, Code and Rush. T-Mo looked at me until I mellowed: "Her mother was an enchantress, her grandmother also an enchantress but her great-grandmother was a midwife."

"Tell me about Grandpa," guiding the eagle's flight from the tip of his hand into the sky.

"What about him? He was a migrant." The look. Folk nicknamed my father Runaway. I relented: "He was a guard from the land of Shiva who, during prisoner transfer and a stopover for supplies, absconded after he fell in love with a local girl, the daughter of an enchantress born in a family where women became midwives or witches and it ran for generations."

Finding himself stripped of the familiarity of Shiva and all its harshness, and rewarded with the jeweled sky of Grovea, its red moon and fauna, marked the start of his impairment. Rather than adore his new world, Runaway could not bring himself to imagine life without fear. The tangent life he lived was removed from normality. A recessive mutation incited an allergy on his skin; it formed what looked like all-over body acne, a condition that later manifested itself in its wildest form in T-Mo. But most about Runaway, I remembered his roar. He roared at everything, the bellow a derivative of fear.

"Why did Grandpa leave Shiva?"

"People move on all the time." The look. Shiva was a harsh place only guards, prisoners or exiles could inhabit. It was a place of rationed food and water, even air, labor in plenty. Everywhere were steel fortresses whose walls were spiked with a battalion of metal. I relented: "Your grandpa was a deserter who traded his laser gun for the love of a woman."

He lived in fear that somebody might one day recognize him and betray him and he'd be carted back to Shiva to face execution for desertion, and he was craven to his death.

"Why did he trade his laser gun?"

T-Mo loved those questions: why, how, when, from where? But he never asked about Novic or his family. Novic was so ancient that nobody understood anything of his past, what brought him from the land of Sayneth all alone to Grovea. I never understood his future either, or his hang-ups. All I know is that the obsessions weren't there at the start. But after T-Mo—no, Odysseus—everything about me except amorous activity was a problem to Novic. A single hair out of place, a missing ladle in a gravy bowl, whatever thing that was nothing, it could bring on a slap.

· 8 ·

T-Mo loved centuries—the color of history.

Hues along our strolls charmed him. He stayed in awe at the rainbow of street music, the blackness of the printer's ink, the lemons and blood oranges of the market, anything grass green or snowy or cerulean or antique.

Before you got to Cozy Place, there was this herbarium of exotic plants. I remember T-Mo's fascination with the ornamental conifer, the withered olive that was the habitat of the paper-making spider, the sweet daisy species, the temple of winds shrubbery, the knotted pond-leaf, the flowering elm . . . all brought as seedlings from other worlds. So strong their scents, you could smell the plants from blocks away. That is where I found Weed.

Weed's mother worked in the herbarium. Hers was more than a green thumb; she was a Botan, gifted with nature. Loaned us her son Weed, a tall, thin boy always wearing a red scarf around his neck and a jacket. He had all over black hair going north, east, west but not at will. He brought along a half-jar of Lycopod spores that grew into dwarf plants with soft, single-veined leaves. Three times a week, he came to the garden to stroke the branching stems. The plants were simple in their forms but they carried presence. He kept them fragrant and flowering all seasons, through winter, spring, summer into autumn. He watered them sparingly, removed dead leaves and tenderly buried them.

Weed knew everything about plants, made sure our garden wore plenty of color. He knew how to get the space right between seeds for maximum growth and spread, understood which plants needed the soil to warm them up and bring out their explosion of pigmentation, call the birds and the bees. He knew which ones mushroomed and rainbowed, flowered and flowered best and without pause when he wrapped their roots in ice. He was friendly enough with T-Mo but cautious with Odysseus.

Weed, perhaps the Botan in him, was one of the early ones to distinguish between T-Mo and Odysseus. Easy for a mother to tell difference, but in time more people could tell. Eyes told the boys apart: T-Mo's carried poems in them; Odysseus and his eyes stayed flat. And smiles: T-Mo's smile was wide as a rainbow; Odysseus had none—just a movement of lips that did not reach his eyes. Later clothing, hair and how the boys interacted with people enhanced difference.

Down Cozy Place to Chirnside and away from Mead Street, as T-Mo and I walked, I pointed out the trading part of the city where you would find Jarvis the blacksmith who was also a goldsmith and a tinsmith, all muscled and wiry; Moriac who sold candles, lanterns and soaps, face like he was born in a wrecking yard; Autry the foundry man who spun metal into anything but was infamous for his bummed-out moods; Berchill who owned a drapery store—the place I bought baby wear and linen for T-Mo when he was a tot, before I could yarn them myself after Ma Space resumed her visits and remembered to learn me.

T-Mo loved best Miss Lill's sweet shop between the grocer and the post office. His favorite was the fish licorice that tasted of honey and vegetable and fish, and held a texture of oatmeal, chicken and liver. I liked the pepper and mint drops, nothing shy in those flavors, real kicks.

Miss Lill, she was a golden woman with sun in her hair, happy lipstick on her lips and laughter in her walk. She never asked T-Mo what he wanted; she just saw us and gladly cried out: "Little Poetry come to visit, bless those eyes," in her sing-sing way, all cultured-like. She spoke good sounds; I could listen to Miss Lill all day. Ultra slender for one who sold confectionery, she would ease the lid off the fish licorice jar, scoop the boy a handful—never charged him what it was worth.

"Manners all impeccable, my little Poetry, remembers to say *please* and *thank you*," she would markedly exclaim to her cap-headed helper named Warun. He was a boy with one lazy eye, lanky arms sprinkled with baby hair and a shop pet named Mate—a yappy but harmless tail-wagger two-feet tall.

By the time the door swung back at Miss Lill's, Mate yap yap yapping, T-Mo had gobbled all lollies. Then his eyes would gobble the city, a place not split into domains—it just flowed. It didn't matter whether you sauntered along the avenues of commerce, where folk peddled aloud their wares, or you strolled in the suburbs on a person-wide track that bordered the elbows of a racing river and fingers of a fattening brush, where a nudge could plunge you into the wet churn: the flow was still there, that sense of seamlessness. Tradesfolk in Bruthen were friendly, nobody littered the street. Further down, shores were pristine not bird-pooped, and wild things and micro things showered the coastline.

But back home, once we reached the doors of the manor or the Temple, T-Mo became uneasy or edgy and then Odysseus would appear. In quiet mourning, I would watch him disappear with Novic into the incense room, and I wondered how one so sacred, a Sayneth priest, could breed something so ugly.

Novic was the homeschooling kind, nobody but him worthy of coaching his son. What-am-a-think? Guess it was okay. The little I understood—carelessly revealed when a priest from the planet of 180C gave homily at our wedding—was that Novic was an itinerant scholar, one who traveled the galaxy, learnt new worlds. Mastered natural medicine at Stillwell, cosmo sciences at Abacus, political science at Panada, cosmology at Greenberg in the land of Vernis.

Apparently he had relatives. An uncle named Deimos: scorched almond eyes alert with observing folk, prisoners more than normal folk, prisoners who stood chained, compliant, sometimes standing in parade or crawling ass up on their knees (in neat rows) upon command. Deimos was commander at Shiva, same penal colony my father Runaway deserted. A cousin named Surrimon who cast herself to the ground in a sudden loss of mind, confined in a madhouse in the land of Sayneth. A nephew named Blizzard, a robber, whose palm was cold, the stare of his good eye appraising—one eye was steel, the other dead as stone. Blizzard had found a fortune, or robbed someone of it, and now reveled in a life of aristocracy on 180C.

Besides homeschooling in the incense room, I often heard their play, the child's squeal of mirth so loud it could break your ears. But when he emerged after spending time with Novic, his eyes were like pinpoints. And then he was dominating, opinionated, deceitful, manipulating, prone to boredom, even cruelty. He was nothing like the infant that Nene, Corio, Anakie, Blanket, Norlane and Ma Space helped pop out of my belly.

Odysseus was cruel to Novic's new wives—Yaris, Vara, Xinnia, Clarin—when they arrived in their separate timelines. But T-Mo, fastest being ever, raced around in play with the new wives' offspring. He liked best of all little Cassius, nestled in his mother's arms, gold coin eyes and a mutiny of amethyst hair. But Odysseus brought Yaris to tears with his unkindness to her child. Pinched it, snatched food or toys away from it. Always like that, mean. Odysseus did things that shook or dismayed everyone—but never Novic.

Odysseus, he would vanish for hours, lie about where he had been, show no remorse for my anxiety. He was secretive in his zippings in and out of the house, finding his true nature.

"Where have you been?" I asked when he came home.

"Nowhere."

"Nowhere has no distance."

I waited a moment to see if he would answer and was about to give up when he answered: "Has an end."

"Seemed a long time coming," foolishly I persisted. "You can't just vanish like that."

"Says who?"

"How about me."

Odysseus cracked my smudge of hope with two words and a soft glow in his eyes: "From *when?*"

I looked at him and wept. Nene, Corio, Anakie, Blanket, Norlane and Ma Space would have wept as well had they been around. But Ma Space was long in the ground. Blanket had opened a restaurant and, when she cooked, you tasted history in her dishes. Corio had migrated with her husband to newfound lands on 180C—who wouldn't if the family was going? There, picturesque islands encapsulated themselves and people initiated escapades and brand new ways of having fun. Norlane—don't know what happened to her. Only Anakie and Nene were still birthing, but they were spending much time catching babies, too busy with midwifery to notice how my baby had turned out.

While I understood that Odysseus was right—from when did I start having a say about Odysseus?—still I questioned. What is a mother to do?

One day something triggered him in some way and he vanished in some other way. In palpable fashion, his absence that day filled me with a sense of dread, the reasons for the tingling in my fingers, the twist in my gut, the itch in my body . . . completely unclear. My body was still unsettled when he returned. His arrival home and my bewildered questioning were just moments apart when the story broke.

It was Weed the garden boy who told me: "Odysseus, he do something real bad."

Odysseus had gone to Miss Lill's and pulled out with bare hands a fistful of heart from howl howl howling Mate. He then flung himself on Warun, swinging over and over at his head a sock full of amethyst rock. Would have smashed Miss Lill's head too when she dashed to help Warun had Jarvis—the blacksmith who was also a goldsmith and a tinsmith—not heard the screams. But it took four men—Jarvis, Moriac, Berchill and Autry—to pry Odysseus, foaming at the mouth, away. Four grown men to rip him from savagery, and he was just four years old.

A grenade went off in my heart that day. There was no more feeling but deep sorrow and, for the second time for him, I wept. I saw with great insight that my son was a herald of death, perhaps the very father of death, reincarnated across worlds, across centuries. And I remembered the curse of his naming.

That was the only time I saw Novic show rage at the child but it was not the striking rage that closes a slap to the cheek. This one moved inside like a pot of simmering soup. If you looked closely in his eyes you could see it. He took Odysseus to the incense room and this time there was no laughter. When Odysseus burst out it was with eyes turned inward. As for Novic's gaze, it did not touch me. He stared straight ahead.

It took three whole nights for my T-Mo to emerge. But when he surfaced, his twinkle for me was back, his eyes full of poems. Smile lines filled his face but his voice was broken when he clasped my hand and said, "Walk with me, Mamma, let's walk."

I took his hand and together we walked and walked to the end of time.

Miss Lill, she sold up. There was too much randomness in a child she had once thought precious, it broke her belief.

· 9 ·

I calmed Novic's madness.

Other than the laughter in the incense room, I never knew what he and Odysseus held common, what they talked about. If I walked into them, Novic slunk off mid-sentence and I knew when night came he would hit me.

Even then, when he struck me, I did not cry out but lay in submission, the weight of his slap not losing its sting. Wasn't long before he crouched beside me, his mane to my face and he would pull back my head to bite my neck in mating. I stayed loving him, even when bit by bit he turned my T-Mo into Odysseus.

I calmed Novic with mundane words, things spoken quietly after the mating. "The kitchen sink needs fixing." That very night he would fix it: the sink, a table leg, a cabinet handle. Then he would slink alone outside and prowl the house. Round and round, the entire circumference of the mansion, pacing and pacing, sometimes leaping like something had agitated him. Often, the sight of Odysseus would calm the madness.

The next day Novic was like quince: acid when he woke up fresh in the morning, soft and tender in daylight. I would have stayed with Novic, cherishing the times when T-Mo emerged. Didn't I stay after his attacks took on a new viciousness and he put magic to dinosaur my skin? Didn't I stay when a red-hot poker rod, not magic, broke my eye? But a look made me pause and think and say: what-am-a-stay-here-for?

When Novic gave me that look, it was not an evil eye or something. It was not the rage that boiled from your big toe to finish at your palm behind a strike. This one came with curiosity hinged so steep, it was a measured look. It was like something small had shifted inside Novic, and it was swirling and swirling into something bigger inside him, forming a decision. The look that sent me packing was the kind you gave a gnat you were plotting to kill.

I walked through the spread of lawns and its rows and fencing of flowers, shrubs and trees. A little bird perched on the branch of a low-leafed tree stopped preening its blue feathers, silver-tipped, and crooked its head to look at me. It was a native bird, not a seasonal migrant like the long-legged, slim-bodied glow-bird, upright and elegant when it perched, often at dusk. Weed was out in the garden and did not turn his head when I ruffled his all over hair as I walked past. But one of the dwarf plants crept all the way after me until I was level with the gate. Its soft stem wrapped gently around my ankle and it hugged me for a moment before uncurling and returning to the garden. What-am-a-know? Weed was a plant whisperer.

At the gateway, I looked back and saw through the liquid in my good eye my sister wives gazing at me from their bedroom windows in the oval face of the mansion, their hands waving quiet goodbyes. The sun was beginning to sink. It was T-Mo not Odysseus who stood hand pressed against his window in one of the three towers of the mansion. He refused to wave but surely he knew—how could I claim him while Odysseus lived?

I turned with a boulder in my heart and put one leg in front of the other, leg leg away away . . . Some of the little children ran behind me a long way before their feet could take no more running. Then I was alone with dusk. For the first time in my life I wanted to take that boulder in my heart, find Novic and bring it down smash on his head.

I left one soul behind to watch over T-Mo when he could step out of Odysseus, who was growing bolder and more domineering. I knew I had done the unthinkable: left my own behind in a place where a child belongs to his ma. I argued with myself over and over that this child understood. Years later it was T-Mo not Odysseus who took the same path I took, leg leg away away . . . leaving behind Novic and roaming the world. He was eleven then, same age as I was wedded.

Tssk. I like this sound.

I did not see fit to say goodbye to Ma Space where she lay, a headstone marking her spot near the northern gate of Creek Point cemetery with the words: *Herein lies a distracted beauty, no will to riot.* Why no goodbye? Perhaps I was fearful that—even in her grave—she might treat my departure with the caliber of levity capable in a person named Space, raised in a houseful of boys named Hook, True, Bone, Fever, Pretty, Cute, Lantern, Comet, Code and Rush.

SALEM

· 10 ·

Yellow Trek was no gleaming metropolis, not even a countrified one.

T-Mo made house for them in Yellow Trek.

"A m-mining town?" said Salem.

"*Once* a mining town," he said.

"An old m-mining town?"

"Why not."

Yellow Trek had seen centuries of gold. Her contours cradled vacant mines, caves, tracks, even ruins of an underground church, now a tourist trap. But this town held no popularity, none of the kind that made people visit. Land was semi-arid, save for patches of farm that grew corn. It was a town safe from change. Everyone knew everybody: from the postman to the dustman to the butcher girl to the four spinsters in the craft shop next to the pick and shovel museum down Fisk Street.

Salem took her time knowing its people, the shop, the museum . . . because she was clutched close to T-Mo's heart the night he swept them into Yellow Trek. Her stomach heaved as clouds chased away, as pinheads became trees then houses. She knew by now she should be used to the flights, but she wasn't quite.

First time T-Mo took her higher than a kite goes, drifted her to a place above the earth's surface, she found herself in a world that shuddered with his halt. It flashed at them something white, perhaps it was lightning, certainly something to salute or dissuade them. When a more vicious light came at them, Salem cried. T-Mo bombed them out of that world, flew them across a river of molten lava, dived and perched them on the edge of a cliff in another that could well have been earth but wasn't. They walked over shale, bits and bits of loose rock. It was like walking along a quarry. Then they stood holding hands. A warm wind, spicy as it was tepid, blew into their faces. Creatures like whitetails headed to some hidden world flew in formation over the skeleton coast, singing a ballad as they soared.

In Yellow Trek there was no diving. T-Mo drifted them to a standstill above ears of corn, glided to approach the neighborhood. He firmed his hold on Salem to steady her as his own toes touched the ground and he coasted into a run along a golden meadow. It shouldered a corridor of bare-leafed trees. The tree line stretched all the way to a township, then there stood a villa overlooking a vista. T-Mo eased his grip on Salem and her toes also touched the ground.

"Holy moly," she said.

"Welcome to our home," he said.

She looked around. "All this."

"All ours." He came from behind, cloaked her with his arms.

While they never talked about money, Salem wondered how T-Mo afforded the house or the metal gleamer he drove, those times he drove—not flew like a giant bird.

"I thought as we landed you might be sick all over our house," he said.

She saw that he understood her fear, how her gut pitched each time they climbed up or dropped from the horizon.

She pushed away from him, faced him. "Are you h-happy?"

"That you weren't sick?" His smile was impish. "You bet."

"To s-settle down," she clarified.

Ancient skin on his face moved. He laughed something deep. "Settle? Why not. You are the one for all of me."

He scooped her and they fell in a roll on the porch.

"It's l-like that?" said Salem. She giggled.

Right there on the porch, T-Mo made her forget any more questions awhile. In the afterglow, their brows touched during a whisper of words that were nothing but full of weight, back and forth words like "I see you," or "Touch my heart," Later, she remembered to admonish him and patted her skirt back into place. "You're a b-bad man."

He shrugged. "I was bred in bad."

"We have f-frightened the neighbors."

"Mostly shocked them, I'd say."

She closed the space and put herself back in his arms. Buried her face in his chest and cried. Fulfillment—this new word in her vocabulary—needed getting used to. She promised herself she would invest in this life, in this relationship.

Salem was a home maker. She set about making the house theirs, and T-Mo brushed away any frugality each visit to the carpenter. He was a chap named Zok with a shop down Hunt Place. He had a weathered look, wore army boots and a two-day stubble. He crossed his arms when he spoke, only to inform you of a pick of furnishings that might suit. His son hovered, a dimpled child with a hooded top. Striking eyes, almost silver, looked at T-Mo. The boy scratched a scar on his left cheek. Salem ruffled tight curls on his big head, but the child had eyes only for T-Mo.

"My daddy said not to talk to any human which I don't know," he said.

"Good," said T-Mo. "You can talk to me then."

"But I don't know you." His voice wanted to please.

"So maybe I'm not human."

The boy fled.

Zok smiled. "What can I do for you?" His voice was full of grit.

"The finest," said T-Mo.

"You've come to the right place. Where would you like to start?"

"That lot," T-Mo pointed to a table of walnut timber, its majestic self surrounded by a set of upholstered chairs.

"B-but it costs—" said Salem.

"And that lot," said T-Mo. He pointed at a heritage sofa suite cloaked with fabric.

"Handcrafted," said Zok, also an analytical man who shared detail. He fingered the fabric, lingered his feel of texture. "Six hundred thread with a mulberry silk finish."

T-Mo was almost impatient in his buying, never once quibbling cost. When Salem hesitated or questioned, his impatience was mixed with affection but he was firm on choice. In little time they had bought curtains of textured fabric, structures of aged metal, rustic fittings, finishings for the kitchen, the bathroom . . . Salem converted the villa to something soft yet manly, cozy yet rugged. The master bedroom was a sanctuary with earthy colors, woven fibers, lime and dust accents, all that reminded Salem of the outdoors.

· 11 ·

She was not too busy with setting house to notice her neighbors. There was Pike and Moni Catch, who looked like the kind of people who would name their children Cracker, Soot or Piston. But there were no children. Moni was the sort you spoke to and felt her gentleness. Not only was she generous; she was a visual feast. If you painted her face, you felt you had painted her soul. But her husband was a cantankerous git, most likely a petrol head who needed work on his fuselage. He was also quite a unit, built like an orc, dumb as a cupboard.

On her way to the township one morning, Salem walked past the Catch household, saw Pike cursing and kicking a timeworn mower in the yard.

"Jus' pull de head, Pikey . . ." said Moni.

"Pull de head, pull de motor, pull de gear. Done all dat, bitch won't stir."

"Maybe . . . she jus' need more fuel."

Petrolhead must have drunk it, Salem was sure.

"Bitch got fuel. Invest coin in dis shit and she don' work."

"Maybe . . . jus' try-n take out—" Moni pointed at the engine.

"It be you I'm a take out if you don' shut up real quick. Need thinkin' in ma head, not womanly holler."

Moni's natural beauty peaked with calm, like when she visited Salem and they sat sipping tea on the heritage suite. In those times, Salem noticed the shape of Moni's face, an even oval, the smile line from her nose to her lips, a perfect frame. Her eyes were completely green and big on that face, eyes that surely would turn to emeralds if you looked at them one moment more.

There was Audax, a big man sweating butter no matter the weather. He was a cheery odd sort, fixing to tell mishap stories to anyone who listened:

"Scoundrel givin' me heaps. Granddaddy rat diggin' diggin' under me house near de foundations all nigh' long. I corners him wit' de sweeper, put de snare round his neck, tell him I'm not here ta club ya. He be angry as hell, swearin' at me in rat holler, den he be pleadin' as hell, tellin' at me he got de missus an lotsa kids. I says, 'I knowed dat nose anywhere, 'tis you been givin' me heaps fer weeks. 'Tis you ate up de wood in me shed two months past, give me a sniff and de bird when I try-n corner you. Repeat criminal, come back agin, we'll see 'bout a club on de head, won' we?' I eases off de noose, let him peddle ta de missus and dem kids. I sees him round de corner, scoundrel has de bold ta stop, sniff and give me de bird afore he bolt."

Salem nicknamed Audax, called him Trotter. His manner of walking was nowhere near a trot, it was a trundle—he used his body to drag a broken foot, so that wasn't why she gave him the nickname. She named him so for the way his mouth trotted out mishaps.

There were Divine, Glory, Sultry and Spring, four spinsters in the craft shop. The spinsters were not in neighborly reach if you were to count households or shop-holds, but Salem saw them as such. She found excuse to visit the craft shop more often than T-Mo could think to keep count.

The spinsters were ocher-eyed stockies. A yellow-red richness in each set of eyes distracted you from the bodily voluptuousness of their holder. They could well have been quadruplets, how like their countenances, but hair told them apart. Divine's was a shoulder-length black; Glory's was a center-parted chestnut; Sultry's was a messed-up gray; Spring's was a close-shaved auburn.

Character also distinguished them. Divine was a tough one to figure out, often ambiguous in her remarks. Glory was hard as old boots; walked with a big, loping stride while the rest walked like they were saving something, protecting energy. As for Sultry, hers was a gentle heart that held sympathy even for her somewhat vain sister, Spring, whose grace lacked depth.

The spinsters sold buttons, zips, needles, wool, wallets, curtains, lace, quilts, pots, candles, soap, beads and food. Salem, who had cut her teeth on church fetes, quickly discovered sandwiches, watercress cakes and whatnots in the craft shop on her first visit, found hilarity in the spinsters' vociferous opinions of who cooked best.

Sultry made the pumpkin spice drop scones. "Secret to dem babies be de temperature. Chill de bowl, chill de knives to cut dem shapes, chill de milk, de egg, even de butter. Bake dem scones 'til deys all gold; one shade more, one shade less and deys ruined. Frost dem still warm, serve dem still warm, split dem open. Add de cream not too cold, de homemade jam freshly cooked jus' right, an' you got bliss."

Divine made the meringue cream torte. "Secret to dis baby be de ingre- dient. Mix mamma's hazelnut spread wit homemade cream of tartar; whip dem smooth 'til you hide dem bumps, an' you got cream torte."

Glory made the almond honey pound cake. "Ain' no *secret* ingredient to dis baby, jus' de *right* ingredient. Cut whole almonds, cut dem right for homemade paste. De butter, she be unsalted. Dem eggs, deys from free roamin' chickens only. A hard squeeze a lemon, an' you got honey pound cake."

Spring made the fifteen-layer crepe cake. "Secret be *luv*."

"Ain' no thing as *luv* to bake *good*," said Glory.

"A bit a luv ain' hurt none, surely," said Sultry. "And yore secret ingredient Glory ain' hurt neither."

"Secret be *luv* or me name ain' Spring. Line dem bakin' sheets wit' de luv, swirl de batter wit' de luv, use dem fingers wit' de luv, layer de crème wit' de luv, fold her—"

"Wit' de luv," chimed the other three, "an' you got bliss."

"I s-see you use homemade ingredients," said Salem.

"Except Spring," chimed the other three.

Salem was a sheltered girl, not one easy to make new friends. But she tried with Moni, with Trotter, with the craft shop spinsters and found it worked. These friends added to her fulfillment. She held them close to her heart. The rest of the townsfolk were neither quick nor keen to make friends with fresh residents, in particular not with T-Mo. They sensed if not saw his unearthliness. Even Salem sometimes felt the weightlessness about him and at times touched him and felt magnets that were more than chemistry. He was magnetic, moved quick too, mind you a dangerous quick. That was T-Mo. By the time he met Salem, the bark in his skin was obvious but it was the kind that aligned itself with mist through trees to take on new forms. He was to her always a mystery, an ultimate mystery. A grand oddity outside her knowing, more than ever in those moments when jungle replaced the space of rainbow in his eyes.

Those same eyes gazed at you in a personal way, passion and stillness in that gaze, as it measured you and determined a fact about you. The fact stayed unclear to you, and all you understood was acceptance, dismissal or nothing. Those same eyes had considered and dismissed Ike's preacher face the day he said to them: *You are both strangers to me. Get out of my house.*

While Salem wasn't too busy with furnishing to find her pick of neighborly friends, she failed to catch a skip in her period. By the time she discovered that a second and then third period had skipped, she also started to notice how much she had "porked." She laughed at the word. It wasn't like she was eating her feelings—she had never been happier.

The sense of emptiness that had haunted her at East Point was but a bad dream. Still, sometimes she recalled church pews that filled up every Sunday, chimed in her head one or the other song from that not long-ago hymnbook:

Give you thanks, Hallelujah!
My Lord, my Lord.

Her Lord. T-Mo. She smiled.

Attributed her porkiness—again she laughed—to the rarities T-Mo brought home after his wind-swirling flights and descents from a seeming softness of cloud. Salem's appetite was undoubtedly healthier. First time he said, "Back in a sec," he was really back in a second. Appeared suddenly and at speed, bedraggled, but back. He carried a carcass.

"Look out of s-sorts," said Salem.

"Me or the boar?" He laid the meat on the table top. Skinned it, chopped it. "I'm your personal butler."

"Can't wait."

"See how I cook this."

"You've certainly t-talked it up."

His cooking was a disaster. The bisque he served looked and tasted like something filtered through mucky socks. Things floated inside it and Salem spat out something chewy, rubbery—or was it elastic?

"Remembered to pull out intestines?" asked Salem.

"What intestines?" His face a calm stone.

"A whole b-boar. Ruined."

"I know . . . don't. Back in a sec."

A whole five minutes passed. Salem looked at the mantle-piece clock, an antique that wore a face gilded in bronze, two dragons embossed on its body looking at you with lit rubies. With a sigh of wind, T-Mo flew in from the northerly west. Looked wrecked but held out something that was half snake, half fish.

"Needs no cooking," he said. "It's organic by neglect, the work of nature."

It tasted like something an animal had shat.

"You're special," said Salem.

"Special as in: *Class, Jake is special. Be 'nice'?*"

"You were home s-schooled; how would you know what t-teachers say in a classroom?"

"So I am special?"

"I d-don't think your cooking will get any better."

He smiled. "Best I could do."

"We'll have to get more f-food."

"Body's a bit rough," he said. "See the size of that boar?"

"Saw the size of the f-fish snake."

"Not going back out there."

Salem took the remainder of the fish-snake, already it smelt like a moth's nest. She pushed T-Mo out of the kitchen and flew through her cooking. When T-Mo hovered, was a nuisance, she struck him with a wooden spoon. "B-back off that little bit."

Her spread boasted color and taste. She had taken the moths out of its natural flavor, replaced them with a blend of chocolate and spice.

"Whipped up posh nosh, huh?" said T-Mo.

"Exclusive l-luxury," said Salem. "Next it's molecular f-food."

"Mozarella di bufala?"

"N-never heard of it."

A few helpings later, he allowed Salem was a finer cook. Not in those words exactly.

"Right now, I am outclassed," he said.

"R-right now?"

"Yes, today. I'll have a bit more—"

"J-just finish it."

Wilderness ingredients worked well for Salem. She had a knack for meats that were neither beef nor goat nor lamb. She didn't ask what they were; wasn't surprised with whichever texture or essence they presented, even when something she thought might be savory came out tasting scorched-toffee.

"Who's the b-better cook now?" she couldn't resist, perhaps with spinsterly influence.

"I refuse to confirm anything."

"T-taught you quality."

"Through personal embarrassment, yes."

After more feasts—sweet, sour, spicy or foreign—Salem looked at herself naked one day in the mirror, saw her bulged breasts, her swelled belly, and begged T-Mo to stop. But the next time he put daylight between him and the universe, he returned with fruits and vegetables of a kind she had never seen. Like the pomegranate thing that tasted of sweet potato, or the apricot that was actually a grain . . . or the caramel-tasting tomato with agreeable impurities of spice that teased your tongue . . . "H-how much for all that?" she joked.

"Sorry, set price. Don't haggle."

One day he found a plant that soon became an important member of the family. It was large leafed, tolerant, wore tints of scarlet and bronze. Salem placed the exquisite thing by her bedside and named it Red.

By the third missed period, Salem knew it was not a simple matter of being porked so she broached the delicate topic with T-Mo. "I d-didn't see the moon this month."

"Been there all the time."

"The . . . b-birds and the bees—"

"Birds and bees gone where the moon is now?"

"The s-stork . . ." she tried.

"Woman," he threw his hands, "storks don't follow the moon. Have you eaten one?"

"A p-pig more likely. I d-didn't get the cycle . . ."

"Right." The blankness of his gaze confirmed it had found no facts.

"M-my period skipped."

"Right." Still no facts.

"Don't they l-learn you anything in G-grovea? We're having a b-baby!"

His jaw dropped, she panicked. Then he laughed, scooped her. "Are we now? How about that. Preacher's gal zapped by a Martian cowboy."

She pushed him away. "It's not f-funny."

"Best news I heard in years."

SILHOUETTE

· 12 ·

The traveling one, Novic had said. Had he anticipated how the roaming bug might crunch not just into Odysseus but T-Mo as well?

How do I know about the roaming? Ma Space was the daughter of an enchantress born in a family where women became midwives or witches and it ran for generations. *Tssk.* I am not a midwife. I always could ventriloquize and levitate. Found comfort on the mansion's rooftops to escape Novic's rages and needs.

Many times when unseen I found him in his roaming, and I wanted to reach out to my son. Sometimes I imagined our reunion, how it might be. Each time, the bearing of our conversation halted me. My first worry: what if T-Mo did not recognize me?

And I said: "Son."

And he said: "You're mad, woman."

What if he met my approach with accusation or derision, loathing that unfurled in his words: "You left."

"I'm sorry," I would say.

"Look like you mean it," his eyes a prohibition.

"I'm sorry." Pause. "Son—"

"Best clarification right there: son."

I would reach for his hand. "Let's talk."

He would shrug my touch away. "*Talk?* Here?"

"Where else?"

"*You* left."

"A part of me stayed."

"I was a child, a *child.*"

"Your eyes were ancient."
"Why return now?"
"To see."
"See what?"
"See why."
"What, why, when does it matter?"
What if we met and spoke with easiness: easy words, easy eyes of friends?

· 13 ·

Where-am-a-go?

I walked alone to the edge of Grovea past a copse of trees, the rising moon a smear in the sky. In a yawn of silence past a small stretch across a meadow, down a vale, up a hillock—three consecutive vales and hillocks—I came into another canopy of trees that pushed me into an alternate world. Literally pushed me: a low hanging branch touched my bottom and, with a tremor, pushed me out of the blanket of trees into a cascade of sound.

Crowned birds cawed and scratched at the ground, pecked for dusk crawlies and hoppers. A flock of yowlers clouded the immediate sky. Chirpers, croakers, laughers, wailers and rustlers lifted the chorus of that noise and ran with it. I saw for the first time the buzzless—Ma Space had told me about these flies, silent as they were bright—and I was grateful for their non-contribution to the godawful din.

The ground was here and there studded with sprouts of olive grass, the rest of the place bare. I walked along the bare patches, thinking of Weed and his care for plants. To take one life is an outrage; to take two in an instant is carnage. I was shaking those thoughts of Odysseus and his bloodthirst from my head when the ground suddenly humped in the middle of my step. I quavered, felt empty.

Empty and alone in all this world. Where-am-a-go?

The ground at my feet had more heart than I did; it pulsed with something that suggested malice and slowed my tread. Soon as I rested my heel on firm ground, it humped or collapsed and made sure that I fell.

A tree rose from a sudden mist to stand solid a meter away. It was black stemmed and wispy-leafed. Weary with walking and loneliness, I put my arms round its trunk and rested my pounding head. A branch caught me and lifted me to a bough. Ahead of me was a sweep of plain, but my eyes were too worn to explore. My mind flitted back to Nene, Corio, Anakie, Blanket, Norlane and Ma Space.

She drop a baby, not her rights.

Yeah. Our job be pull out her baby, not her rights.

I hated Novic for a whole moment, how his snakelike self stayed stealthy and coiled, striking without notice. How he manipulated things, beings—*who* gave him the right? Thoughts of Odysseus hurled in from nowhere. Where did he go when he disappeared? What if there were other bodies, tidied away or left abandoned for scavengers? I willed my mind to easier thoughts, like the sound of a wilderness full of life; like the sight of the buzzless, silent as they dazzled as Ma Space taught me; like the plain that returned an echo of chirpers, croakers, laughers, wailers and rustlers.

As night closed in, the bloodred moon against a sooty firmament gave this world a mauve backdrop. I rested my cheek against the bough. The tips of the tree's leaves gyrated like dancers. I smelt rain before it poured. I gazed for signs of its onset in the sky and found instead the face of my T-Mo.

He was my . . . rainbow. My spectrum of light in the sky. With T-Mo I felt illuminated, full circle. With Odysseus I felt shadowed, full broken. My eyes sought T-Mo's megawatt smile in the sky but in its place was . . . nothing. I prayed that T-Mo would not harbor resentment of the kind I might guess from Odysseus, whose distance from me had grown day by day into a weapon. I considered the strength, the clarity of his rejection, so flawless. So transcendent it was deadly. What-am-a-do?

I understood now that I never knew how to relate to Odysseus. He never approached me with a need, a request. Never sought motherliness as a child. And he snatched my T-Mo.

T-Mo could turn into Odysseus inside a sentence.

• • •

Odysseus once tripped on his leg at the top of a staircase in the northern wing of Novic's mansion. I was dusting and Odysseus was flicking a penknife with the skill of one who knows the use of a blade. My dusting cloth followed the fine fingers of the balustrade, a glimmering palisade that curled in stable craft and profound refinement, weaving itself ground up to my chambers where

Novic completed his fixations. I had reached a column of fingers that locked into fists to command an elegant post when Odysseus tripped.

He rolled downward headfirst in fetal position, down and down. I flew after him, leaping several stairs at a time down and down. We reached the bottom jointly and I leapt, skidded, avoided a land on his head. My impulse was uncontrolled when I fell to my knees and cradled him to my breast.

His stillness frightened me. I put a finger to the side of his head and found a pulse. I searched his face for evidence of life, and found life. While already I knew that his knowledge about people and their feelings ran on minus, I wanted to know how the boy saw me. I wanted recognition from him that I was his mother. His eyes froze me, pinpoints bright as crystals and lifeless as doornails. Puts a shiver down my back even now thinking of it. Suddenly I was ice—frigid, dense, unclothed.

Without a word he peeled my fingers from his body and rose, crystal eyes avoiding mine. Like my own ice, his touch was frosty on my skin. My mouth opened and closed; no words could bridge what had just happened. First I saw a blur, thought I might faint. *Might?* Like it was a choice! I didn't faint. Then the dusting cloth I had moments ago flung onto the floor so I could cradle my boy—*my* boy?—grew visible until its brightness hurt my eyes.

For want of activity, seeking something to clutch in the place within my arms where I had held Odysseus, I lifted the dusting cloth, embraced it. Odysseus stood. The blade sticking from his thigh came into view. The penknife had stabbed him. He followed the horror in my eyes to the blade in his flesh and the first sound, a rasping sound, escaped his lips. It was a sound of annoyance, not pain. "The hell," tongue click. The casual way he pulled out the blade strengthened my concern.

No blood oozed from the gap. Not a drop of blood anywhere.

I gazed at my hands still holding the dusting cloth. My eyes ran along the lines of its pattern, noticing where threads intersected in a crisscross of white on yellow, noticing where they fell apart. With a cry, I stumbled to the bathroom and retched and retched until I could more calmly breathe, and my impulses were more controlled. That was the last time I dared put a finger on Odysseus.

• • •

I roused to find myself in dawn. Bad thoughts had lurked through my sleep and now tangled my mind with the completeness of the child's rejection—set in stone in a way that physically hurt. Rejection was rejection. Full stop. You couldn't garnish it. I slapped myself to whip it out, that demon of a past taunting me with memories of the day I took an estranged child in my arms.

No rain had fallen.

An arrow of light guided my eye toward morning—shy, uncertain and wooing the sky. I looked down the plain and found in my line of sight a hut full of shadows. I blinked. The hut moved. I blinked again. The hut had moved, the distance surely wrong; far closer this time. As I stared, it vanished. I blinked and there it was again. Even nearer.

I climbed down the tree, kissed her trunk, thanked her for showing me kindness. I did not think Weed's plant whispering had followed me all this way.

As I walked into dawn a cloud churned with malevolence above the plains. The land still fought, shifting its stomach to conflict my tread. So precise the malice of its reasoning, it knew exactly where to find my next step and a calculated hump would upset my foothold. I mislaid my heel and hit the ground. Glimmers on my head just then falling from the sky affirmed the ungodliness of this world.

Rain. Omen or blessing? The glimmers gained fury and madly poured.

The hut was waiting for me. It held no entry and disappeared like a challenge. I realized that I was undrenched in the downpour, water touching everything but me. The hut was now behind me, a sudden door open.

Right on its threshold lay a grumpy tail-wagger, long-furred. A fringe of shiny hair fell across one yellow eye. The beast rose on its paws, snarled. Without moving my face, I returned a throat growl. The animal primed itself to lunge but my second growl found its thoughts.

"I'm not here to harm," I said.

"Not afraid, are we?" it said.

"You have a beard and a mustache but, no. I am not afraid. Where's your companion?"

"You are . . .?" It came close to sniff me. I scratched its neck.

"A friend." She spoke as quietly behind me as she had arrived. She was of fair build, her hair short and receding. Her face . . . I noticed her face the most: the length of it, the brooding in her eyes, the downturn at the corners of her lips. Hers was a kind of face that depressed you to look at.

"Such misery in so youthful a face," she said, mirroring my thoughts of her. You looked at her and you felt sad, old. She walked in a forward slant like she was about to topple. Life sat heavy on her shoulders.

"Here, Ball," she said to the tail-wagger in a sound that was song not misery. The sadness was an illusion, unhurried in its unveiling.

"You are . . ." I said.

"Eccentric, my dear. Completely potty, yeah. My whole family is bonkers." She wore an amulet on her wrist.

We laughed, easy laughter, hers the bring-the-hut-down kind.

She was bare-chested, unashamed of her nakedness. Shells dangled from strings of her sisal skirt.

"It's a bit—" I said.

"Rude barging in like this? Yeah. I got food going," she said.

"What-am-a—?"

"Say? Thanks."

"Giving food to—"

"Strangers? No. Then you must be a friend, yeah." She turned and entered the hut where she stirred stirred a pot on a three-stone-hearth fire that contained sootless smoke. Bark dolls with straw hair hung at a window. I watched them dance upon a creep of wind. A bottle full of pendants stood on the mud floor. Another jar held little turtles, floating upside down and dead in water.

I listened to the silence of the ladle on clay, spoke: "What if I broke this—?"

"Silence? Whatever's comfortable. Talk. Touch. You want a hug?"

We laughed.

The leg of a dead turtle kicked in the jar. The creature came to life, flipped. It dove to the bottom. The other turtles danced alive. A jingle turned my eye to the bark dolls jigging in the wind. One winked at me, another smiled in its sleep—it was the smile of a baby. Another stared at me with the pupil-less eyes of death.

This world meant me no malice but it meant to test me.

Without prodding, over wild boar soup and roots of turtle grass with their transparent membrane, I told Potty about Novic and Odysseus. I spoke of how they always shared something between them: a glance across a room, a brush of cloak past a corridor. I spoke of the heat of Novic's desire, the lightning and primitive kind. I spoke of a visiting high priest from 180C—a land of such beauty it confused the boundaries of propriety and a man could take liberty to covet his neighbor's wife. He was a thoughtless priest whose gaze lingered a moment too long on my face, whose envy sent Novic's mood to scarlet. His rage took out my eye with a scorching poker rod. I spoke of what I had left behind: two little persons—same but different.

She slept on the hard floor, leaving her straw bed for my head. In the morning, she baked river crab.

"But where is—" I said.

"The river? My mother taught me to smell for crab."

When she wasn't swallowed in enfolding laughter, I found dignity in her speech, always finishing my sentences.

"I was a silly little—" I said.

"Thing fascinated with grandeur, yeah. Novic knows how to get into someone's head."

"I never knew—"

"What kind of Sayneth priesting he did. What you came to know was the chaos he bade when he introduced a notion."

"Will it hurt—"

"Every time. Every time you think of T-Mo it will hurt. Until you learn to remember that pain, my dear, is a state of mind."

Although her hospitality had no time attached to it, I knew in the morning that I must leave, that my destiny was elsewhere. I also knew that when I left, time would grow between us for a while.

She gave me an amulet before we parted. It held the face of a rook. "Give you comfort with the shadow self, yours and that of the other," she said. "No ghosts you never want to meet. You can sit in the shadows until you seek to be seen."

Back on guard, Ball the shiny coated tail-wagger lay with a lugubrious sigh by the hut's threshold. He smelt like old ladies. He opened a yellow eye as I passed, like he half-remembered me. A wild wind got up and teased his beard and mustache.

The same wind shoved me as I walked. The hut vanished soon as I reached my friend, the black-stemmed and wispy-leafed tree. I turned and walked toward the rising sun, parallel to the edge of the world. Wind pushed into my face. She whipped at the rest of me, blew at shrubbery until it bent. I staggered. This time the live ground was innocent at my feet, having long determined that my examination was complete. No more humps, or collapses, displaced my tread. A cloud of flat leaves fleeing the wind strayed into my face. I peeled away their frantic kiss and they trembled at the seams but surrendered. I watched them chase away, the wind ardent and close behind.

An eagle called overhead, his high-pitched scream finishing with layered notes. I was no longer hollow inside—thank you Miss Potty—just perplexed about living. And I still questioned: where-am-a-go? Nettles spoke at my feet, told me I was barefoot. I clutched the amulet to my breast, decided to wear it. Lifting my eyes to the now turquoise skyline, I willed myself to levitate.

· 14 ·

I found Miss Potty in every world.

When I set out hunting T-Mo after he went roaming, there she was, Miss Potty, in the lands I visited.

I found her on Earth. She was unmistakable. Always there: her quiet appearance, the life-is-too-heavy walk, the fair build with receding hair. Her face . . . always her face I noticed the most: the length of it, the brood in her eyes, the downturn in those lips. But I already knew the moroseness was an illusion; staring at it, I did not feel gloomy or ancient. I also knew that the bring-the-hut-down laughter was close.

I stayed long enough to learn this world, and its fascinating creatures. Always Miss Potty had a companion: there was one called a jaguar, another a lynx, then a turtle, an owl, a crow, a mustang, a spider, a raccoon, a turtle, a bat. Once she was at sea, riding an orca.

"Tell me—" I started to ask, leaning across the rail of the ship that sailed me.

"About the companions?" she finished. "They bring wisdom. They see roads within chaos. They bring sight that is psychic. They guide you to the unseen. Soul memory—they have it in different forms, depends on the animal. The jaguar is a shape-shifter, he brings no fear within darkness. The orca frees the soul from the body, he controls rainfall on earth. The crow guards a place before it exists, he brings light to dark souls. You, my dear, need a mountain lion to balance your power, your intention, your strength. Most of all, you need him to free you from guilt."

We had an air of ease between us, always, Miss Potty finishing my conversation. Once I saw her in an open-air restaurant in Delhi; she was dressed in an orange sari. *Bhangra Kitchen.* That was the plaque on the stall. Miss Potty sat on the pavement dipping roti into a tin plate that held something the color and texture of mud.

"What's—" I began to ask.

"This that I am eating?"

"Perhaps now I am afraid to know."

"Fear is an art—it is enhanced and holds meaning. Only fools are afraid of curry, vindaloo or chick pea gravy. One of these is what I am eating."

Swinging a playful trunk beside her was a baby elephant.

"Tell me about—"

"This companion? He moves heavy objects," she said. Bring-the-hut-down laughter. She sobered, adjusted her sari. "He understands complexity."

"And the mayfly?" when I met her in Macedonia garbed in an embroidered dress, fully national it included a vest, a collar, a headscarf, red socks and blue shoes. "What about—"

"Him as a companion? He is intense; he lives in the moment."

Of the dingo in the Australian outback, she spoke about loyalty, about understanding silence. Of the goat in South Africa's Jericho, she spoke about sure-footedness, about a quest for new heights. Once I saw her driving a tuk-tuk in Phuket, riding free with her companion: a cock. Or was the cock dinner and the raven soaring behind the tuk-tuk just outside its exposed back the companion?

"No sign—" I shouted as I waved.

"Of T-Mo in this world? Not the tuk-tuk kind, I don't think," she yelled back.

"See you—"

"Again? I hope not," she said, laugh laugh laughing.

Miss Potty. *P, P,* a voiceless sound. Lips together, try to blow air through the mouth, a surge of pressure and the sound explodes.

She was my soundness, my reasoning. She poured on me her wisdom. In her presence my heart calmed.

"Go further," she would say when I was fretful, giving up on finding T-Mo.

"What if I—"

"Find him?"

"What if he—"

"Does not recognize you with that new hair? He is your son. Unless you hoodwinked yourself."

By this time, my hair had turned, the dinosaur on my skin had intensified; and my broken eye had sunk into itself.

"Believe in success," said Miss Potty.

"What does—"

"Success look like?" Bring-the-hut-down laughter. "You will know when you see it."

When I left Novic, inspired by Miss Potty and the exotic worlds she visited, I learnt exploit. I hiked an iced mountain in Siberia, trekked a rain forest in the Congo, strode barefoot across planets like Bianca, Lithium, Tharsus, Nexus, Sic'bel, Sic'defi, Haabains, Fosoids. Even Tiptirons, Solobs, Tafou, the Nether Realms, Hibar, Thierrie, Toguls, Pabs, Pifsers and the Moorlands. T-Mo never forsook my mind through all these escapades. Friends I made new, never found old—nobody I knew or remembered from Grovea came to these lands.

I found my friend Moth in the land of Sic'bel. He scarcely conversed, felt no incline to chit chat. I use "he" to circumvent a "he/she"—Moth was sexless. His voice was sometimes velvet, sometimes full of husk. Freckles, as did baby-soft fur that caught light, peppered ashy skin that matched his eyes, his hair. In a moment of fondness, he caressed the back of your hand and you squirmed—his palms were sandpaper. Moth opened me to the diversity of species. His raised ears resembled clubbed antennae, parted wide to allow a flourishing comb. It was gelatinous, lined with zigzags and swirls. Slender feet supported a sturdy upper body, like the rest of his kind. Moth was a typical Sic'belai—extremely shy, socially unskilled, unable to handle stress and then suddenly affectionate. When I cajoled him from reticence, he would speak of the cousin planet, Sic'defi. Moth shyly described it in his limited language: "Far more than Earth is and sun is and wide cloud is." My description of Grovea left him unmoved.

I found Tambo in the Moorlands when my eyes snapped open to a night as timeless as it was unsociable. The Moorlands were barren, inhospitable, motion in them—let alone barefoot—near impossible. Several times I found a need to levitate. My first sighting of Tambo was all eyes in the black night. When dawn filtered, I discovered her lips were a little rose. Very young looking, she wore a short crop that resembled tea leaves on her head. Her toes she must have stolen from toadstools but they did not deter her athletic sprint. It was Tambo who told me of a place called No Good in the land of Hibaar, where the ground was tough as a whore and filled with a peculiar shimmer of light that came from the north-east.

I found Nuntin at Hibaar, a humpbacked galactic island, its vast ocean of rocky ground speckled with black mountains in the horizon. Nuntin's eyes, white as pearls, sat on the back of her head. Her hair was surely borrowed from steel shavings, pulled forward to make those eyes big, eyes she did not appear to use because she looked by touch. I do not mean to say she could not see; her large fingers probed you feeling (your mouth, your face, your chest), always feeling to know you, fingers clearly shaped in a sausage factory. She took me to the Nether Realms where a neon fire in the sky gobbled the moon.

I found Hunt—his pupils woven from gold dust, hair the color of sunflowers and cut in a helmet—in Fosoids, neighboring the Nether Realms. At first I was convinced that no life forms could flourish in that derelict place, and no wonder—not with the barking wind that felt our approach before it died. But we came across a knot of trees, clustered round like a fence, something of an enclosure, and saw three toddlers in loincloths and legs that waddled. Honey-yellow tufts of hair soft as fairy grass moved with their eyes when they saw us. They were pale, almond-skinned babies, moonstone eyes round as saucers.

"Ma'amm! Ma'amm!" they cried softly.

I gazed at the younglings, endearing and helpless, alone in this place of what-knows, and my heart skipped.

"Ma'amm! Ma'amm!"

I thought of T-Mo who once toddled arms spread, how seeing him opened my heart so he could closet in it.

"Ma'amm! Ma'amm!"

I dropped to my knees and the younglings fell into my arms. Up close, the babies' angelic smiles revealed dimples along tribal grooves on scored faces. The almond skin was not as powder-soft as I had imagined and I was astonished to notice not a set of perfect baby teeth but rows of fangs.

"Ma'amm! Ma'amm!" and the first youngling pulled out claws.

I staggered back, levitated, blended with the shadows long before claws were out for the other two. All three younglings loped (no longer toddled), softly chuckling as they leapt, toward Hunt. From the labyrinths of vagueness, something Ma Space—quite a historian—had told, I understood. Those beatific blue-eyeds were not magnificent babies but Tot'lins, a tribe lost to history.

Centuries since any of that race had been seen.

• • •

The Land of Fosoids was once coveted for its peridot stars, particles of which fell as objects from the sky and fetched money as jewelry. Scholars never understood the phenomenon of falling stars; nor could fathom the vanishing of the Tot'lins, fast, powerful and ruthless, a vanishing that journeyed to the shadowlands of myth. It became a rumor, often contested, that Tot'lins were an evolutionary breed of Moorlanders originally from the land of Solobs—or was it Sepples?—or some other planet that started with S. They colonized lands, annihilated citizens of Breathing Rock, of Random Rock, of the Land of Many Waters, until abruptly the peridot stars stopped falling and the Tot'lins went extinct. Or so history has it.

• • •

I was yet to learn my powers as an enchantress. I knew only to levitate and ventriloquize. My friend Hunt I could not save. Ma Space had only midwifery to show me but that was not my calling, and the amulet Miss Potty had given me, the one with the face of a rook that brought me comfort in shadows, was unusable against the gluttonous feeding that sank Hunt's screams. A leg twitched long after he went silent, then all that was left were his pupils woven from gold dust and a scatter of his sunflower hair on the ground.

I recount this story because it is a memory of my quest and it leads to how I found magic.

The amulet kept me unseen in the shadows until the Tot'lins, chuckling and replete, bounded—not toddled—away. I lurched barefoot into a whooshing wind, my eyes filled with tears, in what seemed like a tall journey to a colorless world that I later understood to be Tafou. While my acquaintance with Hunt was short-lived, the tragedy of losing him in so merciless a manner drew me back to the solitude of my existence, rekindled my harsh longing for T-Mo. The day I walked out on Novic, left my child, I walked out on a part of me: a lung, a kidney, a chamber of my heart.

Each step from Fosoids enhanced the searing in my throat, knifed my heart anew. I found a cliff that had a ledge protruding like a tongue above a howling bowl of water that sighed and roared, water that bucked untamed. The wind that humped the water also whipped my face, tugged the tendrils of my hair. Giant hearts beat in the stormy bowl with such impulsion, froth jetted up like volcanic ash.

I sat legs down, adangle at the cliff. I wept for my lost childhood, my lost child, Ma Space. Sobs heaved my breast, my ribs felt as if they would crack, but even tears could not scatter the bulk in my chest. When my weeping was done, jolts of fierce hiccups should have thrust me to the roaring jaw, the water's fury, but something stayed me. This water did not want me, the abandonment absolute.

Long after the heaving in my chest subsided but my throat stayed raw, I found another emotion that reminded me of Miss Potty and her reliable laughter. It was then I realized that night was a black wall, indifferent to my state.

I thought how, betrothed from infancy, I never bonded with my brothers. They were just . . . my brothers. I had no special childhood memories to reminisce about, no clear names to warm my heart. My siblings remained a blur wrapped in a noun: brothers. *B* a soft sound, lips closed. Small *r* with a strong tongue; a tight throat, no trill—just a straight sound. Even the *th* is smooth not popped, tongue just behind the front teeth. Brothers. That is what they were to me, situated sounds. Rusty, Hedge, Dash, Kit, Blaze, Footloose, Bluey, Tiny, Boxer and Donzo. Not objects like doors or windows or chairs because a door or a window or a chair has a reason. I had no reason for my siblings, and they had none for me except when they took advantage of my being the youngest. *Bring me, give me, fetch me, get me* and *sod off* in the end. That's the little I remember of them. They also wrangled, boxed, wrestled with each other, never me, because unlike me they were free to childhood. Destiny did not hand-pick them from a cot.

Novic, he was my destiny. I remembered the glow in his eyes when we were wed, how he measured me, black gold in his eyes. Did he wait to consume me, consummate the marriage (such fury in his taking), out of respect for Ma Space? Or was it so no one could accuse him of being a child taker? I remembered the pale champagne of my wedding dress, its intricate folds, delicate draping, floaty fabric light as air. Ma Space beside me put a hand to my shoulder, guided me to my spouse at the altar. It was the beaded straps on my shoulders, not Ma Space's touch, that burnt.

I should have felt beautiful inside those crisscross threads that left my back naked, inside that empire waist so tight I could feel my heart and my throat. The gown was designed to give curve to my boyish frame before birthing gave it form. A train of silk fell down my back past the invented curve to conceal my bare feet. At the altar, Novic eye's swept from my feet up the pleat and sequin embellishments, rested at the padded breasts, then up a bejeweled neck collar to find my trembling lips. Our eyes never met.

Never before had I been the center of such attention. Even Ma Space glowing in her green crepe and a gold belt did not command the eyes I got. Another priest from 180C sanctified our marriage. It was the same thoughtless priest who returned to visit and took liberty to covet me, and a demon flowed out of Novic—he put a sizzling rod in my eye. The Novic I wed was a priest and a demon, one entity. A creature of the kind to throw a grenade, and do so without curiosity or bemusement, just potent oblivion to the aftermath. Someone else would be curious, excited, scared. Not Novic. Outside the oval windows of the temple, soft rain gentle as a dove gave way to a thing of monstrosity that clasped hands with thunder and clapped and roared its way from the clouds straight into our hearts.

Legs dangling, tear-washed eyes peering into giant hearts in the water, I wondered whether I was ever anything to Novic, the lustful brute, anything more than a soft pleasure with a womb. I remembered how at first his distance when he did not crave me was solid like a club until I learnt to be solid back and match it. I pondered my life and the lacking, the absence, the missing initiated by the vagueness of Ma Space, sustained by the absence of Runaway—my migrant father unable to match his new sanctuary, amplified by the disjointedness of my marriage, sealed by the puzzle of T-Mo and Odysseus. Miss Potty, she understood the missing. She taught me with her dependable laughter and offhand words to reorient myself, to unpick the solitude and embrace it, to untether the pain that was a need and revive it to a fullness that was enough.

There, right there, on the ledge, I finally unhooked from my past, resituated myself and found a place complete inside me. So complete that I ignored the warmth on my nape, the waft of shifting smells around me, the crisp thinking in my head that drowned into formless thought. So complete that when a shadow stirred to my left and grew more shape until I saw her where she stood, a tall figure one and a half times my length, a tot on her hip, I ignored the apparition. I curled on the crag, closed my eyes and slept to a scent of storm, to a darkness that no longer felt foreign.

I woke to waters now mute, to a colorized world alive with chirruping, squealing, groaning. I cast an eye to the night's howling bowl—it was calm. A rainbow of fish, a magnificent brilliance in their sidewise eyes, swam in the waters below. Rock stumps wearing the faces of gargoyles guarded the water's edges. A stunted tree, also on the edge, climbed giant-like and I could touch its leaves from the ledge. Above, the sky was an azure sheet and a flock of butter-colored birds followed another flock of striped birds. Out yonder, a volcanic mountain coughed smoke above a labyrinth of trees into a rising sun.

And there she was again, to the left of me, a tall figure with a tot on her hip. There was something unforgettable in the ridges and contours of her thinned face, calm lips, flat nose, and her nakedness that was as natural as dawn. I moved my eyes from breasts perched perfect on her chest and found her gaze that went and went into my soul.

Without planning to do so, I found the child's eyes and felt no heart-wrench. Because he never relaxed his eyes he *did* remind me of T-Mo. This baby had wide, never-blinking eyes on a pockmarked face, eyes that were white as white and full of snow. Despite his stare, his body was playful on his mother, hands clasping, legs flexing, chin dimples dancing, mouth forming sounds and shapes. A flutter-fly startled then amused him, he burst into big laughter that finished with squeals and a hiccup.

My gaze returned to the tall woman, who also had a pockmarked face. The pupils in her eyes were full of pulses, diamond dust in them. Her dark skin glowed as if reflecting the sun. There was a dignity about her, in the set of her jaw, the angle of her chin, even the way she held Baby. A well-shaped elbow hooked Baby to her torso. The texture of skin on it . . . such beauty on an elbow . . . Her mouth stayed calm, soft as the diamond dust in eyes that contemplated me, the coveter of elbows. Baby moved his fat hand to clutch in a possessive way the handsome elbow.

Silently she approached, touched my arm. It burnt where she touched, something inside me doing flips. She wore a scent of tree, something oaky, not harsh. And then she smiled. It was a smile that made me think of something exotic, of a mirror full of flowers, of Miss Potty and her exotic worlds.

Keera of Tafou. She taught me to use magic.

SALEM

· 15 ·

He refused to admit it, but for once, this pregnancy thing put T-Mo out of his depth. At Salem's insistence they went to prenatal: the Tambo Clinic. Quite an eyeful it was, limewashed walls, graffiti all over. It could well have been an artists' hangout. The clinic stood three stores from the pick and shovel museum on Fisk Street. The graffiti on its walls comprised images: an old man's head on young shoulders, lips smoking a cigar, giant lashes on a woman's eyes, a model on a catwalk surrounded by a mischief of rats. It had words in tear-drop art, stamped-art, stained ink art:

> *Peace train for your ride*
> *Conked out, yeah*
> *Staple my fingers*
> *Ghetto is a state of mind*
> *Cringe to touch*
> *Fixin' to mess you*

It had names scrawled rebel style, boasting an artist behind each work: *Con. Plate. Hammer. Willow. Homie. Diag. Anarchy. Comet. Vigil . . .*

As if the graffiti were not enough, the Tambo Clinic had artists for practitioners. The doctor who ran it had a sentence for a name. He was a man with a goatee and a pair of bright shoes, and his smile was all teeth. Miss Louden—the nurse, the midwife or both—was a gypsy with big everything: hair, scarf, earrings . . . She touched Salem with worker hands, poked her with busy questions: *Last period? Miscarriages? Abortions? Genetic conditions?*

Salem looked at T-Mo.

In a room labeled "Birth without fear," Miss Louden prepared tools for screening. She wanted urine, didn't want stool, charted height, weight . . . She was slow like a sloth in her examining but prompt as a sneeze in her lifting Salem with strong arms onto a hospital bed. Firm hands (big) pushed aside Salem's modest hands but the examination turned out to be fully external. A slow rub of gel, now she administered ultrasound.

The waiting room enclosed more artists: a teen toying with a purpled braid across her shoulder, her bare midriff branded with tattoos; a boyfriend with loud sunnies—looked the type who wouldn't talk until Christmas; a very pregnant woman with skimpy shorts. The woman with shorts made it her mission to size up T-Mo. So he prowled the room, then took himself to a window. He stood watching outside. Tilted his face to the wind, stood there, a presence you couldn't ignore. It wasn't the length of him or the honest shoulders or eyes that offered up little on a face that shouted scars. Perhaps it was the liquid in his motion, the oddity of his stillness. He was a radical man of extremes. Whatever it was, it made people edgy and they yammered, like the woman in shorts now did.

"Eatin' fer three," she said. "Twins secon' time. Deys hungry all de time. I eats eggs, chickpeas, popcorn—it got de fiber. Walnuts—deys allergy feed, ain' givin' dem dat. You an' yore missus: new folk?"

T-Mo's gaze stayed level.

Inside a private room with a poster that read "Bellies to babies," the gleeful doctor whose name was a sentence confirmed what T-Mo must have known. The bub Salem carried was not a tadpole of a thing but something big and moving, by human standards it was growing triple rate.

Listening, T-Mo's gaze shifted. His eyes glowed.

· 16 ·

Salem wondered: other than the obvious, how much role she had in getting pregnant. You know . . . how a thought planted, you fantasized about it, then your body acted it out? She had wondered how it might be having a child with T-Mo close to the months it happened, then it happened. If she hadn't nurtured the thought, she pondered, would she have porked? Again laughed at the word.

Baby kicked any time, dusk or dawn, T-Mo touched Salem's belly.

He forebade her from drinking tea, anything fizzy, whatever thing liable to bring headiness.

"How w-would you know what pregnant people should or shouldn't d-drink?" protested Salem.

"I know."

He went all jumpy if she approached certain mollusks or fish, in particular the fish snake. He was fully picky with his wilderness treats. Still came and went, an object in the sky, flying at speed from stillness to return with hover and a sackful. Sometimes he flew east until out of sight, and Salem would watch from the patio as something pulsed in the sky, changed color from cerulean to bloodshot. Sometimes he flew out in a flame that made static noise, like the one some electrical things made, then he streaked out, formed an orb and disappeared. But his modus operandi was speeding out in spurts, taking off fast and leaving no tail in the sky. When he flamed out, his whole body blazed like burning cotton, and suddenly—without noise or lights in the sky—he reappeared with "soul food" as he called it. Things like jolly berries from the Nether Realms to indulge her cravings.

He stayed discreet, reflective, each visit to the Tambo Clinic, when Miss

Louden talked them through Salem's exercises, including the breathing ones. The doctor with sparkles in his shoes, whose name was a sentence, made sure baby was maintaining the rush to grow. Salem, amenable to most things, would hear nothing of testing the bub for genetic abnormality when the cheerful doc suggested it.

"Abnormal?" She cradled her belly. "Something that k-kicks like this?"

The baby was alert to T-Mo, communicated all the time with him from Salem's womb. When he spoke, a limb stretched in his direction. The devotion was reciprocated. Never minding carpenter Zok, T-Mo built a rocking chair and matching medicine cabinet for the nursery.

Salem, who by now felt more than porked, her body was a dumpling, protested: "The child has your constitution, why plan it to be s-sick?"

Pending fatherhood sometimes befuddled T-Mo. He frazzled over the color of the nursery, the furniture to put in it, the diaper pail that worked best . . . It didn't help that Salem's new friends, the neighbors, visited multiple times and brought with them multiple opinions.

"We bake good," announced Sultry, holding out a sweet whiffed hamper. "Couldn' have did a better job. Dem spice scones make de baby boy."

"But I'm not h-hungry," said Salem.

"Follow yer hunger woman," said Glory. "Honey cake make de baby boy too. Sweet food for de boy; savory food for de gal."

"I don't m-mind a girl."

"First boy bring luck."

T-Mo fumbled around the neighbors, was too discomfited to pick out details on their faces, to determine a secret fact about each of them. To one or the other he said the wrong thing, stated the obvious. When the spinsters came to gift Salem with new baking "for de boy," T-Mo got everything mixed up. Thanked Divine for her pumpkin spice scones, Sultry for her meringue cream torte, even mistook Spring for Glory.

The spinsters ignored his discomfiture, made themselves at home: they ransacked Salem's kitchen, confiscated the melons.

"You silly or bluffin'?" said Glory. "How you gone push big baby head if you gone eat melon?"

"She got baby brain. Clear mind out de window."

"Good thing she ain' got squid in de kitchen," said Divine. "It twist de baby cord."

"Why you talk 'bout squid, bring bad luck?" said Spring.

"Yeah, we all knows it twist de cord!" said Glory.

"I jus' says she ain' got none—how dat bring bad luck?"

Having settled that quarrel, they ran Salem a bath, nearly drowned her with opinions:

"Secret be de temperature."

"Water bath too hot, it burn baby lips."

"He get cleft lip."

"Burn baby bottom too."

"He get witch mark."

The other neighbor Moni—Petrolhead's wife—also had ideas about the baby. "Stomach dat low, she a gal. See how down de belly button sit?"

As if the looks they gave her were not enough to shut her down, the spinsters gave a good go at more:

"You dumb?" said Glory.

"Been drinkin' more like. Belly button sit like boy," said Spring.

"Stomach dat low be nothin' but Salem holdin' farts," said Divine.

"Let deys fart go, gal," said Sultry.

"Shoot dem out."

"Hold an' de burn give baby de mark."

"Burn big as dey farts you hold."

"Worse'n cleft lip."

"Worse'n witch mark."

"C-calmer you are, the better," suggested Salem to gentle Moni who the spinsters had managed to ruffle.

The spinsters were not a cheap laugh; could be funny but their words carried loudness and opinions, as well as bite. No wonder Moni found reason to escape as soon as they arrived. "Might push out now," she'd say.

Trotter, who was always smiling it up, surprised Salem. She couldn't tell if he was a pal or a pervert when he looked at her fat stomach and said, "Kin I haves a feel?"

First time the spinsters visited, they gave themselves a tour of the house. Found Red the plant, even saw with loud bewilderment that squeezing a leaf made it sing.

Ye la freak squeak ma leaf
Buttons cartons pots bored
Spinsters sweetsters freaksters
Ye la freak squeak ma leaf

The plant seemed to know something about its squeezer. Chimed about kindheartedness for Sultry, bigheadedness for Spring and a tune that went *"Ol' boots hard as boots"* for Glory.

When the spinsters stood to take leave, T-Mo fumbled with doors, mumbled, "Leaving us for the shop?" like it needed an answer.

When they were gone, Moni Catch returned with those A-list eyes, emeralds shimmering in her pupils, and helped with household chores so Salem could rest.

Trotter, bless him. He had a cousin with a face full of beard who was an itinerant peddler. He unwrapped from a boxful of boxes diapers with a pee pee bell, a fanned stroller, a set of feathered britches and a reusable burp bag.

For all preparation, the baby did not wait for a neighborly visit before it started pushing down, come out say hello. Birthing a baby would be a simple thing, you would think, but it wasn't. Breathing exercises . . . who did that breathing when the pangs hit? Wasn't time either to practice how the nurse, Miss Louden, positioned Salem to lean on a birthing ball, to rock and sway the baby down the birth canal. No time for T-Mo to use the rolling pin (a spinsterly gift), roll it up and down gently on Salem's lower back to ease her pain. No time for the rice sock (a spinsterly tip), frozen for when Salem got hot.

T-Mo soared mother and child (head crowning) to the Tambo. There, the doctor whose name was a sentence enlisted the help of Miss Louden. In the private room with many bright lights and a poster that read "Bellies to babies," they hauled, Salem pushed. She had followed the spinsters' opinions: Salem had eaten neither melon nor squid. But the bub was not easy coming out. Doc inserted curved tongs, cupped the head. Yet it was the giant cup that sucked the baby out. For all medical intervening, tongs and vacuums, the bub refused to breathe. Gave cause for doc to administer vigorous stimulation. Profound slaps on the bub's bottom, on its heels, stirred nothing, even repeat upside-down dangles. Nurse Louden held it by its feet. The doc rub rubbed with two hands like how you kindle a fire . . . But this was no ordinary bub; it needed T-Mo to call it. He said, "Wakey, young'un," and the baby coughed, spluttered to life.

T-Mo had told Salem the story of how he was born looking all beautiful: big brows, full lips, smooth skin. His bub when it was plucked was all squished, looked a mess. It resembled a fur ball that a monster had spewed. Unfurled, rubbed and dried, turned out that—for all the spice scones, cream tortes, layered crepes and honey cakes Salem gobbled—baby was a blue-haired girl. She did not cry but stared at them, and saw them, one by one with onyx eyes full of curiosity. The eyes settled on T-Mo. With a pleasure-filled burp and a happy squeal, fat legs kick kick kicking, she held out her arms. He scooped her and she purred and kroo-ed on his chest.

And while he knew naught of the making of hair lockets, of the softening of baby bottoms with hydrangea dust . . . T-Mo learnt. Same way he learnt the meaning of a gurgle or a whimper, which one was joy, distress or simply talk.

· 17 ·

Silhouette . . .

I was born in a family where women became midwives or witches and it ran for generations. Keera of Tafou. She taught me to use magic.

I saw the earthly girl in East Point a week before T-Mo plummeted from his roaming. That was before their worlds collided at the IGA.

Salem.

Same S as in Sayneth but this girl was no snake. I thought she would settle him but roaming was his thing. T-Mo was never a homed being, despite seeing the birthing of his young'un with vacuums and tongs. Even got it to breathe, took so long he had to call it and wake it. In Grovea, the right poke in the midrib from a sharp midwife—one like Nene, Corio, Anakie, Blanket, Norlane or Ma Space—the bub would be squealing inside a moment.

The trip to Grovea happened when the child turned four.

T-Mo's face was a calm stone that night at the table when Novic's wives prepared and laid out a feast. Salem's face was something glowing, unprepared for sunset when it happened. She found dusk in the one she called T-Mo. The one whose love for her once lit him more than sunshine. This same one was as deadly as he was charming because in a flash his heart had turned to petrified wood.

Giving context, are we? I speak for myself when I say no words could fix this. Him saying, "My love," over and over in that smothered voice—nothing could fix this. You ask how I know; of course I know. I make it my mission to know, to make Keera swelled with pride at my mastery of ma-gik. I glided through doors, levitated behind an invisible cloak like a leprechaun, saw them all, every single one, watched them for a reason.

Trouble started at the dinner table. T-Mo was suddenly a stranger to Salem. He *jeered her every move, shot a barb for her every sentence. She went silent, as did everyone at the table. Only the cutlery spoke. A crying child, perhaps it was Cassius or Amora—or was it Tor? One look from T-Mo and the crying clipped to quiet, to fog that had entered the room. T-Mo kept up his goading. At one point Novic said: Odysseus!*

A strange word to Salem but it appeared to quieten T-Mo. He retired with Novic to the incense room. Salem took leave with her child to her rooms. When T-Mo reappeared with the stealth of an assassin and a weapon in hand, a bottleful of grog, she was sat on a bed reading a bedtime story. The child was at her feet, hair blue as blue, coal eyes dancing dancing. Myra. M, M, M. I like that sound. I press my lips together, make a circle. M, M, M. Such elegance, such complexity in one so young. It seemed, very much it seemed if I remember this right, that Salem looked up one moment, saw T-Mo, and a flicker touched her eyes.

Was his act a pulse of drunkenness, or was it bedevilment? The man Salem knew, thought she knew, was at speed by her bedside same time as the bottle crashed. She paused, mid-sentence in her reading, as he jerked her arm and the book fell. Her hand was tender on his chest, her look gentle. And she said, "Please, no." Perhaps a cloud of sadness entered the gentle look when he groped her, when he ripped her garment to bare her tit. Her lips parted as if to speak to him lightly but it was the child's, not Salem's, sound that came. The child's face went all wrong, her arms gnarled. The sound formed shape on her lips before it came, and when it did it was animal. It was the guttural howl or scream of a creature. It trembled windows, made my core freeze.

Before I could do something—I couldn't let him take her, rape her in front of the child—I saw Novic. My chant was already forming, its spell swirling to blind T-Mo with a burst of light, to cast paralysis upon him, to unmake his intent, when Novic arrived in a pummel of gust. He stood by the doorway, eyes ablaze: Odysseus!

T-Mo went still for a moment. His whisper of horror turned to rage. Then he fell to his knees, put his head in his hands and looked broken. "My love," over and over he said in a stifled voice. Salem knelt by him, pushed his face to her breast but her expression was flat as a pretzel. Tension never left her neck so you knew something was working inside that pretzel. You had to guess, could only guess, how she . . . mentally explored, interrogated territories of cause, found something or nothing to explain it.

"My love," he said one last time, before he was no more able to speak. A spell of silence had homed.

Salem's head was tilted, her eyes fixed to a distant place. There was no definition in her gaze, no heave in her gut, no kick in her chest, nothing to tell you of her state. Finally she faced him. "Delusion—," she chose her phrasing. "We—all s-snap at some stage."

Novic had a shining for the child; perhaps it was something in her adventurous spirit. Or was it her restless spirit? He took Myra, lifted the skinny thing, her face puffed up with temper, her clumps of sapphire hair damp with tears. She closed her eyes on his chest and slept long after he tucked her, slept three whole days. The image will not leave my mind; it repeats in slow motion: Novic walking barefoot on bottle glass, robes and hair flowing. He scoops the child, presses her face to his mane. He is tall as tall, walking, walking away and away from me, like always.

What-am-a-say? Played us all, Novic, like a masterpiece. Was all his doing; he created this. Odysseus was his finest art. How could you look at T-Mo without wondering if whosimawhotsis was gonna show?

Ninth year of T-Mo and Salem together, that's five years and a four-year-old child, T-Mo was gone. That night in Grovea, he resembled a man who'd lost all cards. The loving he tried to show afterward didn't last more than a month because the spark where it came from was already dead. Same month they returned from Grovea to Yellow Trek, he fell ill. How? You should ask, "Why?" Don't you see? Something in him had clogged, perhaps dissolved. Something had surely shifted. Was it the entrance of his new hate? It was the kind that came with knowledge that he would never be free while Odysseus lived, that those he loved would never be safe as long as Odysseus was. What was it like to know, I wonder. To know that Odysseus didn't come in pockets; that he arrived full gear. Same one—two people. Novic created this. When T-Mo vanished from a sickbed, people took it he had died, disbanded as an otherworldly might.

The night he took off, before he took off, the child—unable to appreciate an immortal father's disease—threw a tantrum. First a shimmering of tears, then a tantrum that came with belly sound. When she calmed, she kept vigil by his bed while her mother slept. At the child's first nod, at a hint of sleep nudging her eyelids, he was gone.

Disappearing like that, he put the earthling, Salem, in an impossible position. Didn't matter that the child they begot proved that T-Mo, when he was that age, wasn't the fastest being. Much as T-Mo had done, when the child mastered the art in her feet, it was startling how fast she moved. Coal-eyed thing had bursts of liveliness, surges of strength, left her mother curious, excited and confused. But leaving a woman with an exceptional child does not excuse the abandoning. In her hooking up with an otherworldly, Salem had sacrificed much. In his breaking loose from the human, T-Mo had fragmented much. He left behind a fragile thing, an already orphaned one. Broke it, left it worse than when he took it. T-Mo had exploited and then protected, seduced and then destroyed. Had discarded a thing most precious.

Poor girl she was beside herself. She moved around the house, putting her hands on anything he had touched. She just wanted to feel, and he was everywhere. In the cushions, in the throws, on the dinner sets, inside the quilt . . . He was in her bath, in the lighting of the house. Beside herself! But panic is a state of mind. What mind do you get when a man takes off at the height of your love, leaves you standing with a ditch in your heart? Turned out that what was simple and complicated was complicated through and through. Worst was the death he faked. And she was quick to believe it. There was no body. Without a body, how do you prove death? She buried an empty coffin. How could she not? She had nothing else to believe. What but death could vanish a man who had once looked you in the eyes, measured you with his own eyes that teemed with wilderness? A man so enamored that his heartbeat said you were profoundly beautiful. Whose lips once said, "You are the one for all of me."

He felt right but was wrong on many levels. He showed her the art of living without the weight of time. Imprinted, rather than showed, how to live a timeless living. He snatched a good person and took her to hell. Imagine what it took for her to leave East Point, to cross the boundaries of what she knew and, with fear, enter a new world she didn't know: his. Even while uncertain of the fate for her it offered. When he left, the weight of time slammed itself upon her. She loved him, loved him, so much. She hated him.

News crept like winter fog. On a day colder than normal the neighbors—Moni, Trotter, Divine, Glory, Sultry and Spring—hands on their cheeks, chests, heads . . . all stood with her as six men lowered the empty coffin into the yawn of a grave. Stood with her to the last (amidst the wilderness of mourners from all over Yellow Trek, people Salem didn't really know but had likely once glimpsed, walked past or smiled at), to the fistful of soil gently sprinkled into a grave on top of the casket. The sound of its falling on wood was an eternal gong. When they led her back to their high teas, to honey cakes and crème tortes and whatnots (someone even made cricket pizza), none of it could go down Salem's throat. Because by then she was speaking in tongues:

Ahmm-bralla-gaither-malu-theologa-umber-trivo.

Pla-ci-te-reciter-spiriniu-printa-go.

Sounded like nonsense but it carried meaning. Her friends, the neighbors, understood these were not words of exorcism or something of the Holy Spirit. These were words, as Salem's tears flowed, that only T-Mo, if he were present, not the Lord, would understand.

Salem wept for Pastor Ike, for Pageant, for East Point and all of Yellow Trek. Then she found silence inside her scream. The explosion of tongues, all that weeping, diminished. An impossible calm took its place.

Dissolving from her life as promptly as he had appeared left Salem parentless, homeless, for what was home without T-Mo? She found herself repeating history. Like me, she had a boulder inside the gap in her soul. Like me, disaffected, no goodbyes. She put one leg in front of the other, leg leg away away . . . from anyone, anything she knew. Left with qualms those neighborly friends who amplified her fulfillment, her definition . . . in the hitherto quiet comfort of Yellow Trek. She clutched in her hand the fist of a charcoal-eyed child who in infancy appeared better able to fly than walk, who never stopped riding on water or wind, unafraid and in her element with nature. A child whose face and hands went all wrong and whose sound trembled the world when her temper flew.

Unseen, I stood with Salem at the bus stop in Yellow Trek, different one from my first seeing of her in East Point. She tried to look independent, determined. But she was unchanged. Salem . . . she was that caliber of woman who never knew, never said, could never say, "I am strong. I am woman." What-am-a-know? Let's talk about this. I was there, in that caliber, once. What might that be, to be strong and woman, I wondered, until the answer came, and I left Novic.

Later, Salem would find a man to sell the house in Yellow Trek, sell the soft-top and split all proceeds four ways: Moni, the spinsters, Trotter, Salem. If the neighbors did wonder about their liberal benefactor, Salem was by then far away in a future where the past was too raw to visit.

At the bus stop in Yellow Trek, she stood unchanged: same pulse of fear, same uncertainty . . . Like me, she found connection with a plant that touched her ankle. Mine had been a dwarf plant that crept all the way to hug me the day I left Grovea. Salem's was a potted plant named Red. It stayed close to her foot, to her present and future. She was no longer bubble-wrapped in sermons and church fetes, no more clad as a nun like the first time T-Mo saw her in the IGA, but still wearing a tremor on her lip and those large brooding eyes. She, who was defined in terms of others, who perhaps had no core . . . a tragedy already without everything else . . . Salem, same S as in Sayneth. She needed padding from the world. No wonder she picked the first blockhead she saw.

SILHOUETTE

· 18 ·

Peaches, his name is Peaches. *P*, the sound is voiceless, no vibration in the throat. Lips together, you mean to exhale. You build pressure inside your mouth, lips together still, you exhale and out comes *P*, an explosive sound. Like the *P* in Miss Potty.

Baby is a loose bundle in his crib, limbs everywhere. Peaches folds and unfolds in his sleep. He coos, babbles, grunts, squeaks. Sometimes he sighs. He is never fussy, his cry a rare thing. When he wakes, he likes the outside barking of rosellumus birds: *Gwa! Gwa! Gwa!*

Gets himself into a sitting position in his crib, pulls himself to a stand, walks holding the rails toward the sound. Head aslant, his ear is keen to catch the twitter of birds. Gleeful, head bobbing, he imitates: *Ga! Ga! Ga!* Takes a few tries for his throat to get it right: *Gwa! Gwa! Gwa!* If it is a Koolah bird, he crawls forward on his belly, copies their lazy amble, croons like them: *Koo-wee-oo! Koo-wee-oo!*

He understands each bird, the sound it makes. When I say: "Look, Peaches, see the rosellumus!" He looks at the tree, points with a finger to the right bird from a flock, makes the right sound: *Gwa! Gwa! Gwa!* "Peaches, the Koolah bird!" He gets into a sitting position, imitates: *Koo-wee-oo! Koo-wee-oo!*

When Keera lets me, I take him further out close to the volcanic mount so we can bounce echoes off the hills surrounding it. When we mimic birds, an outcry from the birds roars back, bounces in echoes.

Often you forget he has no brows because his eyes command everything on that face. When I first met him, took me awhile to grow accustomed to this child who never relaxes his eyes, who reminds me without heart-wrench of T-Mo. Having left my own child, I search but cannot find reason to close myself from this baby. Sometimes he creeps on you silent as a startle; tickles him silly when you jump.

I adore his liveliness. One minute he is crawling forward on his belly imitating ground-worm play, next he is proceeding with purpose on hands-and-knees to find insects, finger-feeds himself fallen wings before he hunts the hiding critter. He finds it, lifts it to his face, but if it is an inedible kind, Keera—ever watchful—reaches him with a few long strides, knocks his fist from his mouth. "*Naw get!*" He understands the warning. Another baby might pucker, howl. This one, happy chappy, looks at his mother with those white as white eyes full of snow and, unruffled, his mouth forming vowels and syllables, begins to test sound: *Ya ya ya. Tey tey tey. Ne ne ne. Po! Po!*

Sometimes I show him pebbles and hide them so he can find them, which he does. Squeals of glee that finish with a hiccup, he holds up his find. *Peb! Peb!* he cries. "You don't say," a shine in my voice. Keera sweeps a glance at us from her hoe, her smile sunny with flowers.

She is good with her hands. The little pocket of land where she lives has volcanic soil rich in nutrients. You can see speckles of calcium in the black. Her hut sits in a cleared patch in a tangle of forest. She hoes, digs up roots for feed, snips off shoots for cure. The day we met on the crag, when she approached me, touched my arm and it burnt, she pointed somewhere in the distance where the sky met the earth in a line of orange fire and I understood that there, right there, was our destination.

"Keera a Tafou, this my name," she said.

"Keera. *Tssk.* I like this sound."

"Keera a Tafou, *this* my name." Her gaze that went and went into my soul. "You name?"

"Silhouette of Grovea."

"Sil-oo-ate." She took a stick, scratched a map on the ground and pointed: "Grovea." Pointed south of it: "Tafou." She looked at me. "How you speak my tongue?"

I met her eyes, something vivid and moving inside them. "I wonder."

"Sil-oo-ate."

"Silhouette."

"Sil-oo-ate. What this?" The amulet.

"Magic."

"You . . . ma-gik?"

"I was born to it but I must learn it before I can use it."

"Me ma-gik—I learn you."

She was out in the garden and I was inside exploring my new habitat, being nosy to be honest, when on a shelf in her chamber I found a book of spells. It was old as a curse. There was no doubt what it was because it said in bold silver on the ebony cover: Book of Spells. Was it something in me, perhaps the amulet I wore, that allowed me to read this language? Already I could hear it when Keera spoke to me, talk back in it when I answered.

I felt eyes on my back, turned and found Peaches, a question in his gaze, or was he waiting for me to say something that would make him giggle? Keera was between us in a wind. She retrieved the book of spells and said: *"Naw get!"* She had no concept of time, nothing was rush, so to her I was an impatient apprentice.

Today she crouches at the edge of the water bowl near the crag, Peaches on her hips. She peers into the giant hearts. Her palm slips into the froth and lifts out a writhing tail that finishes with the head of a fish. She places it in a bucket bedded with weeds whose scent knocks the fish out of its writhe in seconds. She peers back into the giant hearts, slips her hand in and pulls out another fish. Her favorite is the rock mullet, its scales large as her thumb. Sometimes she pulls out a fish, strokes it with a prayer, returns it to the water bowl.

"She no good, sick."

"How can you tell?"

"Eye tell a disease. This fish cloudy eye."

She pulls out another.

"She good fish, lively eye. It skin shine too."

She shows me I can close my eyes and tell a good fish because smell matters. A healthy fish smells faintly of seaweed. A sickening one is strong, fishy; you feel it and its scales are dry and gritty. You unclose your eyes and find discolor, sunken eyes, and you know the nose was right.

She puts Peaches to the ground so she can scale the fish. She holds it firmly with a hand, scrapes from tail to head with a knife. But before the scraping, she guts it.

"Inside go rot, spoil the meat."

She inserts the tip of her filleting knife into a small opening at the tail, cuts with her hand through the belly toward the intestines. If the fish is female, Keera unfastens roe from the intestines, rinses it in a separate bucket. Sometimes she fillets the fish, sweeping strokes from head to tail, flip, and cleanly debones it. Sometimes she cooks it whole. Sometimes she skins it so we can later snack on crisped skin rich with smoke and a rub of spice.

"Tell me about the child's father."

"Taken."

"Who took him?"

"His name, Taken."

"Taken of Tafou?"

"Taken a Tafou. Spirit a fire." She mutters a prayer. "He clan a fire. Me clan a land. No marry clan a fire, clan a land. Me defy, he burn."

What-am-a-say? Keera made child with a non-enchanted, a defiance that cost Taken his life—they tied him to a stake and burnt him.

"He clan a fire, come together with blaze. In fire, I see him spread, become spirit, his soul float in horizon. No more touch me but protect me."

The day she spoke of Taken, feeling unmapped from her face. Her countenance went plain. Her eyes did not become a world of hurt as you might expect. She said it matter of fact, like a narrator without personal claim. But Peaches showed interest. He halted mid-crawl, sat silent and faced us.

"They take from me him. Later, much later, secret, I take ash. When they outcast me, ash make land fertile. Taken not deadened . . . Taken"—she beats her chest—"here forever."

Peaches clapped, big laughs that finished with a squeal and a hiccup. Keera went silent, said nothing two days straight.

That night I sat alone at the crag. Suddenly there was a rook and then a panther, gleaming eyes, beside me. "Together we know the dark," they spoke as one. "Death and rebirth, remember this." I looked back and in the distance where the sky met the earth in a line of orange fire, Taken was there.

When Keera broke her silence, she also broke her nakedness. She approached me, garbed in a flowing dress splotched with flowers. She drew me to her chamber. The skirt spread when she sat on the floor, the book of spells between her legs. She caked my face with a scarlet paint, then striped it with a white paint. Her chant, most bewitching, put Peaches to sleep. Light from her lantern danced and cast a circle around us. Our bodies swayed. Keera's chant found my throat so I hummed.

She learnt me the ways of her ma-gik. I can cast a fizz of spit to ward off evil. I can detect lure placed on a thing, and dispel it. I can cast light into a creature to blind it, charm it to obey me. I can protect myself from evil in a barrier. I can hear thought and remove fear. What-am-a-feel? That night curled in Keera's arms, her long frame holding me in a spoon on her bed, every inch of me burnt.

"My name is Silhouette of Grovea," I spoke without sound into her hand cradling my face.

"Sil-oo-ate," warm breath on my neck.

"I am an enchantress."

"Mine . . . enshant-tress."

MARGO

· 19 ·

Folk nicknamed them Fidget and Sprinkles.

Fidget and Sprinkles were born in robust households full of kids. A parent in either household must have decided the secret to a vigorous child lay in throwing the tot out of the house. Neither Fidget nor Sprinkles wanted for a healthy dose of wind, sun and rain.

Ken was Fidget and Margo was Sprinkles. Fidget wore a gummy grin and was the bouncy, animated one—whoosh, off he goes again! Sprinkles wore a head rather big for her. "Skinny-balinki long legs," as Fidget liked to tease.

The nickname Sprinkles came from a lolly with sprinkles at Cindy's Blow Pops down the road, and the name was all about the little girl's big head. Cindy sold all types of suckers, from chewy types to bubble gum center types, hard candy shell types to soft fruit-flavored shell types. Sprinkles preferred sour lollies that came without wraps and sold at half price. Fidget preferred blue raspberry ones.

Despite clear confectionery differences, the children found friendship at the local kindergarten in Sheepwash Creek. Every child but Sprinkles was uneasy with the boisterous little boy in dungarees who climbed tables and roared: "I am a dragon! Put out my fire!" Only Sprinkles neared enough to try and put out the roaring dragon's fire.

Fidget continued to unsettle other kids with his fueled play. Everyone but Sprinkles huddled away, and this was despite the presence of a number of helper mums in the classroom, adults equally bewildered by the boy who must have gobbled a bag of jumping beans.

Soon after she met Fidget, little Sprinkles did not wait for her mother to pour her out of the house. She tumbled out of her own volition, yelling as she raced, "I go play wif Ken."

Fidget's father was a carpenter, and his nimble hands provided mobile objects carved in wood, objects that the children pedaled with fierceness that sent dust and roosters flying. The timber objects transformed as the kids grew older, from tricycles, carts and scooters to wooden bicycles.

Fidget and Sprinkles were competitive in their sportiness. Prize ribbons for cross country, athletics, netball and hockey—the only sporting activities in the local community school—decorated their walls. Neither child went on to secondary school after finishing early learning.

From the time Fidget and Sprinkles were little, folk always joked about the two of them being together and predicted they would grow up (as if that needed predicting) and marry each other. No one imagined that one day they actually would.

Fidget quickly learnt his father's trade. When he outgrew outdoor playing, one would find him gluing, clamping, bolting, drilling, gunning, sawing, sanding, and then some. His special talent lay in softwood. He was deft at making bowls, trays, racks, buckets, blinds, cutlery and toys. In no time he mastered cedar and black walnut, and expanded his crafting to chiffoniers, beds and boats.

Sprinkles had a father who was a landscaper. In time she too picked some of his trade. She amused herself with paving, decking, concreting, water featuring and turfing . . . mostly in other people's compounds for paid jobs with her dad. What she enjoyed most was the gardening. She also loved being out on the farm with her mother. She was diligent in trying to learn her mother's animal whispering and green thumb, and her mother was equally attentive in trying to teach her tomboy daughter these skills.

In time Sprinkles (who by now had grown into her head and preferred to be called Margo) found herself increasingly drawn to Fidget (who was still restless but preferred that people called him Ken). Margo admired Ken's uninhibitedness, his confidence and amusement with life. His coffee eyes were always smiling, and each time you looked his way you became certain he was tripping to release a chuckle.

With her siblings way older than she and no longer living in the homestead, Margo took to discussing Ken out loud with herself. She also conversed about him with her mother's favorite white oak at the edge of Sheepwash Creek. The tree was one of much age and squat appearance, and its gnarled roots insisted on poking above the ground. When Margo sat on its roots and talked to the tree, she was convinced that the white oak thought it was favorable, if not prudent, for Margo to try and kiss Ken. But Margo didn't know how to initiate the kiss. Each time she thought to try and bring her face close, Ken merrily bounced away.

While they still chatted like dear friends, adolescent Ken became gentlemanly with Margo, oblivious to the lusting for a kiss. Their moments alone continued to be seemingly innocent.

While his unreachability kept her hungry, Margo found a new worry: Ken was showing interest in traveling, and his talk conveyed an increasing restlessness. When her mother died suddenly of whooping cough, it was Margo—not her siblings—who inherited the plow, yoke, axe and winnower. She did not inherit her mother's green thumb. Her mother also left her a cased record player with red velvet in its interior.

"I'm sorry about your mother," said Ken.

"It's not like she was in my pocket," said Margo. But she grieved.

Perhaps to distract her from her mother's death, Margo's father taught her to drive. One day he simply tapped her elbow, led her to the truck and rolled it into an empty paddock. He showed her how to move the clutch and gear, pointed at the brakes. He switched to the passenger seat and Margo took the wheel. She turned the ignition key. The engine started and the truck jumped and rolled forward. Soon as it began to speed along the dirt, across the grass and over horse poop, Margo's father pulled his seat and leaned backward, put a hat over his face and fell asleep. He opened his eyes when the engine turned off and the truck was maneuvered back into the garage.

"Cracken hell," he said.

This is how they both understood Margo was good with trucks.

With her newfound responsibilities in the garden, on the farm and with the truck, Ken's suitability as a kiss recipient and someone greater became more and more unlikely for Margo.

• • •

One day when Ken was twelve or thirteen, his mother, who was nursing a newborn that later died, was astonished to find that Ken had pulled out all his bedding including the eiderdown.

"What's with the bed?"

He said nothing.

"Accident?"

"Yes."

Later, as she sorted the washing and found no smell of urine, she tackled the delicate subject.

"When boys arrive at your age they get wet dreams," she said.

He said nothing.

"Heard of wet dreams?"

He nodded.

"Your body is forming and it's ready to make babies, but when conditions are not right it shoots out breeding water."

He nodded.

"If the body doesn't shoot out the water, you might hurt some. This is why sometimes boys like to touch themselves. "

He nodded.

"Your father does it. He pulls himself all the time."

Ken fled.

• • •

Perhaps nervous of the babies Ken might make with the landscaper's daughter who drove trucks, his father sent him off to a carpentry apprenticeship with an uncle in Middle Creek.

· 20 ·

Ken loved the apprenticeship, and Uncle was generous in his teachings. But Ken was torn because he also loved the moments when he came home to visit. It was no surprise that, when he did visit, he and Margo found themselves together in her barn, their backs on hay as they faced a corrugated iron roof that wailed when it rained.

One afternoon he reached for a straw of hay, put it to his lips.

"What shall we get to?" he said.

"I've got a few ideas," she said.

He was not discomfited when Margo's conversation meandered into prattle about their future.

"Lots and lotsa kids," she said.

"Four," he said.

"Lotsa them."

"Four."

She jumped and faced him. "Seven."

He took her face in his hands and kissed her.

• • •

They tied the knot a month later in the same barn, decorated with blues and yellows.

• • •

Ken's father allocated his basement as temporary housing for the couple.

The night of their wedding, Ken made music with his hands, chanted while Margo danced. She moved her body freely, but froze when he took her in his arms and unzipped her gown. For the first time in their lives they found themselves awkward with each other. But Ken's playfulness steered them out of the odd moment and drove them into a merry jousting that culminated in a rubbing of toes.

It was on the second night that the couple discovered a giving and taking that left their bodies pulsing. It was as if this was only a beginning. Indeed, satiation quickly peaked to a new hunger that intensified to a necessity.

The baby making when it started was a playful curiosity. While the couple wrapped and unwrapped themselves in linen, as they giggled and grunted between sheets and the softness of the eiderdown, they began to speak of the seven children they would raise.

"Four girls and three boys," said Margo.

"Four boys, three girls."

Three miscarriages later, they started to lose their fun. Thermometers crept in as a precursor to their play. Ken discovered that Margo was at times agreeable, but often when he neared, she clawed at him—unless the thermometer said conditions were right. When it said so, one look from Margo and Ken took her hand, and led her up the stairs.

It was the thermometer that also said Margo should stop eating corn and spreading butter on her toast. Instead she gobbled ghee, honey, avocado and eggs, and drank nothing but water, raspberry leaf tea and nettle leaf tonic.

"Urine color must be right," she said.

The thermometer also said no beer or smokes for Ken, but more salt to his dinner. Margo also gave him lots and lots of grapefruit juice and insisted he drink it all.

One night after their duty-filled routine in the bedroom, Ken said, "It's a full moon—tried walking on your hands?"

"Now you mock me," she said.

"But you sit on the roots of the white oak, wait for birds to shit on your head. Who really is the mocker?"

"For luck!" she yelled.

She was doing dishes the next morning when she broke down and hurled a plate. "It's all your fault," she sobbed.

"Mine? Why!"

"You're not taking it serious."

"But I am."

"I don't think so," she hiccuped.

"Really, I am." And he put his arms around her.

• • •

Without spoken arrangement, Margo started waiting for Ken on the front step of the porch and, soon as he emerged from his carpentry, she took his hammer and put it away. Then she took his hand and led him to the bedroom.

No matter how tired, how could Ken find voice to say no, with grace, to a coupling? He recrafted himself to a new version: dutiful husband.

The heaving bed provoked unease in both, but Margo did not seem to notice. She kept her eyes to the ceiling beyond Ken's head until his duty was done. Their coupling continued to be a simple yet complex experience that left them both dull.

"It is what it is," she said when Ken broached the subject.

"Perhaps we need a plan for the plan," he said. "There has to be a more effective way—"

But she shoved his protest out of the way and rolled off the bed. "Too much thought doesn't make babies. All you'll find is a devil in the detail."

The devil was in the detail—intercourse left them as childless as ever and sticky with distaste. Sometimes when the deed was done Ken reached out a hand, but Margo rolled away.

She agreed to see Dr Ace.

• • •

Margo climbed into Ken's light truck about noon. The truck was perfect blue in color. It was a four-door truck with a tow bar. Ken called it his simple workhorse. Its sparse interior and capable carrier gave no hint of the truck's stubbornness: it ran out of fuel, its gear was shifty and the carriage wobbled. This was a car Ken's father and grandfather had both separately owned, and in all that time no one had thought to fix the smell of burning that rose from within its engine when it ran.

The Shadbolt Clinic was right in the middle of town, off Orion Street. The clinic stood between a bakery (Milly's Crumpets) and a butcher (Sirloin and Shank), opposite a blacksmith's shop (Horseshoe) and the Antique Bookshop.

The odor of alcohol in the Shadbolt Clinic overwhelmed Margo. She counted hand cleansing gels (eleven pump jars) from the doorway, past the reception to the doctor's room. Its sole nurse, who was also the receptionist, wore a white apron and pale green gloves. Inside, all rooms were completely white and blinked with light. All floors shone like silver. A sign on a wall overhead said: "Toilets for use only by patients."

Dr Ace was the only doctor in Sheepwash Creek. He wore braces and rim-less spectacles. He was a general practitioner, and a bone and heart specialist. He was a fresh face from some overseas college and brought along brand new knowledge of unconventional medicine. His client base was largely sporadic, if not outright negligible.

Ken and Margo on their first visit were relieved to find the doctor was agreeable to tackling matters of fertility, and of animals, it turned out. When they arrived he was attending to a sad little boy and his mother, both sniffling over a rabbit the good doctor had euthanized.

"Human behavior flows from three main sources: desire, emotion, and knowledge," Dr Ace was saying to the distraught duo. "These are Plato's very words. You desired for your rabbit to live. Now you show emotion at its death, but you have knowledge that my action today has eased its suffering. This knowledge will guide your future behavior."

When he rid himself of mother and son and got chatting on fertility, he squirted gel into his hands. "Animals matter, " he said. "Did you know that man (or woman) is a civilized animal? Plato said this." He faced Margo and Ken. "Now, what can I do for you?"

Ken explained.

Dr Ace looked at the couple for a moment, hand on his chin. "The beginning is the most important part of the work," he said. "This is what Plato himself said. You have come to me for intervention at the right time."

He prescribed Margo two sets of pills: a bi-colored capsule to swallow with water every morning before breakfast, and a bloodred pill that tasted like beetroot or blood depending on what part of her tongue the tablet touched. Margo was to swallow the red pill three times a day in the week straight after she finished her menstrual cycle.

Ken and Margo had many questions but, before the good doctor could answer all of them, a man burst into the clinic carrying a fur-splotched puppy that had been mauled by two canine brutes.

"Will he make it?" asked the man.

The doctor adjusted his glasses and stared for a long moment from above the rim at the man.

"He is a fighter," said Dr Ace, and went on to resuscitate the pooch. "He will pull through."

"Have you treated many dogs?"

"A good decision is based on knowledge and not on numbers—Plato's very words."

• • •

The bicolored and bloodreds did nothing for Margo. After swallowing pills and regulating coupling for seven months, one morning—it was wet season—Margo and Ken looked at each other across the table.

"Cereal?" she said.

He took the container and poured.

"Milk?" she said.

He took the jar and trickled.

She rose and made toast.

"Butter?" she said.

Their fingers touched in the exchange.

When they locked eyes, something in each gaze was like a mirror suddenly visible, and it reflected the scale of their discord. This was not the life they had imagined. Without words they examined their motives and wondered how stupid they had been. That night they cradled against each other and freely breathed.

"Can't imagine you put up with all that," said Margo.

"The right is always right. Got to know where your bread is buttered."

"Cream doesn't always float?"

"No," he said. "It doesn't."

Longing for each other coursed through them thick as life.

Margo remembered something she had already realized years ago: that Ken, this man who was a carpenter and did not know how to sit on a horse, was her paradise. She could behave young again with him. She offered herself up to him and, in that abundance, by some fooling of fate, or a consequence of it, or perhaps it was trickery, the womb that had closed itself like a solid bean and refused to nurture a child opened itself.

• • •

It was a delicate pregnancy. Nausea, fatigue, heartburn and anemia assaulted

Margo. It didn't matter what she ate. Still, she avoided spicy foods and allowed Ken to cover her belly with ointments from the clinic.

"Ah, salmon oil. Let's rub the tottie," he said.

"Happy tottie," she said, bedroomed on a dark, wet day.

• • •

Three times during labor Margo nearly passed out.

Dr Ace pulled out a pallid baby. Its tiny mouth on Margo's breast had no strength to suck. When Ken put a finger to its nose, he couldn't tell if the tot was breathing, until its ribs moved faintly and its lips parted to let out a faint whimper.

The child's health increasingly failed all the way from the clinic. But at last, at last! There was baby noise in the house. The child would not stop whining.

The tot continued to be feeble. He was colicky and his bowels pushed runny fluid. He turned white when he slept, so white that Margo had to roll a towel and place it under the cot to raise his head. Three months later it was hard to tell whether he was teething or had an earache because he was ceaselessly whining and rubbing his ear. His fingers were so tiny they did not close around Margo's thumb.

He had acquired the indigo in his pupils from Margo. Despite feebleness, Ken couldn't help but notice the startling blue and gray that shifted in the tot's eyes. It would be years before his weak nose and lips gradually shaped to take Margo's handsome form.

By this time all of the child's remaining grandparents had died. The baby was Ken and Margo's problem, no one else's. Matter of fact, Ken was more and more taking on other clients' work from near and far, so the tot was largely Margo's problem. She thought it was a temporary difficulty because, frankly, she and Ken did not think the baby would live. They could not bring themselves, or perhaps, with all the nursing they just had no time to bother, to give him a name. They simply called him Tottie.

For his business, Ken needed a reliable truck that did not leak engine or refuse to start. They sold Nibble, Margo's favorite horse. Gradually they sold the rest of the horses to pay the doctor's hefty bill each time Tottie's health sank.

Twice Margo harbored ugly thoughts of snatching Tottie from his cot and swaddle and dumping him under the white oak tree for the gods to decide his fate. Twice she abandoned the idea. What reformed her mind was less of panic about how she might present the abandonment to Ken when he got home, and more of acquaintance with the maternal tug in her chest.

When the child's stuffy nose refused to clear and he lost interest in eating, only Dr Ace stayed optimistic.

"Of all the animals, the boy is the most unmanageable. Plato said this. I have the very remedy for this champ. Lots of music," he said.

"People will think I am mad!" said Margo.

"Opinion is the medium between knowledge and ignorance, Plato's very words. Plato understood that music is moral law. It gives soul to the universe, wings to the mind, flight to the imagination, and charm and gaiety to life."

Margo wished Ken was present, but he had bought a new truck and was up north in Nuntin Creek, building a house for a client. Bewildered and on impulse, she left the clinic and entered Milly's Crumpets. She bought a rye cob and a few plaits. She stepped into Sirloin and Shank and selected some sausages and ham. She found herself wandering with her groceries and droopy baby into the Antique Bookshop and its dim inner room.

At the counter she approached a young female with braids and purple nails. "Music?"

The girl pointed.

Margo put her baby and the groceries on the floor. She trawled through a box of records and picked out a few labels: classical, folk and something called "progressive."

The drive home was without hiccup—the truck did not stall.

Margo retrieved from the attic the record player her mother had bequeathed her. She took it from its case, lifted the dust cover and set it aside. She positioned a record onto the turntable and played the classical and then the folk and then the progressive music, which turned out to be drums and melodies that built up and troughed.

Tottie ran a new fever in spite of the music. He trembled with chills. He flopped and whined when Margo put him to her hips. When she tried to settle him in his cot, sporadic crying accompanied his disrupted sleep. His forehead grew hotter. Slowly he sank into delirium.

Margo climbed back into the truck with her baby, and this time the car wouldn't start. She opened the hood and found nothing. She got back into the truck, wiggled its gear, tried the engine and it turned over but didn't start running. She took one look at her dying baby, found a plank and hit a piece of metal inside the hood.

As she struck the damn thing, she thought about how comfortable she was with her father's truck. It drove as though she and the truck were one. It understood her intentions and flowed with them. She had only to look in a direction, and the truck followed. She had only to will it to halt and its wheels slowly rolled until they locked to the ground. But this . . . this . . . b-beast of a truck! It roared, it bucked, it charged when it was not in comatose! Now it was taunting her. Now? Now! Her baby was dying. Tears flowed—Margo's and Tottie's. She whacked at anything in the truck that looked like it might be the problem.

Finally when she tried the engine this time it started. The truck jarred forward, shook as it took the road, but it ran. Halfway, Margo stopped and investigated an acrid odor from the bonnet. She lifted it and a blast of steam nearly scalded her face. One glance at her baby, and she jumped back into the truck. The engine agreed to start, but the gear stick refused to move. Margo found a plank by the roadside and hit the gear until it slipped. She drove to the hospital with service lights on.

"We are twice armed if we fight with faith," the doctor said. "This boy is a fighter, and you need to be one too—Plato would have said."

Margo found herself in a room partitioned by glass from another that housed an anemic kitten dying from a parasitic tick. Next to the kitten was a broken-limbed baby goat that an eagle had snatched and dropped.

Sharing her room were two women wrapped in shawls and scarfs. They looked like a mother and her daughter. The women talked recipes over a gray child with a grandmother cough as it lay. Their words floated into Margo's nightmare: *Fold in the egg with a spatula . . . Almond meal in chocolate cake makes it moist . . .* Twenty-two minutes after the child's cough stopped, twenty-two because Margo had counted, a nurse came and pulled a sheet over the child. The women abandoned their recipes and went berserk with grief.

Despite the frail heartbeat she felt on Tottie's neck, Margo panicked each time a nurse approached. Each time she was relieved to find the nurse was not carrying a sheet to pull over Tottie's face. By now Margo was certain she would not walk out of the clinic with her boy.

But she did. The boy refused to die.

Perhaps nudged by his near-death experience, Tottie actually began to thrive. It was then that Ken and Margo decided to name him.

"Vida," said Margo.

"Vida?" said Ken.

"It means vitality."

"In what language?"

"The boy is a survivor."

Vida toddled at the age of four. His joints were tender and his legs started off bowlegged. The good doctor at Shadbolt Clinic gave him chicken bone powder for strength in his feet. He prescribed lime green tablets for his weak heart. The doctor would have continued recommending other remedies but, soon as Vida could voice it, resist it, he declined further visits to Dr Ace. Nothing Margo said or did would nudge Vida to undig his heels.

One day when Vida turned five his dad gave him a chessboard. It was a hand-crafted set, meticulously polished. Ken meant for Vida to play with the wooden figurines as one might play with toy soldiers. He was taken aback when Vida set the chessboard on the coffee table and suggested a game.

"These are knights," his father pointed. "These are bishops. This is the queen. And here is the king." Ken arranged the pieces on the board. "This is your army. And this is mine." He looked at Vida. "Your goal is to get my king."

Vida did.

This is how they both discovered Vida was exceptionally good at chess.

In time, his knees straightened but his body remained frail. Ken took to calling him his "little alien"—an alien because no one in Ken's or Margo's family could possibly have passed on such a doubtful constitution.

Margo, who had never before taught anything but lettuce, cabbages, chicks and foals (she taught them to grow, and they grew) took to homeschooling.

· 21 ·

Pale-complexioned, frazzle-haired and completely sport-poor, Vida sometimes believed it was true: he was an alien. His fragility rendered him unminded when he was not being homeschooled. He noticed how his parents handled him gingerly, as if he was a hummingbird's egg and they were frightened he might break. True, sometimes he played chess with his dad. But those games were only at night when his dad got home, because Ken worked all days through weekends.

Vida became the boy who played alone. He forged friendships with lettuce and cabbages in the garden. He befriended the white oak tree and its birds at the edge of Sheepwash Creek. Often, surrounded by a friendly tweeting, he would put his arms around the tree's waist and listen to what he chose to think was an alien colony inside the tree. One day creatures would emerge and the rest of the world would dissolve around him in embryos of light, he determined.

At night from his bedroom window he would look closely at the stars, and search for kindred spirits. He would roll his eyes toward the heavens, roll them far back as he could until he found a pulsing black star north of his eyeball. Sometimes he saw a creature inside the star, a creature that was nothing but eyes on a float of brains.

What if, he often wondered as he took his breakfast, what if the clock on the kitchenette wall stopped, and fluorescent beams entered the house, a magnetic field surrounded his parents, and unconsciousness took hold of Vida until he woke up to find himself cushioned in rotating lights, mingled with kindred spirits, aliens like him? Often he looked at his bowl of cereal, expecting it to talk to him.

Because he did not attend formal school and was mostly alone, Vida played with marbles when he wasn't out in the garden or conversing with his tree. One day he taught himself to make fire using a magnifying glass and focus rays from the sun. That night he curled on his bed and sought sleep, but it evaded him. He looked out the window at swaying branches of a lofty pine tree against a deep blue sky. As the pine's leaves shimmered, one after another, he wondered whether, if he looked hard enough, he might see a spaceship inside the shimmers.

He angled the magnifying glass to the moon, focused it until a steady stream of light through the window clasped the moon's shine in a straight beam. To his astonishment, inside the steady handshake of light Vida heard voices: Clicks. Tweets. They formed syllables and he understood the . . . talking. He had no clue who was talking, but he understood what they said, understood it so well he laughed.

He angled the magnifying glass toward the moon differently. Again, a straight beam fell from the sky and into his room, then clicks and tweets, voices whose words he understood, words that made him laugh.

During the voices, sound changed to a cacophony and a tremor shook his room. Vida threw open his window, leaned out and skyward. A dazzling object *swashed!* an inch from his nose and crashed down below. He trembled for a while in silence. No sound came from his parents' room. Vida mustered courage and peeked out. All was still. After another wait he slipped out the door, along the corridor, down the stairs. He pulled the bolt and stole outdoors into a blast of tepid wind. The ground was equally warm, increasing in temperature around the house.

He examined the ground outside his window, but there was no crater two meters wide. No debris and certainly no dent on grass or soil. Instead he saw a square tablet almost hidden from sight but for dazzle. It was cool to touch, oddly cool given the heat it caused around it.

Vida wrapped it in his pajama top, took it to his room and studied it. The tablet had black, silver and gold squares embossed on its face.

What a find!

He stroked the tablet, laid it on his mantel, gazed at its blaze. A handshake of brilliant light fell from the sky. The light grew thicker, whiter, stronger. It too dazzled.

Suddenly there were military choppers, soldiers dropping from the sky into the front and back yards. More militants marched in formation along the streets outside Vida's house, a brigadier commanding the squadron.

A noise, shrill and harsh, came from the lit sky. It changed in pitch and resonance. First, there was a rise and dip of garble, and then sirens, gurgle, more sirens, more gurgle. Cacophony became floating sound. And then, in an invasion of silence, the beam from the magnifying glass to the moon transformed color from blinding to radiant.

The vessel that appeared was serpent-like, but it had legs. It grew large as it neared ground, and the military men sprang. They grouped, advanced. The craft's surface grew more luminous. A door slid and soldiers on the ground fell back. A staircase dropped in a trail of light from the doorway. It lowered until it touched ground.

Cluck! Cluck! Tweet! Tweet! Sound from the spaceship.

A brain with eyes emerged. It floated at the top of the stairway and regarded the ambush.

"Identify yourself," the brigadier shouted from a mike behind a car.

Garblegook. Garblegook.

The brain floated downward along the carpet of light.

"Step back," the brigadier. "We'll shoot! Step back. We'll shoot!"

Light bounced off the brain. Compound molecules within translucent skin squirmed and shifted.

"It's radioactive," somebody cried.

Garblegook. Garblegook.

Vida watched the proceedings from his room.

"I know what the alien is saying," he said.

His mother, now in the room with him, began to say something, but before she could utter the first consonant of her word, Vida grabbed the tablet and ran out of his room.

Sirens. More cars and choppers arrived. The helicopters circled the luminous craft.

"Final warning. Step back," the brigadier. "Warning, we'll shoot!

As boots advanced, just then, on the edge of eruption, Vida snapped the door open, jumped down the porch. He raced at his best to the brigadier.

"Please. Wait. Don't shoot."

The brigadier stalled the launch with a hand.

"Boy, you crazy?"

"I know what the alien is saying."

The sentient being had almost reached ground on the staircase of light.

Garble. Crack. Gurgle.

"Salom," translated Vida. "Bring no war."

Garble. Garble. Crack. Crack.
"Lower weapon Earth being. Bring no war."
Crack. Google. Garble. Garble.
"In Universe we accommodate together. We no war."
The brigadier gripped Vida's arm.
"Ask it," he demanded. "Ask what it wants."
A new wave of light fell from the craft.
Crack. Crack. Click. Tweet. Zip. Zip. Gurgle. Gurgle.
"What is it saying?" the brigadier.
"Give game back please."
The brigadier stared.
Vida drew his hand from his back and showed the tablet.
Crack. Crack. Click. Click. Tweet. Zip.
"Give chessboard back please."

• • •

Vida stirred from sleep, rubbed his eyes. His mind felt torn between dreaming and reality. He looked out of the window and there was no brigadier or spaceship. His parents when they emerged from the bedroom were their normal selves, unstirred.

That same year of the spaceship, a great-uncle Vida had never met died and left Ken his carpentry business. Ken drove the truck all the way to Middle Creek and the family settled into the uncle's two-tiered weatherboard house surrounded by a thicket of trees east in the valley.

Middle Creek had such amenable air; it made possible remarkable improvement in Vida's health. It was only a matter of time before Margo made an unshakable decision to prod him out of homeschooling and into the local community school.

But other children did not allow their play to touch him. They circled him and left him out. They treated him like an alien.

"Malformed species," said Dale Hocking. She was a divine little girl with russet tresses and rosy lips that curled like half a ribbon.

When she said it, called him misshapen, and an alien for that matter, the other children laughed. It didn't take Vida long to figure out the children put up laughter like walls. Each time they wanted to insulate themselves from his oddity or fragility they laughed. Once, Vida tried laughing with them. He pulled his lips and let out a sound. He chuckled with them and tears ran down his cheeks. Someone clapped him on the back and another roughed his hair, but his laughter did not shatter the walls. Vida did not belong. He was still the outsider.

Yet oddly it was the children's laughter that sounded alien.

Garble. Crack. Gurgle.

Garble. Garble. Crack. Crack.

And this alien speak was in a language Vida did not understand.

Crack. Crack. Click. Tweet. Zip. Zip. Gurgle. Gurgle.

So one more time Vida resigned himself to his dreaming, or reality. This time he took to sitting by a river and watching its tides rise and fall. Unlike the tree this river was not a friend. He was too frail to swim in it, or out of it, if he fell.

One day he saw a naked girl with topaz hair swimming in the river.

MYRA

• 22 •

Silhouette . . .

    I watched Salem in her wooden soles. She stood at the bus stop facing a howling wind. She held the hand of a child whose hand needed no holding, or was it the child holding Salem's hand? Some people are ancient before they are young. T-Mo lived in that child. Salem stood helpless and needing rescue, bait to a prowler, even as it began to rain. It rained hard that night, churning waters, almost viscous, that rose to their shins. It was a yellow night, moonlit. As it gushed relentless, a flattening rain that was also blood-warm, it was the child who finally tugged her mother's hands, who led her through the rain, through shimmering waters, away from the bus stop, to . . . where? To a clock whose hands moved slowly. To the nearest place out yonder.

    Salem picked the first prick she saw, a cashed-up prick, in the first car that threw mud in her face. It was drifting at speed, all four wheels sliding. Prick drove it like he stole it. The wet road roared as the car took a corner, as it drove past, stopped, reversed, and pulled up alongside mother and child pushing through the torrent. Perhaps it was the heart wrench inside Salem's eyes or the sense of a crushing pressure inside her head or her stance of guts like concrete . . . whatever it was, it took ill meaning from the driver.

    "Headed someplace?" he said.

    "W-waiting's a bitch," said Salem. Her face was wet with tears or rain. "If it's not too m-much to ask, could you, would you—"

    "Hop in."

    He was a skinny man with cut jeans and oily hair. His name was Tonk. Must have been fixing to score a wife because Salem, at that moment, was no unfolding beauty. She wiped her nose with the back of a hand in the passenger seat, her child alert at the back seat, but still Salem must have looked very shiny as a possibility. And Tonk staked his claim. He drove mother and child away from spitting rain, from the liquid and roar of foul weather, from roads turning into rivers, into a canopy of trees. Red, the potted plant, never stopped singing. "Tonkie wonkie dastardly prickie!" it chimed. "Skinnie mannie cashed-up drinkie!" They drove into a dark world that finally found starlight. Trees cast flitting shadows into the car as it raced, all the way inland past Fortrose, Shaving Point, Crotchety . . . to Middle Creek.

Middle Creek was new suburbia from what was once rural and bordered the towns of Sheepwash Creek up north, Coulthird and Lockwood to the west, separated from Middle Creek by the steep falls over rocky ledges of Little River. A new bus line ran all the way from Passings Lane, Seal Rock, past the community school—with its focus on integrated student learning, problem-solving and a range of support programs for its youth—and traveled all the way to just short of the Forest of Solemn further south. But Middle Creek still wore on its landscape remnants of wheat, rice, cotton and cane. It was in panic not fondness that Salem allowed her knees to be softened by a rich chap, a tart meanie with a comely face. Should I have cast a magic barrier to protect her from evil? But Tonk wasn't evil; he was just arrogant. Polished too, other than the torn jeans of their first meeting. His world was dressed with money, with charm if and when he chose to. But his choice of charm was rationed, his shoulders mostly stiff, and his eyes at most times level with disdain. His humorless countenance must have made him incapable of wooing anybody sensible or unburdened.

Not that Salem was insensible, but she was burdened. She was still uncertain how her world had so changed. She was forever uncertain of everything. Oh, the tragedy. Tonk offered possibility to a heart driven with survival. A new marriage was sealant for the rip in a woman's soul, a woman whose stammer for weeks before the altar had got more and more pronounced. When Tonk first took Salem in his arms and asked her hand in marriage, she pulled from his embrace, looked past him to a point somewhere in the distance and said, "Y-Y-Y-Yes." Having spoken to the shadow, the one in the dance, and announced her intention, then and only then did Salem sag back into Tonk's arms.

Standing there at the altar in a fishtail gown and a choker—her fatherless child a sweet-smiling assassin in an open-backed cape dress (according to Tonk, who disliked Myra)—Salem seemed the kind of woman who was lovely but useless on most counts, too fragile for meaningful companionship other than one of a protective nature on his part. Nevertheless her exquisiteness was unmissable and, strong and stubborn as Tonk was, he had an eye for beauty. Tonk was a moneyed man with a penchant for drink, but no patience for complications. Yet Salem was a complexity he could simplify. He waited until she stopped looking at the end of her shoe eight hours straight, until she no longer woke fragile and wide-eyed from sleep with T-Mo's name on her lips, until her stomach appeared to stop dropping and her heart was less littered with scars. When her deep grief appeared to ebb, he figured she was ready to move on from T-Mo. His natural tartness, the ill manners that a silver spoon from birth encouraged, mellowed enough to permit wooing and the asking of Salem's hand in marriage. And she said yes.

It's not like she forgot. She missed the disaster of T-Mo's cooking, how he cooked something and it smelt and tasted like a truffle a dog had spewed. The badness of his cooking was the very thing that made his efforts special. She missed how her stomach dropped and when her eyes opened she was high above the contours of Yellow Trek and the topmost tower of the pick and shovel museum down Fisk Street was nothing but an ant. She missed how he loved lollipops and remembered the day he put a hand in a jar at the craft shop and pulled out a blue and yellow lollipop, unwrapped it and his eyes shone like a shooting star before he closed them when he popped it in his mouth. But out on the street his brow curled, his skin darkened and he spat the lolly into a bin. That night he told her about Miss Lill and how she used to say "Little Poetry come to visit, bless those eyes," in her sing-sing way, all cultured like. Sometimes Salem remembered T-Mo differently and she couldn't filter her memories, which ones were real and which were dreams, or perhaps longing. Especially when she saw T-Mo in her mind like how he wasn't, head bent at the kitchen table as he read the morning paper, slowly chewing toast.

With Tonk's money, Salem found a penchant for hosting other people as this brought escape from being alone, from time that did not forget. Poised like jewelry on Tonk's arm—wearing gold, pearls, emeralds or sapphires in tiered rings, cluster bracelets and bib necklaces that Tonk generously gifted without stupefying his wallet—she swallowed her panic as guests entered the house up the hill, a manor that climbed, open to the stars.

• • •

The lens of time remained undead eleven years after the fragile beauty and unstained simplicity of a pastor's spawn astonished a man who wore a rainbow smile, a magical man with gator skin whose teeth were pretty as baby ivory. His blood was still alive, never fragile or simple, in a wild girl named Myra. By and by, young, mutinous Myra caught the pubescent eye of a boy named Vida who later became a tutor and a Cosmo scientist, but was best as a dad.

· 23 ·

It started with a name. And ended in a swim.

Russet tresses framed Dale Hocking's face. Smile lines formed a faultless triangle from her nose to the corners of lips half curled in a ribbon. So young, bewitching: Dale was divine, no doubt, Vida Stuart knew. But he was drawn to Myra Lexus. Myra was blazing, unreachable; her kind of beauty rarer than a comet. She electrified him, stirred things in him that bewildered. And it was not just the sapphire hair splashed with light, or skin ever so fluorescent to behold; it was her secret.

That spring morning when Vida saw Myra naked as dew in the river, hair roped with weed and dripping wet, he knew she was a river child. He watched from the crag as she glided back and forth, hundreds of miles just about. Each blade of her hand cut smooth and powerful against the white tide, her swim far different from his splash and furious paddle. He watched even as it began to rain, a slow clap. It swelled into a pounding storm, mightier and mightier swirls that loosened pebbles. Myra swam deeper, further out. Water closed over her head and he panicked.

Something caught his eye in the direction of the Forest of Solemn to the west, behind shrubbery just before the valley. He could have sworn it was Dale but she couldn't be here. It was insane to imagine Dale might be watching him and Myra in the wet. The imagery and thought fizzed from his mind, turned to vapor by panic for Myra under the tide still. So he hurled stones into the bobbing water.

Plop. Plop. Plop.

As his fear grew, so did his hail of stones.

Plop, plop, plop, plop!

Then there she was, stepping out from the deepest belly at an impossible coast, beads of vicious waves and rain, fresh still, on glowing skin. And his heart staggered.

She climbed (dressed) to the crag and sat wordless beside him. He had seen her nakedness; now he was discomfited by the watching of it. But she didn't care. And it didn't seem to matter that he uttered no word.

Plop!

Her stone.

"So you come here." She spoke without turning.

Plop!

"Some." He wondered at the scratch in his voice.

"And you swim?"

Plop!

"Don't mind a chill now and then," he said and hurled a pebble. "Why?"

"I hope you chill better than you throw."

"Nothing's wrong with my swimming, and chucking pebbles is a breeze."

"Course," she said, sly.

Her stone whizzed and bounced twice in the waves.

His dropped short.

That was all they ever spoke – until the day Dale Hocking brought up a name.

• • •

Prep. The class hummed. Myra's head was bent as her pencil moved on drawing paper. Dale turned from the front row, ringlets of her mane tossing.

"Your dad—" she said jauntily. "Is his name really Tonk?"

Myra, pencil moving, ignored what had been building at the small community school for a while now.

"His name really Tonk?" Loud.

The pencil stilled.

"Oops," said Dale, tone syruped. "I forgot. He's a fake dad. Your stepfather, isn't he? Your real dad's a *Grovean*."

Humming died. Dale had said the unspeakable—talk of otherworldly beings on Earth.

The class stood on nails, many curious, some discomfited, most seeking a glint in Myra's eye. Vida sensed impatience around him, a serpent-like eagerness for something that had been growing like an infection. But he wanted no part in it.

"My father's dead," Myra said with impossible calm. "Leave him out of this."

Dale looked unruffled. Her mouth pushed ruthlessly on: "Let me see: Grovean father, human mother—that makes you a *hybrid*."

Vida cringed, for he too had been called a hybrid, and not for Grovean reasons. Malformed species, divine Dale had said. Her digits determined the conduct of her behavior. She looked at her nails and became horrid.

"Hy-brid," she was saying now, rolling the word. "Know what that means, Myra?" Her toss of mane followed nervous giggles in the class.

"Ha bloody ha," said Myra. Her voice did not shift an octave.

"See, Myra. It means that I don't like hybrids."

"You're stupid."

"Blooming heck," Dale, syrup making her voice softer. "Not stupid like you; spindly legs here"—chin indicating Vida—"for a boyfriend."

The class roared. And then they were yelling, jostling, surging forward for prime view, for Myra had shot straight at Dale. The two girls rolled a meter, rolled and rolled again. A teacher weaved through the sizzle and snatched Myra and Dale apart. A bubble hovered in the class still; Mrs. White calmed it with a hand. Heads lowered and eyes turned downward.

"No more of this nonsense, now," she said. "And you two"—hail in her glance—"with me to the office."

Nothing more was said of the incident, even when Dale returned surly to her seat, and Myra with a quarter smile. Both had been punished. But Vida remembered the laughter long after it settled; long after the chair that had swallowed him released him, and the burn of crimson left his face.

· 24 ·

The first peal of bells went. Bustle, as people moved. The class streamed out. Vida walked, as did Myra.

She fell in step alongside him.

"Ta," said Vida, awkward. "What you did for me—"

"Were you hanging out the whole day to say that?"

"N-no . . ."

Icicles turned on him. None of the magnet that drew him; these ones glittered with tones of bad temper.

"Why *think* it was for you?" she said.

"Wasn't it?"

She swirled. He stopped too, and looked at her with a worrisome eye, his focus not on blazing sparkle but on a northern point on her forehead.

"Your legs *are* spindly," she said. "Remember that. But you are *not* my boyfriend."

"All good." His eyes shifted to her grazed chin.

"*Is it?*"

They walked in silence to the fork of the road that separated them: one path up the hill where Myra lived; the other down to the fold of a valley where Vida lived in a weatherboard house surrounded by a solid thicket of wild trees.

"Until then," he said, parting.

She nodded.

He was well on his way down the vale when a pound of feet chased him.

It was Myra.

"I thought, maybe," she paused. "Maybe you wanted to come to the river with me."

"No sweat."

She started running, surging into a warm, chaffing wind. Her claret tunic lifted and sank with her knees. He ran behind, too slow to catch up, duffle bag too heavy, the path too cobbled in parts. And then they were out in sprawling fields of wild grass that led to the river, away from the knot of trees surrounding Vida's house far east. Myra was swift and lithe, looping around shrubbery, gunning for it. Her laughter made melody in the whistling wind. He laughed with her as they ran, his own sound utterly rusty and scratched.

Finally she spun around. They almost tumbled in a heap. They lay face up, arms spread, fingers almost touching, eyes cast at a spotless emerald sky. Myra smelt of fennel.

"Dale's a bitch," she said to the skies.

"Class was wretched," said Vida.

"Wasn't your fault. Girls are bitches."

"Aren't you, Myra?"

She looked at him.

"A girl?" he clarified.

"You crackers?"

"So you really are then . . ."

"Grovean?" she helped.

He was going to say *hybrid*. "Are you?"

"And if I am?" Her gaze lingered.

He flushed.

"Tell me, Vida." She knew his name. "What if I am Grovean?"

"People talk."

He had caught snatches of hushed conversation, sometimes from his parents. All harmless talk, really, but sometimes anxious words, frightened even.

"*. . . move with velocity of light . . .*"

"*. . . switch through time, between worlds . . .*"

"*. . . never die, not normally, anyways. Wonder what happened to T-Mo?*" Myra's father, her Grovean past.

People tried to place her: "*Is she a mammal?*"

"*Don't know.*"

"*Then what?*"

Her mother, Salem, was wide-eyed and tear-prone. Fully mortal, as was Tonk: steel, brisk and dapper. But even his arrogance could not shield him or his wife from the shadow of the Grovean mantle. Though it was not explicitly spoken, young children were forbidden with a glance, a tug, a furrow of brow from entering the house with misted windows on the hill. A manor that climbed, open to the stars.

Now Vida's curiosity overcame him.

"How come he died?" he asked. "What happened?"

Grass trembled slightly. A torn leaf, desiccated and useless, raced along the ground. Myra did not ask whom.

"You miss him?" he tried again.

She faced away. "How old are you?"

"Eleven," he said. "You?"

"Ancient."

He sat upright. "What do Groveans do anyway?" Bolder now.

"Slay people."

"Really?!"

She eyed him as if he deeply amused her.

"Can you?" he said. "Kill people too?"

Her expression altered. "What do you think?" A voice within a voice, distant.

The glint in her dark eyes was almost difficult to catch. His brow lifted. His heart sang. He blinked, and she kissed him. His world swelled with shadows and light, distinction, restriction, temperature, ice, salt, earth. Texture, promise, complexity, integration: all trapped in an instant. His knees jellied, his hips blazed. His hands lost sensation. When he opened his eyes to find his brittle fingers on the rise and fall of her chest, he knew not how to lift them to the velvet smoothness of her face. At first, he could not define the borders of what he felt. Then in a breath, Vida was new and old and happy and deliciously in love.

Myra jumped and skipped away, her laughter uncomplicated. She threw her head back and the glitter in her hair, a sapphire waterfall, bounced. He climbed to his feet, brushed his khaki shorts and chased, fast this time, running at his best until his heels sang. Elation touched him; the significance of the moment. Strangely, with wind on his face and a big, clean sky above him, he also felt . . .

A surge of purity.

At last they came to the swell and swirl of the river. They stood on their crag, the sacred place of their first meeting. Vida's heart leapt at the sight of a figure in the water. Although Myra was half-close to a smile, her face was pallid. She gazed in silence at russet hair moving in silver waves below.

"Is that you-know-who?" she said quietly.

Vida processed the scene before him. It was Dale Hocking. Swimming in their river. Not as effortless as Myra, not as clumsy as Vida, who was wary of the water's belly. But there swimming, nonetheless, spoiling their fun.

"Come."

The touch of Myra's fingertips was frost.

"Where to?" Vida hesitated.

"You know where."

"Why?"

"You know why."

"No. Myra, I don't."

Still, he followed, as if in a spell, knowing she was plotting something.

"You shouldn't—" he froze his feet a little, resisting weakly.

But she pulled him, the light in her eye too keen. And in a wink she was gone. Vanished. She had literally thinned in air. Next he saw her, she stood silent on a northbound shore, naked; skin aglow; half-formed breasts alert. His breath caught. Dale was still swimming, free, shameless, playful even, oblivious of added presence.

Not a ripple broke the water's surface with Myra's dive. She slithered, gliding like a water snake toward her prey. When water closed above Myra's head, chill touched Vida's flesh. Suddenly Dale was gasping and choking; soundlessly flapping and splashing. Then water covered her head too and it fizzed, bubble after bubble foaming and floating on the water's face. Endless bubbles broke the calm surface one after another. Then the bubbles stopped.

Even then, Vida wasn't convinced.

He sat and hugged his legs, waiting. Night fell whole and silent. Shadows awakened and crept. Wind pulled water from his eyes. A yellow moon, hostile, sinister, stalked across the river. A wave slapped at the raised crag, and ice-cold spits struck his skin. Somewhere in the distance, inside the silence of night, Vida heard the crystal ping of a calling bird. He caught movement behind him and there she was—Myra. She slipped, fully clothed, beside him. She smelt of seaweed. Her face looked weightless.

They sat very still. If, disoriented, he wondered . . . nothing was said of it. How and why he spoke nothing, he didn't know. Perhaps it was a method to madness, or was it his acceptance of Grovean . . . codes? he silently asked himself. Myra hummed. Her low song carried something surreal and gray and wistful and sweet. He listened without melancholy, a part of him both frozen and thawed.

"Better head," she said calmly, when at last she spoke.

"I guess."

His awareness of her reeled his mind. He stood up, abrupt.

She watched him, head tilted. Her moonlit face was tender, ever so soft. Bewildered, he turned and ran, chased by a pounding of heart. In a flash, Myra's weed scent flew past him—up the ridged footpath, swift as a spear. Dusk swallowed her litheness.

He surged behind her into spreading darkness, running further and harder than he ever remembered. He closed the space between them, madly laughing as he ran.

· 25 ·

Transition.

So they are. Vida and Myra. She is half-alien to his humanness. Her Grovean mantle is strange, it is shifting, sometimes disquieting. Sometimes it is intense right there. It is that Grovean thing that makes people talk. But Vida doesn't care.

• • •

Myra took him to the house on the hill, the manor that climbed. Took him up ironed balustrades, C-shapes and S-curls. His hand followed the curves and twirls all the way to Myra's bedroom. Despite her denial of femininity, *Girls are bitches*, she had said, she *was* a girl. There were mirrors and frames, shelves and hooks. Whimsical lights gave the textured wall a muted hue that cast a soft gold upon the geometric pattern on the floor rug. The bed had latticed pillows and throws—fuchsia, lavender and taupe—petal-edged. By the window, beside a floor-to-ceiling drape—ribboned—a large-leafed plant with tints of scarlet and bronze brought the room to life.

It was a jealous plant named Red, and it was very territorial. Soon as it saw Vida accompanying Myra, it started to wag, swell up and clack. And then it sang, morosely, for Vida:

He's a jolly keen fellow
Oh, jolly keen fellow,
Deny, deny?

Jolly keen fellow,
Deny, deny?

"Stop being petty," said Myra. "Vida's not replacing you."

Red turned to a wilt. Took an hour before it responded to Vida's touch, and when it did, it squirted dye on him.

"You really have to stop this," said Myra, and Red promptly went into a *Spindly Vida, Leggedy Vida* song. It sang in a baritone. Its sweet, harshless music of ascending and descending melody was weak and airy in parts, before it swelled to slapstick flourish, operatic. *Spindly Vida, Jiggety!* Red extended and held the last note.

• • •

Myra and Vida sink into a courtship of the young, one filled with inexperience and unfussiness, a courtship of the kind before adulthood bends down to catch up with it.

Today, they lie side by side in their sprawl on a glen that is yellow by day, muted by night. The sun's heart is right there with them. Vida wonders what it is about Myra that stirs him so. Is it her kinship with water—how she spears into rolling waves, immerses without effort into rapids that are twenty-four seas, that howl over her head? Or is it how she wriggles a toe just so, enough to bring pause to the heart of his sentence? Or how she throws her head and light splashes in the spray of her hair? Or how she puts timbre in her voice in a special sound for Vida? What he feels is not lust, but something close.

The first day he saw her swimming naked in the river, her skin a dark caramel, her baby breasts just coning, his interest pitched. Like clothing, it slipped off his body to follow her scattered garments on the shore and spread its curiosity like mist. He could not move beyond it, his notice of the girl, her newness and secrecy as she swam, possibly mad, unhinged in uncontrollable waves. The scene before him was glorious and astonishing, and he sat hopeless—or was it hopeful?—on that bleak cliff. He watched and watched Myra until his yearning heated the wet blue of her hair and she swam into a fiery sapphire in his eyes, until the pound of his heart eclipsed all sound of the untamed river. He became a boy with dreams, arrow sharp. Hers were loose. He could tell from the way her smile was just so—private—when she rose from the black waters. She stepped indifferent into a charcoal wool skirt whose color matched the somberness of her eyes. When she straightened, topless and open to his scrutiny, he uncurled from his hunch to rake fingers through his hair. Perhaps it was the liquid in her eyes, or the loudness in her silence, or her bare back to him as she pulled on a flame orange shirt, hippy and bold . . . His throat caught. Just then, just so, as silver from the stars bathed her hair—she tossed a pebble and it bounced several times in the waves. And she spoke to him without turning. "So you come here," she said.

Now Myra gets to her feet, holds her hand out. "Come, Vida."

He wants to finish his story, the one he was telling before adulthood caught up and, somehow, somewhere, without warning, his voice broke right in the middle of a consonant and a syllable.

Despite the way Myra walks, the way she tilts her chin and allows him a glimpse of the woman she might become, despite her ancientness, he understands that her adolescence is steps behind. His is early.

A gang-gang cockatoo swoops from the sky and perches on Myra's shoulder. A hurricane of yelps, and more cockatoo hover in the horizon.

"I feel mature," says Vida.

Myra stands there without response, guides the gang-gang bird to the skies with an upward stretch of her hand. The cockatoo walks the length to her palm, rubs his beak along her finger, and lifts off.

"Mature?" Now she looks at him. "Why say that?"

"Don't you? Feel it too?"

"Whatever you're on about." Her mirth leaves him inadequate with words.

How does one voice the antlers that make him feel things a boy shouldn't? He doesn't mind some grownup thoughts he experiences. But he minds the fierce searing; the one that sometimes accompanies those other thoughts. When he tries to collapse the thoughts, contain them before they spread to his hips, he finds he cannot catch them.

"Why so serious?" And she is off leaping and burrowing in the glen, skipping over cowslips, dancing with trees. "See, Vida. Chase me."

Ah, heck.

Vida lets loose before that grownup thing returns to break his simple world of cowslips and dreams. He is cool with the grownup thing, as long as he can retrieve his childhood afterward and race about the fields, carefree and wild as she. They are all knees and elbows, giggling with a carpet of dahlias, banksias and kangaroo paws.

"Look, Myra. A moth butterfly."

She leaps sky high to catch it, dispatches it with a kiss. She speaks to nature in the language of a humming bird. The dahlias respond by bending petals her way. A bumblebee eyes her from the tip of an olive blade and sings his sultry tune for her.

As nature's corsetry lifts to reveal apricot and white petticoats, Vida knows he would do the same if he were a plant. Now, right now, it is just wonderful to be. But sometimes, as they lie stretched on cool grass, their bare feet open to the fingers of the sun, something creeps upon them unbidden. It slips in the memory of one Dale Hocking, of her small face and russet tresses (sopping wet). Dale, pushed to the river's bed and it became a tomb. If anyone at Middle Creek Community School wonders what happened to Dale, how she vanished, nobody wonders aloud. But the children, the rest of them, the way they look at Myra is different now. And their look has rolled on to Vida.

• 26 •

He found her growing on a tree. Not Myra, but a woman with hair the color of a cartoon. Right there, at a fork of two roads, one leading up a hill, the other back to the river, she was hoisted on the branch of a tree that twisted downward. She had a short crop on her head and vacant miles in one eye. Her good eye was sharp as that of a lynx, filled with moonshine and a hint of morning, intense and interrogating. The way she rested her cheek on the bough, she looked like she was growing from it.

Vida stopped in his tracks and blinked. When his eyes opened the tree had moved. The woman raised her cheek and he noticed that half her face was disfigured. The disfigurement was old, dead tissue mangled and pasted like a mask on her face. He lowered his gaze, to respect her space, but his eyes drew back. Her smile was a thing left over from a memory; he wasn't sure it was real. Everything about her was like stages of a dream where her face was familiar, yet she was a stranger. When she moved, like when she forgot the hug of the tree and set her pose, arranged it for him, it was as if he were seeing her inside a mirror of reflections, a dream within a dream within a dream. The tree and her body overlapped, intermittent, in hues of black and white.

She made a sound then, a sigh, it was deep and halfway to a groan, but trapped in something else. The sound bounced like an echo off the tree. It vibrated in the air toward him, then silence swallowed it.

Part of him filled with trepidation, and he wanted to retreat. The other felt emotions of a strange kind, and he wanted to reach out and squeeze the woman's hand. But fog took hold. When it ebbed, the woman with one broken eye and one gobbling eye was gone. What stayed were a strange sound in the air of sad music, and a floating in the wind of wet and moss and fur and oil. Later, not much later, he couldn't remember what she wore, if she wore . . . All he remembered was one side of her face smooth as cream, the other covered with trail. And the perfectly round eyes: one a broken portal to a faraway place, unusable and indeterminate in its form, the other interrogating and vivid.

And though, far as Vida knew, Myra was unconnected with the odd woman and her equally odd appearance and disappearance, Vida thought of Myra. He didn't know who he was without her. All he knew was that he should know.

• 27 •

Rain crept nearer, as did dusk. Vida and Myra ran all the way to the woods, inside a fold of land that leaned toward the river.

Vida loped several lengths behind Myra. His duffle bag that held three textbooks skipped and bobbed on his back. A chafing wind on his face carried the backward float of Myra's laughter that was a soft tinkle of bells, a rustle of leaves, a deep-seated stomach purr. Her sound scattered in the breeze. When she stopped, breathless, her face—the perfection of it, the mystery of it—caught sapphire shimmers from her hair as light bounced in it.

Wind and drizzle fell backward. Air warmed and dusk swelled. Myra spoke of places she'd been, worlds that burst with color, places whose horizons filtered rainbow through a silhouette of trees. She spoke of dropping valleys that whispered, climbing hills that blazed, spitting volcanos that touched the sky, singing water that solidified at her touch.

"Tell me about the land of morphing stars," Vida begged.

"I thought you liked the land of the brass witch, ageless as the moon, whose eyes are like desert sun."

"I like them all. Perhaps you've told me everything."

"Not about Amaharti."

"Go on, then."

"Well! Amaharti has wriggly-wormy creatures that talk. Its winter is a grim fog that lurks, that waits to do terrible things to people. Its summer—"

"Nh-nhh," he said. "You're making it up."

"But I'm not."

He held her fingers. "Making it up. I know the lands you've traveled and Amaharti is not one of them."

She leapt to her feet. "How would you know?"

"Just would."

"Hah bloody ha."

"Would."

She started running. Not fast enough, he noticed. He caught up, and then they rolled on grass, oblivious to shapes that crouched in the woods, cloudy gray shadows prowling between hanging branches and fat tree trunks.

When Myra folded in Vida's arms, she was a perfect fit.

His heart pounded *ba-boom! ba-ba-boom!* a perfect beat.

The sweetness of her flesh, the warmth of her lips, tossed him to a vagrant mood. He groped, awkward: hands on her hair, on her face . . . on her breasts, up creamed thighs inside a claret uniform . . . She pulled away and sat abruptly. She looked straight ahead.

"I'm sorry—" started Vida.

"Did you see that?"

"See . . . what?"

"Light. Through the trees."

"What light?"

She had already jumped, was cutting diagonally into a cluster of trees.

"You stay, Vida." Her words rushed at him across a shoulder.

Stay. Like a dog.

Vida stared at his hands, helpless human hands. Wind brushed his neck, reinforced the swell of night around him. Fog seemed heavier. It clung around trees a meter out. Thunder. A clap traveled and shook the hill above him. Movement in the trees. A flicker of light swept behind a Banksia a couple of yards away. A shape, a body. Night carried shadows in droves, Vida assured himself. Or Myra was playing games. In the dusk she was shadows and a glow of eyes. No, he wasn't a dog. He would not stay. So he followed.

Myra's shadow slipped from tree to tree, further and further, deeper into the woods. It stopped when he stopped, moved when he moved. Dampness caught his throat. Light never touched fully on the shadow's shape or face; just a silhouette, then it vanished.

Vida swirled, aware of a presence. The shadow had slipped closer. It was not Myra. It stood tall as a human, three yards away from him. Breath floated from its nostrils like silver shimmers in the blackness of the night.

"Who are you?" Vida managed.

The heart of its eyes gleamed blue and bold and powerful.

"Who are you?" Myra this time.

She stood beside Vida, fingers clutching his. Together they faced the intruder.

He stepped out of the shadows, an ice blond male, almost Scandinavian in looks.

"Al," he said, confident. "My name is Al."

"Why are you following us?" said Myra.

"Look," he said. His hands spread. Balls of flame bounced from them, leapt into the air and chased into the sky.

"Fire," said Myra in wonderment. "You make fire."

"Lightning," he corrected.

Vida watched the flames turn crimson, then blue, then orange. Fireballs shot from the palms of a boy, or a man, named Al.

As Al flicked his fire, as his eyes swallowed light from the flames and danced from crystal blue to purple to an in-between shade of green, Vida struggled, besieged with anger. His hatred of the incongruous man-boy who was much focused and very accurate with his lightning-making was instant. Al continued casting light from his hands, tossing it through the trees as if that was all it took to woo a girl. It *was* all it took. Myra's coal eyes warmed. She half-smiled at the boy with iced blues that carried no soul. From her laughter, a tinkling sound that deepened and sank to a belly cough, Vida saw just how well the tossing of light worked.

". . . can make patterns," the blazing idiot was saying.

Myra listened, nodded, wide-eyed and curious, accepted without question the fool's ability, his guileful presence.

And just like that, they were walking home. All three together.

At the fork of the road that weaved downward and eastward to Vida's home in the valley, he shifted his weight on a foot, waited for Myra to say something, anything.

She didn't.

"Walk you home," Vida offered.

Myra cast a glance at Al. "Be fine, you go."

"Where's home?" asked Al.

Vida started to tell him to mind his own business. Myra pointed.

She *could* take care of herself, Vida assured himself.

· 28 ·

Mrs. Featherstone's voice droned in the classroom. She wore a short crop, masculine, and a neat boyish figure inside her woolen skirt. Always it was something woven. Her nose, the size of it, the shape of it, was hard to ignore. On and on she spoke in a monotone about Tigris and Euphrates and the Ziggurats of Ancient Mesopotamia, until the bell went.

"Al pester you last night?" Vida asked Myra, way before the clip of the teacher's heels had gone cold behind the door.

"Don't know what you mean." She busied herself with books. "Mr Hall's coming," and burrowed into her algebra book.

• • •

". . . the endpoints of this Circle are X—in brackets, minus five, seven," labored Mr. Uriah Hall behind a tangle of hair. His chalk-hand moved, furious, on the board. Vida was far from focused. His mind was scattered. He had *nothing* to worry about, he assured himself. Nothing at all. But it was with disquiet that he eyed Myra. She sat, pencil in hand, eyes on the board, in blissful absorption of algebra. But her mind, where was her mind?

". . . to determine the coordinates of the center, C."

It was no secret that Vida was a mere human; frazzled hair only burgundy, not blue or white or blond. His legs were spindly, not as fast as hybrid or supernatural legs. His pale skin self-tanned in splotches at whim. Al, on the other hand, with his boast of fire play, was clearly another breed. And if he stalked his raggedy ass down Myra's way, there was no telling–

". . . origin or midpoint formula. Vida! Quit dreaming."

• • •

Myra bounded for the woods soon as the first peal of the bell went. Normally she would lunch with Vida. He followed, raced nervous after her, jumpy, for something assured him he had not seen the last of Al.

Sure as dawn, there was Al in the woods wearing cool denims, tossing fire from his palms. Must have been expecting them, certainly expecting Myra, because he said, "I brought sandwiches."

"Oh," said Myra.

"Anchovies and cream cheese."

Vida's good sense and fortitude held back his words. He rebuffed Al's sandwiches for his own almond butter and jelly ones. Myra accepted Al's offerings with giggles.

Vida sagged against a tree and watched Myra and the world fly away away . . . from him. He scratched up soil with the lip of his boot. He caught snatches of Myra and Al's engrossment:

". . . this blue and yellow rosella perched on my finger . . ."

Al was leaning back on elbows, vamping Myra with his eyes as she shared with him her time travel stories.

". . . giant clam with big wavy lips, and this bronze eagle with a three meter wing span reeled upside in a flip and drop, and snapped the clam from the seaside."

Myra's knees were pulled up, her face surreal. Vida had never known her to be indifferent to him. Not when they tossed pebbles in the river first time they met, and hers whizzed in a rapid hail to bounce several times on the river surface, and his dropped way short. She had *faked* indifference.

Vida moved to another tree. A nesting bird with dull plumage and large eyes jumped squawking from a branch. He elbowed it and missed; poorly coordinated was he. So he continued to scratch up soil with the lip of his boot, but could not dissolve the corpse in his gut. His kick connected with a stone on the ground. He picked up the stone, tossed it at quavering branches, but was surprised when it actually met and tore a bunch of leaves.

"Who cares!" he yelled.

On the way back to school, Myra caught him in a hug without reason or warning.

Her scent soothed him. "You wore perfume," he said, wondering.

"Clover!" she laughed.

• • •

The faraway look in Myra's eye perturbed Vida. Her brooding was obvious all through history. Every now and then, he caught her gaze casting out into the fields, wandering beyond the woodlands, the misted hills, the folding vale.

When Mrs. Featherstone turned to board and chalk, in a breath Myra was gone.

• • •

Two hours of misery. Vida waited until school was over.

Lick-a-tee, lick-a-tee. He ran at his best to the sleeve of the woods, inside a creep of wilderness. *Lick-a-tee-tee-lick-a-tee.* He stopped at the sight of two people kissing. It was Myra and Al.

But wait.

Now Myra was pushing Al. "You fool." Slap!

"If spindly legs can do it, so can I." She tried to slap him again, but he gripped her wrist. "Get away from me, you, s-sick unit, you."

Al moved. Sudden fire engulfed him and Myra. The flame's belly throbbed white, its lip orange as ginger, ardent as lust. When the flames settled, Al was gone.

Myra sat trembling on the ground. Her face was furious.

Vida approached, too afraid to understand. He took in the ruffled tunic, buttons off, bruised breast half-exposed.

"What do you want?" Her voice was hostile.

"I'm going to sit down," he said.

"Why?"

He slipped beside her anyway. He put an arm around her shoulder but she shrugged away, jumped to her feet. He tried to keep pace but the anger in her walk took her further, out toward the river.

Up on their crag, Vida saw him: flammable Al. He was watching them, smiling. A dam in Vida gushed. He tore yelling toward Al. But even as he surged and closed the space, Vida had no plan. He was unclear about what he proposed to do when he actually reached Al. It mattered that Al was unperturbed by the sight of a shouting human chasing toward him. Closer to the rock's edge above the river, Vida faltered, realized too late that Al would step aside and let the river do its work.

Al did not move.

The impact echoed wide. Both fell, spiraled in a tangle into the black river. Al's back slapped the water first. The splatter caught Vida's face. He splashed blind in the deep womb, yelled, but his words got lost in spray. Tide clasped his feet, its hungry belly sucked at his knees, tugged at his body. Vida swallowed gulps of water. Many ideas, mostly of death, rushed at him. Then Al's head bobbed to the surface, his eyes rolled to white.

"...can't..." he gasped. "I... can't... swim."

Vida struggled with a pull of current at his feet. He crawled, dolphin kicked but lacked muscle. He bellied up, scissored his legs. He forced his body to relax, to stay afloat. But his breathing was tense. He looked at the sky and took a deep breath, held it for a moment and exhaled. He pressed his weight on his shoulders, relaxed his head as if on a pillow. Again he inhaled, held it, exhaled. Now he kicked gently, gently, alternating leg movements, kick, kick, kick. Water warmed in a circle.

Vida looked, and saw Al's eyeball had loosened. Al was melting.

"...ghelp," Al gurgled.

Vida's calm, his idea to float on his back, to bit by bit kick, kick, kick to shore, that composure ebbed.

On the jutted lip of the crag, Myra did nothing. Hands limp by her sides, she watched. A worried wind whipped her skin the color of dark caramel with its strands of blue hair.

"...ghelp." The roar of a gargantuan wave closed above Al's dissolving head, and it vanished, then was visible again, skin, eyes and bones. "...ghelp."

Vida at once understood—Al was a fire boy: water broke his composition. In a forever split of hesitation, as Vida wondered if he could save him, Al collapsed into skin and hair, into a spread the wave's jaw swallowed.

With a cry, Vida flipped himself belly down. He stretched arms to a breaststroke, pulled knees to his waist, and cycle kick kick kicked away and away from Al. His strokes were labored, messy. His arms were too high, the cycle in his kick too short. Something knocked softly against him. It was the porridge of Al floating on kelp. Vida tore to the water's surface, coughing, spitting, to the firm but soothing touch of Myra's hand. She hauled him out of the water.

Vida ripped his clothes, lashed at them with a foot. They flew to a distance. He yanked his hair, matted and wild. Nothing could rid him of Al's river broth. The hero had avenged the damsel. So why was he crying? Tongues from the river splashed at his toes. Why, oh why hadn't stupid Al moved? The man-boy had underestimated Vida's assault and wiry frame; even Vida had underrated himself. Sure, he wanted to take Al out, as in shirt-front and head butt, but not, not... this!

Myra wrapped her arms about him. Her body was gentle and strong as she cradled him and they exploded into the night. The horizon neared and fled. A glowing moon swelled and burnt a fierce orange, as they soared into space, time and stars, to a place he could find solace.

· 29 ·

Pedestrians give way to buses, read the sign on the road.

Vida and Myra stood at a crossing. A Passings Lane bus ground past, same one whose doors had moments before trembled open and shuddered shut. Vida had gone with Myra to check out car sales. He was now eighteen and had his sights on wheels. He didn't know what he wanted, what make, engine or model, if he would go new or used, whether it was a coupe, truck, sedan, van or wagon. All he wanted was to look.

Look he did, and there was much to see. Still, he was undecided until Myra ran her hands on a convertible. It was a black sapphire metallic with 83,057 km on the clock. Owned five years, a six-cylinder 3.0 engine car. Limited edition, manual gearbox, the salesman said. He was in his low twenties, the type to wear little dick togs at a beach, Vida reckoned as he studied highlights in a sidewise brushed fringe.

"Look," Dick Togs said. "Active bending headlamps. And the wheels: eighteen-inch alloy." The intensity of his lake green eyes deepened with each sales pitch.

But his interest was fake. Myra and Vida lost him for a moment when a woman with a bold forehead, such red hair and white skin, wanted a bigger car, a more expensive one than the black sapphire metallic. That sale pocketed, Dick Togs ignored the man with a pancake nose who did not throw up a clue as to the size of his wallet.

There was something bold and handsome about the car. Stock clearance and sound car finance made it affordable, enough for Vida to find excitement with it. He would collect it in a couple of days.

"Are you going to be a polisher?" asked Myra.

"Grief no," said Vida.

"One car and you're beginning to sound like Tonk."

When they got off the bus, Myra was wearing her important face, but not for car sales reasons, Vida realized.

"You must declare your intentions," she said.

"To whom?" his glance was cautious.

"I'd like to bring you home."

"But I've been."

"Formally," she said.

"Why?"

"You must speak to Tonk."

"But why?"

"Aw, shut up."

"When?" he conceded.

Her face softened. "Tonk is like a barking dog that does only that: bark."

"He's also a prick."

"He has his moments."

"So he's not a prick?"

"How about a small one."

He cast her a look.

"Maybe a big one, then," she said.

"Darn."

"But Salem's a magnificent cook."

"Better be, if I'm to suffer Tonk."

• • •

A blazer or a coat with tails?

He struggled between Party Specials and Fashion World, major clothing chains in Middle Creek. He settled for a suit with tails. Nipped in waist and a somber tie, not the cashmere slacks and polo shirt. All dressed, he froze at the last minute. Pulled out an old blazer, accompanied it with a bow tie. He licked his palm, shone his hair. That should put Myra's step-dad in fine disposition, he said to the mirror.

But Tonk was in a fit of ill temper. "Messing with my gal, boy?"

"Oh, no sir. I have no intention—"

"What *exactly* is your intention?"

Salem changed the subject. "Tell us what you do, V-vida," her voice falsely bright.

"Final year in college. I'm studying cosmology, madam."

"M-madam makes me anxious. Call me Salem."

But Tonk was on a war zone. "Cosmetology? Not keen on a chap bent on beauty services. Hair, skin or nails?"

"Sir?"

"Do you do hair, skin or nails?"

"Pardon me, sir, not cosmetology. I meant cosmology, study of the cosmos. I learn about the universe."

"Could have fooled me," said Tonk. Poured himself another drink, gulped it in a swallow. "What grades?"

"Sir?"

"Last semester. What grades did you get?"

"I . . . uh . . ."

"Speak up, boy."

"I'm eighteen, sir," said Vida.

"I asked a simple question—did you pass or fail?"

"Mostly A, sir."

"Sure fooled me."

Myra's face was a death mask.

"B-be nice to the young man . . ." begged Salem.

"Why?" snapped Tonk.

"He . . . just . . . because . . ."

"I'll settle for because. Myra brought him to my home for a reason, namely for vetting. I shall do exactly that. Vet him."

"M-maybe you should . . ." Salem tried again.

"I should do nothing of the sort." Unseasonable eyes slid back to Vida. "Give me six reasons"—icy as he was appraising—"why I should let you betroth my gal."

Vida could manage only two: "She . . . um . . ."

"That's reason enough," barked Tonk.

"I sorta like her."

"Hrrumph."

Later, Vida could not remember a single food or drink item that was served. Celery or chicken? Baked or souffléd? Water or wine? Pikelets or quiche? All he remembered was how burning his cheeks, how taut his tie, when Myra unmasked her eyes to address her stepfather. "The one time I think to bring a boy home for your—"

"Exactly! A *boy*. Bring him back when he's a man."

A blazer not tails.

At first Vida blamed his outfit. Then he realized Tonk would have picked him apart no matter what. The man would have found reason. He would have pecked pecked pecked until Vida crumbled.

Blazer or tails: it didn't matter. Not for Tonk, it didn't.

· 30 ·

Silhouette . . .

First, they had secrets. Deep, dark secrets buried in the depths of a river. One secret was named Dale, the other was Al.

Now Myra and Vida had a lifetime.

A trail of light chased them beyond the Earth's atmosphere into a new world. Wrapped in Myra's strength, Vida savored a moment both sacred and historic. Night sped behind and stars fell like meteors. There, right there, south of the constellation Leo, in a place beyond time and space, his skin glowed. His consciousness expanded into a higher state that was clear of singularity or polarity, as he and Myra sank into a web. There, he surrendered to an ecstasy that combined awakening, exploration, initiation, abandonment.

Amalgamation!

• 31 •

Before the honeymoon there was a late afternoon gala in the little town of Middle Creek. The normality of Ken and Margo Stuart grew apparent at the wedding feast. For the first time since Vida's betrothal to Myra, his parents shared a table with Myra's folk. There, at the peak of a misted hill, inside a manor that held several views to the waterfront, Ken—Vida's father—rubbed his chin in thought at one end of the table, building amusement. His coffee eyes were full of smiles, his face eternally tickled. Ken, uninhibited and a picture of good form, was a whole head shorter than his wife Margo opposite.

Vida's mother Margo had indigo eyes that sometimes shifted to blue-gray on a face that told nothing. She carried well her cool head and handsome face. Looking at Margo, it was clear to anyone without searching closely where Vida obtained his wiry frame and striking eyes.

Salem's hair over the years had turned fine and curly as a poodle's. This day she drew it in a tier dazzled with glitter. Vida thought how fragile her beauty, how visible the flutter of her heart on her temple. She was more nervous today than she was the first time Myra invited him home to dinner, when Vida was all knees and elbows, more in charge of his broken voice, but still a wreck under Tonk's piercing eye. Now Salem sat fidgety.

As for Tonk . . . this man whose public arrogance and ill manners were familiar as jeans, he *gazoozled* (Myra's word) the rum. He waved at a servant, who came running, almost tripped. Freshly watered, Tonk glanced at his diamond-crusted watch. It was a statement; Vida was not fooled. Tonk sought less to indicate there were matters of greater concern than Myra's big day and more to flaunt that half a bank had been thrown at the wedding without denting Tonk's purse.

A prudent waiter thought Tonk had imbibed enough and took it upon himself to switch the neat alcohol with lemoned soda. Tonk hooked his hand into the waiter's elbow before the man could whisk the cocktail glass away, and said, "Darling, I'd like my drink back. Now fuck off."

A young woman with boozy eyes giggled. The ruddiness of her lipstick matched the color of her hair. All around, the chitter chatter of Middle Creek folk:

"My husband wanted to give the maid a roasting but I said to her, three strikes you're out . . . We got to five strikes . . ."

"I said to the mechanic, hello pops—how much is that two hundred dollar job for the car? He said five hundred . . . These tradies make the bucks . . ."

"We scoured the streets, even down the river bank, the kitten was nowhere and the kids were going crazy . . ."

Mysterious and distant, exquisite in an ivory dress with Grecian pleat, Myra appeared oblivious to gossip. Vida thought how far different his wife looked from the woman earlier who, straight after the officiating, was keen for the honeymoon. "You, husband," she had murmured, fondling his lapels. "How edible." He had grinned, clasped her hand before it undid a button. An usher swept them along a hallway into an open dining area of Myra's childhood, a spacious hall held aloft by four marble columns. Each pillar was sculpted with the cameo of a stallion whose emerald bit shimmered with light. Teardrop chandeliers hung precariously overhead from a gilded ceiling stretching several rooms long. Lavender and cream swathed walls and tables, accentuating and radiating luxury.

Guests who had come to observe history shared canned laughter. They toasted each other, good crops, wealth, health. Men calmed their stomachs and nibbled, not gobbled, enriched canapés and sweetmeats that fitted snugly to their palates before melting like snowflakes. Bread carried the taste and texture of barbecued chicken. An assortment of sweet, sour and spicy dishes, so moist they redefined the meaning of tender, stood in silvered bowls alongside magnums of vintage wine. Women moved past curiosity at the unlikely interspecies alliance to quietly assess each other's outfit: silk, chiffon or a synthetic mockery? And jewelry: diamond, rhinestone or glass?

Mauve and gold azaleas, bird of paradise petals, and tall white lilies spread heady scents that did not distract from these appraisals; Tonk's affluent display, achieved with ease, merely exacerbated it. Now he turned to Vida who was leaned over a plate fingering food, gobbling.

"Who would have thought it possible?" he said. A harmless enough statement, if one did not know Tonk. Today he was off his head on something; Vida didn't think it was the rum.

Vida's smile was bland. At nineteen and married to Myra, he felt ease. He leaned, offered Tonk a platter of wafers.

"Grief, no," said Tonk.

Vida passed on the snacks, wondered whose idea had placed him at his father-in-law's elbow.

"You have made an honest woman," Tonk said.

"And she is lovely as paradise," agreed Vida.

Opposite, hand on chin, Vida's father Ken watched them. He was poised on the edge of laughter.

Tonk accepted yet another refill of Sir Edmund rum from a uniformed maid. "Make it a double." To Salem's consternation, he rose. Conversation hushed. "My gal," he slurred, tipped his glass in the direction of Myra, "is today a woman."

"Couldn't fault that!" an excitable male piped from the crowd.

Myra's face did not stir.

Vida sought something else to pass around. Ah, blueberry puffs.

Tonk downed the glass, stretched for more rum. Guests half-listened to the speech, all the while discerning the freshness of ingredients in their food, most of it new and original, the rest of it complex. Waitresses brought round silver platters of olive wraps, forest mushroom, yogurt nibblets . . . Baby sips of wine, luxurious and delicate, introduced people to something as mysterious as the bride.

Vida could taste fresh dill, a hint of mint, pepper and lemon in a small bundle of meat and rice wrapped in grape leaves. He understood that much time and labor had gone into the deceptive simplicity of the snack. He also knew that Salem had a hand in it. The harmony and versatility of flavor cultivated an indulgence that bordered on rarity. Raw, lightly cooked, sautéed or grilled, delicate, slippery, textured or meaty—everything carried a range of delectable possibility to the investigative palate.

". . . when I rescued Salem from that Martian," Tonk was saying, poison-laced words calmly imparted.

Ken Stuart roared, as did three dozen people in the room who knew about Myra's Grovean past. All three dozen also knew that only Tonk would be haughty enough to refer to T-Mo with such contempt. The crowd teetered in anticipation.

Vida obliged. He rose to meet his father-in-law's height. "Martian?"—looking straight in Tonk's eye.

"Not that tone with me, young man."

"*This* tone when you are drunk or stupid."

"*Everybody*"—deliberately—"knows about that Grovean fool. What Salem ever saw in the freak—"

A shatter of glass, a blink of light and Myra stood beside Tonk. A lifetime of aversion condensed to a moment. She dangled Tonk, tuxedo and all, with a single hand. Vida, only Vida, could halt her from hurling a sobering Tonk through the ceiling.

• • •

Before the wedding gala, there was an argument.

"I will not have Tonk take charge of our ceremony," said Myra. "I'd rather marry you in Grovea."

"Tonk is your father," said Vida.

"*Step*father."

"He is still family."

"As is Novic."

Vida couldn't fault that. Novic, the Sayneth priest who had fathered T-Mo, was true blood.

"My folks would never travel to Grovea for a wedding," he reasoned.

"Neither would Salem or Tonk. Makes us even."

"I didn't think you cared much for Grovea. Now you want to embrace that past. Now, Myra?"

"Now's as good a time as any."

Things escalated. She yelled. He yelled back. He removed himself from the conflict, but she followed him to the bedroom.

"What would you rather me do? What?" she yelled.

"What Myra always does! Isn't it always about you?"

At the heart of disagreement, she snapped. Her roar sent shudders through the house. Vida's galaxy map, a rare gift from Myra's interspace flights, collapsed from the top of a chiffonier. A snap of doors, and Vida left his house.

He had no answers, just a terrible need to walk. A street cat gave him a soft meow and pushed out its tail to brush his leg as he went past. But a bird on a fence further out screamed at him for no reason. After the cat and the bird, he walked blindly, the need for pace, for space ... pressing him forward. His cheeks were wet. Somehow he found the river.

Chin on knees, he sat at their crag. Wind tugged his hair, river spray whipped his face. He thought of Myra and the twenty-one ways she tossed her head; the thirty ways she lifted her face to the sky and spread her arms in surrender to nature, her wilderness hair afloat; the fifty ways she mapped her forest scent every place she touched, in the bedroom, in the kitchen, out the front yard; the hundred ways she swelled other women's admiration to envy, and then hatred. Men's eyes reflected wonderment, desire and respect. They appreciated her radiance, but who knew what went on inside her head? What she was capable of? There were rumors ... They understood that hybrid Myra was bigger than they were, that she held powers exceeding human strength, and that her eyes sparkled brightest for Vida.

The river's whisper announced Myra's arrival. She sat, knees pulled, beside Vida.

"Hey skipper." Her gaze was an apology. She took his hand. "Our way is this."

"Not the fighting. That's the closest we've been to hell," said Vida.

"Only the foyer."

"And that swirly windy roary thing—" he indicated with a finger.

"Never again."

"Let's do it. Do you really want to get married in Grovea?"

"No."

• • •

Should have been Grovea. Though the chandeliers survived, the flower patch outside the dining room window didn't. For all Vida's intervention, perhaps Tonk's curl of lip had something to do with the outcome. His sling and neck brace made Middle Creek gossip three weeks straight, only interrupted by the crash.

• • •

A flaming shuttle spiraled from the sky to smash into the river. Survivors swam north, east, south. Didn't matter where really; all they cared was to swim. And when they found land, they stayed. Took Middle Creek by surprise, opened it up to otherworldlies. They were prisoners from the land of Xhaust on the way to Shiva, the penal settlement. Guards, murderers, whores and their offspring, all spilled into a forgiving river. They all survived.

Mayor Jenkins liaised with government. He was a puppet mayor, despite the metal in his eyes. His photo-on-the-cabaret-ad sort of face, something suave, almost contemptuous, and his ten carat smile told his true mettle. As did those soft, clammy hands, damp as a toddler's.

What to do with the off-worlders? Camp Zero, government determined. The encampment was built at the sleeve of the forest, not far from the river that had brought them. Free tents or hastily raised log houses. If the new migrants glanced wistfully at the sky, that was all there was to it: a wistful glance. They never thought or mentioned aloud Xhaust or Shiva. How could they? Why would they? Xhaust had cast them out like garbage; Shiva only promised rationed food, water, air . . . labor in plenty.

So, not part of one thing or another, exiles became unruly and bordered on dangerous. Males and children were prone to ferocious bursts of fighting that left some crippled or dead. Women pilfered. Middle Creek law rangers were hazy on how best to handle the growing breed, for government had stressed diplomacy. The exiles carried leanness and muscles, thicket brows, savage eyes and prominent cheekbones; it was completely impossible to forget they were technically Xhaust.

And war with Xhaust was out of the question.

Headed from Middle Creek to outer space for an intimate family moment one new moon, Myra stopped mid-flight. "Look, Vida."

He followed the direction of her gaze. "Birds?"

"Not birds."

They drew closer for a better view and hid behind an Oort cloud.

"Space jets," Vida said first.

"Soaring around Earth's orbit."

"Perhaps seeking a landing zone?"

"Or awaiting confirmation to land."

"Perhaps it's been denied or the pilots have changed their minds," said Vida.

Sure enough, each of the four jets, one by one, catapulted, arched and speared high and away from the solar nebula. Myra and Vida watched in silence.

· 32 ·

With a degree in interplanetary law, a hybrid herself, Myra became a perfect candidate for the newly formed Migrant Council. She bustled between worlds in nanosecond beams, mediating for refugees, seeking better homes for them. Occasionally she was lucky, placed one or three, even ten. Croft, 180C, Sapphire or Selenium, all beyond Earth's orbit, stayed viable options. But it was not an easy task, she found, for Xhaust or Shiva or government did not concede funding. When repatriation shuttles ran dry of fuel, Myra enfolded entire families (sometimes extended) to explode them to destinations beyond stars. She would return home exhausted, falling to comatose sleep.

Under that circumstance, it was a wonder she even fell pregnant. But she did. And Vida couldn't deny it—the moments of intimacy they snatched between Myra's interorbital flights and his research fellowship at Techno Institute left his toes pulsing. If he had thought Myra was wild at the honeymoon, she was wilder at new moon. She guided him to the river's belly and swirled him in uninhibited moments whose power and wholeness left him gasping.

Pregnant Myra did little different. She ran barelegged and swift in nocturnal flights, vaguely aware of her condition. She swam naked in the river, ported to the stars in diplomatic missions, exported exiles to new homes, brought food or medicine back to Camp Zero.

Her skin glowed with the life she carried, so much so the skin became a life form in itself. The blue waterfall in her hair grew wild, her eyes wider. Her lips swelled to a softer fullness that enhanced pending motherhood.

One evening Myra was reading the paper in bed. Vida was on the floor doing sit ups, badly. He was never athletic. Strain showed on his face, incoordination in his hands and legs.

"It says here," her finger on the page, "naked chin-ups are the way to do it."

"*Sure,*" he puffed.

Myra smiled.

"I feel like a new woman," she said.

"So do I," he teased. "You've just never allowed it."

She knuckled him on the head but their rough play turned to something else. Her coupling appetite had tripled. In one wilderness jaunt, they flew backward in time into a cosmic weave whose energy guided them through the universe. Vida, at the verge of evolution, heard Myra cry out.

The baby!

Vida plucked his mind from Eros and into Cosmos Medicine to aid the birth of his child in the wilderness of 180C, through portals of time outside the Earth's orbit. He pulled out the head, cleaned the airway, clipped the umbilical cord. His eyes shimmered as he cradled the baby's head in his hand. In the distance, a red bird soared, circled Myra, Vida and the child, as the world rolled by in an expanse of sky. The umbilical clip did it. No wonder, then, the storm in the child's eyes when she was born, her loud indignation at everything she had been forced to endure, the memory of her time in the placenta wiped. That was the only time Vida knew the bub Tempest to cry.

Despite the cry, the birthing was nothing like he had imagined. Everything was too efficient for the rawness he had believed of an actual birth. The pangs, the crowning inside the brightness of a white-as-white hospital room that did jack all to dim the brutal sounds of childbirth . . . How a doctor might reach forward and grasp the baby's mucus- and blood-coated head, pull the baby dangling by the neck to place it skin-to-skin on Myra's clammy chest.

He marveled under the intense gaze of the horizon, surrounded by unbroken landscape. Light from the sky dimmed and the red bird vanished into remote blackness.

· 33 ·

Silhouette . . .

Myra came along nicely, full circle, from the day she stood naked as a pole on a river's coast and saw him, a skinny, spindle-legged boy. The sight of him filled her with something that made her show off her swimming. He had watched her immaculate dive but even then, as he watched, face alight, she didn't know. Only later, much later, when she sat next to him on the crag, and found he couldn't hurl stones for the very life of him, couldn't whiz or bounce pebbles on the water's face, only then did the knowing come. It was remote and found its way through her like a spell. She looked at his bandy legs, unwieldy hands and the uncertainty on his face. The way he tugged her heart, she knew that she would follow him to the end of the earth and marry him. Vida.

They were unlike other couples, never egged each other. He had a way of driving, of moving the steering with one hand, his whole palm flat on the surface. And while he drove, he had this way of putting his free hand over the back of her hand rested on her lap in the passenger seat, the solid comfort of his weight a rock to Myra. He was her bulwark. She didn't mind that he nodded like a sage, agreed by saying, "That's right," even though he didn't get a word of what she said. That he took magazines to the bathroom throne, left sprinkles of his morning stubble in the ivory sink, as puddles of his shaving foam blossomed around the en suite shower room in his wake. He didn't notice that she talked with dinner in her mouth when she got excited about her work in the Migrant Council. That at times her eyes became inaccessible and she nodded but didn't hear a word he said and, when he took her to bed, she snuggled between sheets and popped little farts with a sigh in her sleep.

. . .

Tempest. T, T, T, *my throat does not move. Not always a soft or a light sound, depends on how you say it. This child was different, grandchild of Salem, same S as in Sayneth. Salem who was no snake, whose green eyes were mostly frightened, spaced wide on that small but shapely face . . . The Salem that wound up with Tonk—a plosive sound "kuh," it stops air into the lips—was a removed self, not the original Salem that T-Mo met. The new Salem rolled her hair, countless curls like a poodle's, way different from hair that lay flat when T-Mo pulled her scarf and saw it. Poor thing. She never recovered from T-Mo, long after his absence seared into heart memory.*

Tempest, T, T, T, *child of Myra.*

I stood over her as she lay in a tight bundle in that crib, newborn, her fingers closed. Red, protective Red . . . even the plant that sang the child lullabies as if predicting a future was silenced by my presence. When I touched the child's forehead she startled, but returned to sleep. A single touch . . . that all it took for my gift to her. A gift of the stepping.

TEMPEST

· 34 ·

The child's yellow eyes switched from one face to the other. The loud gaze held more curiosity than baby softness, an expression more questioning than accepting.

Myra spoke fondly, brushed with a finger unruly hair the color of ruby.

". . . your pappy would sit right here on this spot, ogle me as I swam—"

Vida listened, nodded, his bare toes outstretched to spits from the excitable river. "Ogle?" he said.

"And I would pretend not to have seen him, as I'll pretend to not hear him now."

"*Danke.*"

"Whatever that means," said Myra.

"It's a made-up word that means extreme astonishment," said Vida. "Because the key word in what you just said to young'un here is *pretend*. True or false?"

"That it's the key word or that I'm pretending? If the latter: false."

"Any other answer?"

They laughed.

He sat long with Myra and the child coiled in her arms at their crag by the river, under a white moon and a blink of stars.

• • •

Nana Salem was enamored—distracted with age but enamored. Even arrogant Tonk thawed to the tiger-eyed tot with flaming hair, a child who was seldom ill-tempered or unhappy, who stood upright in her crib at three months to watch the world in silence.

One day Tempest was asleep in her room, on her knees and bum up, cheek on the cool of her sheet. Vida leaned on a chiffonier in the bedroom he shared with Myra and took the occasion to raise a topic.

"Happy we can spend a moment."

"We always do," said Myra.

"Not when you're immersed in work. You have to be bleeding out of the eyeballs to take a day off."

"I'm here, aren't I?" Myra.

"A stolen moment. I worry."

"About what?" said Myra.

Vida watched as she applied primer on a face that didn't need any, gently dot concealer with a cosmetic sponge all around skin that held no blemish. She used the point of a brush on her nose.

"About *who*." Vida indicated the door with a chin.

"Rubbish," said Myra. She ran a film of lipstick, kissed her lips together, kissed them again to certify the lasting gloss would stay, and smacked Vida fully on the lips. "Love you and leave you."

"You are a practical wife and mother—"

"And there's a *but* somewhere in the heart of that sentence?"

"You have this outrageous lack of attentiveness around the house when you're embroiled in intergalactic affairs—"

"Yep, stuck into it."

"Did you notice Tempest doesn't perk up any more when you fly in with that windy roary thing of yours?"

"Good. I am glad she is bonding with you and Red. Exceptionally."

"Tell me the last time you read her a nursery rhyme."

"Why, I wouldn't begrudge Red who sings the song of everything in that mesmeric baritone—"

"Your presidency of the Arbitration Assembly is a noble thing, given the complexity of the migrant question, and Shiva battling for its prisoners. So don't get me wrong—"

"Then what, Vida? What?"

"The child never cries."

"Should she?"

"Normal babies—they cry."

"The child is normal," said Myra. "I'm normal—don't raise your brow, Vida, it's not time to be chucklesome."

"What brow?"

"I'm *normal*, but if you asked Salem, she'd tell you I never cried."

"Children jump. They blink at noise. They coo, squeal and gurgle. They make soft *eh ah* noises when you talk to them."

"So she knows what we mean. She doesn't say *hooroo*, doesn't shriek at a stupid face or a *boo*—"

"My point exactly."

"And that's supposed to mean . . . what? Vida, the child is not a nitwit. Margo told me you weren't either but I'm beginning to wonder now."

"And that's you exasperated."

She sighed. "I'm sorry. Didn't mean to come at you—"

"Horrid like that?"

"Yes." She pressed her head on his chest. "Now, my good man, I really must go."

• • •

Two days later Myra flitted home, a stop-over on the way to a repatriation meeting.

Vida gripped her arm. "Tempest *spoke*."

Myra sank into the nearest settee. "She did? Not *hooroo*, I gather. Shattered I missed it, but you're clearly stressing about something."

"She *spoke*."

"Okay . . . And?"

"At three months?"

"Talk me through it."

"Rr-right. I sit her on a rubber mat. I give her butcher paper and a crucible of paint. She dips into the paint, draws with a finger instead of smudging with a palm, as *normal* babies might." His face was a statement. "Then she cuts out a shape, an immaculate shape. *This my spaceship*, she says. *I drawed it and snip it for my migsy.*"

"Migsy?"

"You're her Migsy."

"I honestly prefer Mum. Migsy?" She is pensive. "Think she'll talk again?"

"You're welcome to try."

"Fool not to." She headed toward Tempest's room, shook her head as she walked. "Migsy . . . Really!"

Tempest refused to say a word and Vida, standing arms crossed by the door, was no big help.

"Oh, you're just going to watch?" said Myra.

Vida smiled. "Glad I could help."

"It's not funny," said Myra.

"You need to listen, not talk at her," he said.

"What?"

She left for work the next morning and Vida was changing Tempest's nappy when the half-drowsy child said, "My migsy tooked my spaceship?"

"Yes, darling. Migs . . . Your mother took the awesome spaceship you made."

• • •

The creature spat like a cat, pulled claws almost bigger than its miniature self the size of a thumb. Yet Myra fetched it from 180C. Absent half the time, she expressed love for Tempest in bits: a ruffle of curls, a snap lift into the air, an exotic pet ferocious enough to confine to a cage.

"This . . . thing?" said Vida.

"You bet," said Myra.

"Present for a child?"

"You bet. And it's not a *thing*. His name is LynK."

The creature's eyes moved in opposite directions, never focused together. It rocked back and forth in chameleon walk toward Tempest, curled deep in sleep around her thumb.

When he awoke LynK gnarled at Myra, but allowed an intimate feed of worm powder and crushed pine from Tempest. In that rare moment, Myra and Vida earned the pleasure of Tempest's tinkling laughter.

Singing plant Red took much exception to LynK. First it wilted and gave everyone the silent treatment. When its leaves fleshed from droop, they arrived with new funnels rich with pigment, speckles and spines. What was newer was Red's wagging, its swelling up and clacking. The launching of spikes was just as new a display and, even in its sleep, LynK turned a vivid green when a spike narrowly missed.

Red also discovered a soaring chorus for the household arrival:

Silly little thing, yeah
Paradox or ghost?
Since when do koalas boast
Padded snowshoe paws?
Tipped ears and cheek ruffs?

As Red belted its freshly arranged song for LynK, its voice registered a new timbre:

Neither one nor the other
I'll have my way with you.

The layer of vocals was breathy, solid, pulsed. It changed in pitch to finish with vibrato.

• • •

Then the riots began. They distracted Vida from concerns at the child's alarming growth. They tossed Myra into yet another line of duty away from motherhood.

Bureaucracy between government, Shiva and Xhaust on matters about the prisoners couldn't be more polished. Xhaust maintained neutrality by refusing to take them, fund them, acknowledge them or reprieve them, but would not sign a Deed of Release for Shiva to get them. Government was unwilling to hand over the exiles without essential paperwork, given the punitive conditions that women and children, let alone men, would be subjected to in Shiva. Because Shiva's economy thrived on free labor and harsh conditions at the penal settlement, a carload of muscle-power lost with the shuttle crash was debilitating, especially when the severity of Xhaust law and familial punishments appeared to discourage potential crime and would-be labor.

When a migrant one day disappeared from Camp Zero, Shiva was a natural suspect. The migrant's spouse gave witness statement that stated she heard rumbling in her sleep, woke up drowsy, then alert, as the tail of a mini shuttle sped out of the doorless log house. Vida and Myra recalled the suspicious jets they had espied as they hid behind an Oort cloud, and wondered if and how they were related to the disappearance.

Camp Zero erupted.

Everybody knew where the migrant had vanished to: Shiva. Why? Shiva was kidnapping her promised prisoners. But why take one, only one prisoner, when there were loads of them? But there was no reasoning with the migrants. Middle Creek law was helpless to control the exiles whose government had not cloaked them with refugee status.

Gun-slinging hooligans with silly boy punks, pitchforks and bazookas demanded not only government protection from Shiva abductors, but citizenship. The hooligans were mostly of mid-grown generation; exiles whose primal instincts bordered on the same bestial behavior that had in the first place guaranteed them or their parents a free ticket to the mines of Shiva, had they not crashed into Middle Creek.

Vida watched over the baby as Myra volunteered in a search party composed of Middle Creek law rangers mostly. And Myra's joining was for good reason. No sooner was she out on a hunt than her hybrid eyes and tracker instinct spotted the missing exile in a ditch not far from Shopping District.

"Drunk as a skunk on half-penny booze," she later said to Vida.

"What of the spouse's statement?" he said.

"A rumbling in her sleep, the waking up drowsy, then alert, as some mini shuttle speared out the hut?"

"Yes, that."

"Bollocks. I'd like to sort the woman myself. We can't have exiles being mendacious and the start of riots." She slapped papers on the table.

"And this?"

"Tact. Government orders. I was going to ask her a few questions . . ."

"Ask?"

"Wasn't going to fist her, if that's what you're suggesting. But government wouldn't allow more questioning."

"That's tragic."

"Pathetic. Diplomacy! Government needs a better grip on these exiles who are nothing but little shits! A logistical nightmare."

"Everyone is confounded about how to help the exiles regain their lives," said Vida.

"Yeah. Just smack me on the head."

"Someone needs to vent." He eyed Myra. "We must approach these matters with sensitivity—"

"I won't be muzzled. I need all the help I can get, Vida. You on my side or what?"

"*Hooroo.*"

"Will you stop that word?"

"I like it. I *am* on your side." He clasped her hand. "Our way is this, remember?"

She sighed. "Long day. Over at last! Someone put a handbrake on it at nine-thirty this morning."

Despite such resolution, the finding of the missing one, Government conceded to the exiles a percentile dole handout to each family every fortnight.

Taxing its own citizenry to feed aliens, people protested.

Another rebellion brewed rapidly, this time from Middle Creek's own folk. Not only had aliens turned Middle Creek into a dog wash, people said, government was rewarding them for it.

The army quietly but effectively dealt with Middle Creek insurgents.

And though all was quiet for a while, everybody knew it was not the end of the exile question.

Nor of Shiva, said Myra.

Two months after the riots, Tempest was tall as a four-year-old. The family prepared for their first holiday together, a reunion of sorts to deepen affection. Nana Margo agreed to watch over domesticated LynK, who surprisingly did not spit at her but climbed her thumb, and the plant Red, that continued belting its goading song:

Feline or marsupial?
A bit rude, yeah
Both get a bum hole
So I wonder, and I really, really wonder

Hunter or hunted?
A matter of time, yeah.
Neither one nor the other
So I wonder, and I really, really wonder

I'll have my way with you (repeat)

Whatever rue Tempest might have felt at her parting with big, solemn eyes from LynK and Red, her mother's enfolding arms and leap into space fixed it. The generally unemotive child trembled in ecstasy as she soared high in a whoosh 297,000 nautical miles to 180C, the land of her birth.

· 35 ·

A bird hops onto a rock.

Myra smiles. She unloads a basketful of Salem's affection: herb and cheese crackers, heritage apples, almond and apricot puffs, cold quail's eggs with flavored salt, black bee honey sweetened beetroot and popping buttercakes. Dear Salem, who reaches up a rung in the pantry and pulls out fragilities packed with flavor, things that melt on your tongue . . .

"Your appetite can handle this?" says Myra.

"Are you offering?" Vida's gaze is on her breast.

"Contain yourself, husband. Wild berry cider in that flask."

"Darn, you can bribe."

"When you put me in an untenable position—yes. You're not helping me with that sort of thing."

"Giving me the stick. Untenable?"

She nods at the child.

"Ah," says Vida. "I misremembered."

"Know your place. Don't mess with me again."

"Danke!"

"Stop it with those words!"

"Hai!"

They share laughter.

180C has put on a beautiful day. She carries an aroma of spice: cinnamon, rosemary, even mountain oregano, in varying intensity. It is a color-filled world, livelier than the botanical gardens between Central Station and Shopping District back in Middle Creek. It is a sound-filled world, awash with the sway of porcupine trees, the *clack!* of sand acorns that transform to hoover crabs and softly mewl or harshly caw.

The pocket of land Vida chose is slanted toward Oorong, a vast lake, alive and powerful. Its thermal waters bubble turquoise. The picnic blanket is spread near a water-licked coast, under an ocean-green broccoli tree that towers above their heads in a bold climb to the sky.

Tempest is fascinated by movement. Her eyes gobble everything. "What a that?" she points.

"That," explains Vida, "is a sparrow-giraffe." He holds the child to his lap.

The red-breasted creature sways his neck in the distance.

"Would you like to see it closer, darling?" says Myra.

"A closer," says Tempest.

But closer is too much for the sparrow-giraffe. He flutters his wings, doesn't fly: runs. Tempest wriggles from Myra's hold and chases, an amazing feat for a child who has never walked.

Vida understands the child's ability and is startled by it. Being precocious is like a plant the color of a crystal, a rare crystal that is luxurious to own, the kind one would find on a necklace or a bracelet or a ring curved by the finest jeweler. Angelite. Topaz. Lapis Lazuli. You stand regal in a meadow of olive green grass. Grains of your celestial blue shimmer like starlets bounded by plain grass. Millennia in your grand beauty, the color of royalty, what an incredible blue, how it transcends you . . . Each reed and creeper in the pasture is outclassed. You are lustrous, a thing from beyond, something whose dazzle is a promise or a wish and way out of reach. Encircled as you are in a prairie, you are alone, fated by your beauty. Your splendor reeks with anguish. The sun throws its light on your ultramarine arms, leaves that sway toward a couple, a man and a woman. They stare at your radiance, at your intensity, your preciousness as if entranced. You see in his eyes that he wants to pluck you and hand you as a gift; he's been wooing her for days, coaxed her to a picnic and now wants to sneak a touch up her thigh with the bribe of your beauty. He forgets to reason that snatching you from the earth, from its texture and temperateness, from its dampness and granularity where you long to be, where you must be if your planthood is to thrive, that such taking will make you wilt and die. Despite her laughter, her tenderness, you see it in her eyes that she wants to clutch you, to possess you, to stifle you in the clasp of her fists, sweated fists full of panic, as she is also fearful of what omen such beauty might bring. Such is the curse of a gifted life, one like Tempest's. Vida yearns to give this child a normal life, but normality is not his to bestow.

He watches as Tempest runs, her race different from Myra's streak of light sweep; this one is lithe. With one big surge and a leap, Tempest is riding the galloping beast now headed for steaming waters.

Myra catches them at the lip of the lake, her chase full throttle by hybrid standards.

"Come, darling." She is breathless. She clasps Tempest's hand. "I suppose you want me to teach you how to swim."

· 36 ·

Tempest soars languid in a clean arc that little breaks the water's surface. She surfaces meters from the coastline, shakes hair coiled in ringlets. The child is as effortless in water as Myra, and one up.

Vida watches them.

Myra doesn't appear disenchanted that her plan to initiate Tempest with gentleness to the water has rebounded. If any learnings are to be made, they are nothing but Myra's own; she understood this when the child cast her clothes at the speed of lightning, raced with the freedom of blowing wind, leapt with the ease of a rising bird and hurled herself into the abyss of the lake.

Tempest has oriented herself. She navigates her swim by instinct. Gold, white and yellow birds soar above her head in a soundless hunt for fish. South of the lake, voracious vegetarian rodents dine in endless warble.

Vida strips to his jocks, but only dips in the shallows. He splashes against heated currents, resigns to a back-float on bobbing waves, frightens a pair of coupling flamingo-eels.

Myra swims naked. Her breasts are pert as ever, unbroken by motherhood. She shimmies like a water snake, alerts Vida with more than eyes to her intention. The hands that fondle his belly are full of curiosity. Vida disengages. Myra's fingers are angling for something he is unwilling to encourage now that he has not misremembered. "Temptation be gone," he says. "Let's just hang out."

"Thanks dictator."

"One can dream."

"Come on. She's dancing with the sparrow-giraffe."

"Who's three times her size." He dodges her fingers.

But his paddle is no match. In an instant, he is captive. Squealing and laughter lend their water play a childlike glee. The lake hums. A distant purr of waves, soft coughs as they lap the shore.

Then all is too silent. The merry singing of birds and insects has subsided. Suddenly there is a crack like thunder, a spear of lightning, and then a roar.

Vida glances up. "Look," he says.

Myra turns her gaze toward a tumble of waves gushing deep into a core, a perfectly round crater right at the point where Tempest was playing moments earlier. "A waterfall?"

"See it before?" Vida.

"Him I definitely don't remember."

A bronzed male, fully-grown and ginger-haired, is stalking the eastern shore of the lakeside.

Vida's eyes seek Tempest. He follows the focus of the strange man who has appeared without warning. He sees Tempest's slender frame vanish with a spit of water into the crater. Minutes, seconds, she reappears at the top of the waterfall as if it were a circle, and squeals in another downward ride. Vida and Myra swim nearer, acute eyes tight at the stranger whose gaze on their little one holds disturbing interest.

Tempest is tall for her age. Her legs are bottle-shaped, not chubby as an infant's. Her hips are narrowed, her belly flat, her navel fully healed and sunken into soft, olive-toned flesh that is as perfectly spotless as her mother's—all plain notice board for trouble in the wrong company.

"If that zucchini-faced hog takes one step closer," says Myra.

"You'd slap the orange off his head?" The question is rhetorical, Vida knows.

"He'll friggin' have that, bronzed pedoperv."

"That's a lot of slap."

Vida climbs out of the water, jocks dripping. He walks toward the stranger, still watching in raw rapture the nimble child with long legs and smooth arms and mermaid power, as she dives into the churn and plunge of a cascade. She tumbles, "Whee!" into the gush as if it were a slide in a children's playground. Inside the blue water's rush, her wet ringlets shine bright as a ruby.

"*Zing ama ha ha*," Bronze Man says. His face tilted toward the waterfall, his voice as metallic as the color of his skin. "*Chillo hu?*"

"I'm sorry," Vida says. "I don't speak 180."

A torching gaze meets his unreasoning eyes.

"Amaz-ing," Bronzie says, his yellow lynx eyes sparkling. "Offspring to you?"

Vida nods. His pulse calms a little.

"Storm in that child," Bronze Man says. Turns camera-flashing eyes back at Tempest, absorbing, memorizing, storing. "She make waterfall."

Myra's cool hands clasp Vida's. "So she did." A pulse of pride in her tone permeates Vida's wonderment.

A run, a swim, a waterfall, he is thinking. One day in the life of an infant. She makes . . . waterfalls.

• 37 •

Silhouette . . .

"I'll have my way with you."

Red finished its song, started the chorus over.

Salem was mindless in her minding, remiss in her observations to begin to guess the plant's intention. But I noticed the plant, which for once didn't wag, swell up or clack when LynK neared, when it forsook all territorial display. I saw LynK shake, sway in his chameleon and toddle walk, as he neared Red close enough to touch.

And I saw the spikes that launched, the ones that seized LynK.

Red's new funnel leaves opulent with tint, shine and spines were a snap-trap, one whose poisoned syrup overwhelmed LynK. So just like that, Red consumed LynK whole.

But Salem never saw. She is still looking for LynK.

By the time Tempest returned from 180C, Red's puff, as it gradually ingested LynK, had leaned. What-am-a-say? R, R. I open my mouth, curl the tip of my tongue without touching the roof of my mouth. R, R, R, the roar of a beast, a soft roar.

Red reminds me of the silent vile in Novic, his charm while manipulating for gain. Ma Space thought the world of him, how could she not? I was a child-bride, but didn't he wait until she found the node of fertility in my collarbone before he debased me? I was a dutiful wife, but didn't he see her in her grave before he put a poker in my eye? His wives Yaris, Vara, Xinnia and Clarin must by now know the real Novic . . . or is his puff all lean?

· 38 ·

It was the gift that led Tempest to the refugee Balmoral in Camp Zero. Her sight led her to his memory.

• • •

First they hurt his daughter, then his wife. Alcohol-emboldened males with laser weaponry, the kind that more than amputates—it disintegrates life forms to states lesser than dust—burst into his two-bed log house at Camp Zero and zapped him to vigilant paralysis. They stood with restless boots and sharpened smiles in a molesting queue, taking turns on his family.

Gagged, helpless, Balmoral watched. His adolescent daughter Jacadi fought each and every one of them, each time. His wife Nickel, simply lay, feet facing east and south, eyes unblinking.

By the time the invaders shackled Balmoral's limbs, by the time he recovered from the numbness of being zapped and they dragged him into night black as tar, he had traveled from rage to impotence, from shame to tears, and finally to a state of barrenness. The thing inside him was inhospitable, too arid for feeling.

His captors hauled him to the north side coast, to a steel wall of shuttles whose glinted metal matched the manacles that ate into his wrists, his ankles. As more guards with lasers joined him with more prisoners, only then did it sink in, his predicament. Those rumors of shuttles that hissed behind clouds, that stalked silent the night sky of Middle Creek Town, those tales of guards from penal settlements out to kidnap labor, now sharpened from hearsay to fact.

The river rollicked in the pale light of dawn. Balmoral sat with men as ill-fated as himself, men inward with thoughts and shames too big to share, men who knew that before long, when enough cargo was acquired, the shuttles would freight them all to a labor camp in Shiva.

At nearly seven years old, Tempest saw all this and more when, at almost dawn, she stepped inside Balmoral's wide set eyes, slit, and shared the husk of the man he once was, and his memories.

• • •

Perhaps the gift started on 180C.

Remember how she curled her palm to clasp wind, how the storm in her fist uncoiled to a giant wave of wind barrels? That was the day she formed a waterfall with her hands.

Or did the gift start when those rowdy boys, hardboiled hoods of town, focused their unruliness upon her?

Dusk was falling, she remembered.

Tempest headed homeward from a visit to Nana Salem who lived in the misty mansion on the hilltop, an affluent manor with several views to the river below. It was not the aesthetic view of her grandparents' house that drew Tempest to the hilltop that day and every other day, not the charming singsong of tinkling chandeliers in her grandparent's drawing room. It was not the fact that there was always food in Salem's house, whiffs of baking, curing meats, simmering broths, roasting trays . . . scents that guided you to the right place—kitchen, out the back, dining room, living room—for a feeding, where Salem and her servants pampered you. What it was—the thing that drew her—was something about Nana Salem, perhaps the fragility in her eyes, her closeness to tears when she thought no one noticed. That certain element drew Tempest to forge a bond with her grandmother, a love only surpassed by a fierce affection for Vida and the wanderer koala-lynx no one could find: *LynK, here boy. Where you, LynK? Here, boy!*

That night, as a red sky gathered in the horizon and deepened from copper to purple, Tempest arrived at the fork of a road whose one trail wound downward to Camp Zero, an exile shelter that had been temporary seven years now. The other track swerved left past Middle Creek Community School to run along Shopping District and beyond.

She gazed wistfully at the school with its brick walls and slant of gray roofs and a chuck-a-dollar fountain outside the principal's office. Northwest stood the gym with orange and blue squares on its windows. The community school was one whose stone floors Tempest's feet had never trodden, whose sea green grass she had never pressed her face against, and whose students she had never befriended. Not that she could but didn't; it just never was. Her father, alarmed by express growth in a two-year-old who looked as though she was four, in a six-year-old who resembled an adolescent, was unshakable on homeschooling.

Vida had explained best he could how she had a thing called "different" and not all people understood "different," especially big kids at Middle Creek Community School.

First time he said it, Tempest retorted, "Why can't Different just stay home so I can go to school without it, and I will pick it up later when I get back?"

"Different is not a pet," said Vida.

"What is it?"

"It's in the blood."

"How?"

"You're just different."

"Can't the doctor at Coulthird Clinic, the one who looked at my new teeth, can't he take out the different or give it medicine?"

"It's not that simple," said Vida.

"Why isn't it simple?"

"Because your Migsy . . . your mother is special."

"Special? Why isn't she different?"

"She's different too."

"Why?"

"Some people, like you, like your mother, are born . . . different."

"Why?"

Vida was as apt a teacher as he was a Cosmo scientist. But he was best as a dad. Yet he couldn't explain "different" and resorted to examples of his green thumb: "See the other day how I fixed Mrs. Bright's tomatoes and they stopped dying? She couldn't fix them but I could—"

"Because you're also different, Pappy?"

"Aha!"

Now, at six years and a half, Tempest was lofty and shapely enough to pass for twice that age.

That day from Nana Salem's, she was inside a yawning field courted on either side by a shadow of trees, halfway toward the community school, when she saw a knot of boys. At first they seemed to be standing, perhaps talking. Then with a shift of moonlight, she realized they were dancing. As she drew closer, she recognized them. It was Rock and his punks, a gang of rare breeds who bordered on dangerous. They were the nucleus of most insurgencies against government, stalking the waterfront and making trouble. They terrorized by day citizens of Middle Creek whose very tax and sweat they effortlessly took in dole handouts, but danced to silent music and welcomed dusk at close of day.

Children piped puns about the camp:

What's the meaning of nothing? / Camp Zero.
Thanks for nothing! / But why, I didn't create Camp Zero.
What is the sum of many numbers? / Camp Zero.
What did Zero say to Eight? / Ate. / Ate what? / Free food at Camp Zero.

Shunned, bored, the boys of Camp Zero danced: a shimmying of hips, a ripple of bared chests (toned), a movement of feet so fast they dizzied.

Tempest was still meters away when one dancer, the one whose shoulders carried the biggest sway, the one with the richest savage face, disengaged and approached. He was top dog Rock. He took another step toward her and, in a stagger of stilling motion, the rest of them stopped dancing, one by one. They milled beside him.

Tempest stood, a sole girl on a woodlands jaunt, facing hard-core hooligans a dozen strong. Rock parked himself in front of her and whistled.

"Look what we got."

A responding whistle came from the back.

"Oh, my, yes."

"Bit brave, ain't she."

"Bit pretty too."

"Ain't she a scone?"

She picked her way, moved to skirt around them but Rock and the crowd shifted to stand in her path. Her hands balled to fists by her side.

"Feisty!" said Rock. The gang roared, merry.

"She the little freak whose mama's a hybrid," a voice in the back said.

A fresh ripple of laughter.

"That true?" Rock eyed her. "You a hybrid?"

"She no hybrid," someone quipped. "She a quarter-brid!"

They roared.

"I never seen a quarter-brid before. Feel like Columbus!"

They squealed, half-baked sounds like puppy yelps.

"Nursing your tongue little girlie?" Rock again.

"Maybe she nursing a spell."

"And she not so little."

Rock licked his lips. "Oh, my. Yes," he said.

With a surge, Tempest soared toward the corridor of trees on the far side. They chased, not fast enough, not slow either. She ran until leafy fringes of hanging trees almost touched her head.

Rock arrived first. His gang, tongues almost hanging, panted behind.

Tempest, squared off, fists drawn. She faced Rock.

"I swear," she said.

He advanced, eyes excited.

The tail of an undead creature fluttered in Tempest's belly. She dropped her hands, stood feet apart.

"Careful boy," someone quipped. "She a redhead."

"Tiger eyes too."

"I warn you," she said, so quiet only Rock could hear.

"Yeah?" He licked his lips.

Perhaps it was the beast in her tone or a sensing of the tail in her belly, for although Rock laughed, fear spread in his eyes. The half laughter behind him was equally uneasy. Then deep silence claimed its space, until scattered little coughs punctured the silence.

Tempest's eyes rolled. She was not sure to this day whether it was the sheet of lightning that cut across her path and sprinted to the end of the world, or the earthquake suspended in her fist that exploded Rock's head. That same thing made the first punk behind him cringe against a tree and then stagger sideways clutching his head. He fell in a heap into the softness of dew. Whatever it was, lightning, earthquake or tail, it dispatched the rest. With spaniel yelps they swayed back a few steps, swirled and fled.

Tempest ran, her face covered in body fluid. She raced past Central as a train pulled up the platform. She did not think to fling herself through its singing doors before they snapped shut. She zipped west and sped all the way home.

There, she hovered by the kitchen doorway where her parents worked, as usual, like a pair of hands. Myra washed the dishes. Vida dried them.

It was Myra who noticed her first. "Hey darl."

"Hey Migsy."

"Hey poppet." Vida.

"Hey Pappy."

"Your face could do with scrubbing," said Vida. "You been burying something?"

Tempest shifted her weight from one foot to the other, didn't budge when Myra snatched a fresh tea towel from a drawer and dabbed at the grime on Tempest's face. "Hell, it's wet. Is this . . . blood?"

"Hooroo," Vida drew her to his arms. "You alright, kiddo?"

Nod. Pause. Shake of head. Then: "Pappy, is hybrid bad?"

"This coming from . . . where?"

"Course not, silly." Myra.

That was when Tempest told them what happened. She clutched Vida's waist, her face pressed against his chest, as she trembled and trembled, a six-and-a-half-year-old once more in her daddy's arms.

So they told her stories. Of T-Mo, her grandfather whose night grew silent. Of a girl named Dale Hocking whose pert face and russet tresses wound up in the river bed. Of a man-boy named Al whose body melted to porridge in the water's wash.

Hearing the telling, Myra's voice inside a voice, and seeing Vida's inward drawn eyes, Tempest understood. These were not stories told to reconcile her with what she had done. These were not right or wrong stories. These stories just were.

• • •

If any survivor spoke to Middle Creek rangers about the incident, no one came to arrest the child. But with that gift, a tail in her belly that commanded thunder, came another: the stepping.

Tempest spent much time with Nana Salem, dashing, when she couldn't telephone her affections, to visit the house on the hill. Perhaps it was that fragility in Nana Salem's eyes but one day, alone together, Tempest looked inside them, and stepped in, just like that. Inside she saw a simple girl with big dreams that permitted her hypnotism by the careless smile of a man with lanterns for eyes. Tempest saw spring and summer, all in an instant. There was color and movement on dampened ground, then a soft prairie carpeted in grass. She saw water whose tide hissed and sighed as it touched the shores. If she'd seen beauty, what she saw was a thousand times more, and then the world darkened.

She saw the fading shadow of an ashy man walk into night. He walked light, gentle, treading on air, giant feet moving away, away. Night could not mask the glitter of his copper hair, nor could it fade the shine of sunglasses perched upon his head. Before he touched a deeper corridor of night, he turned and waved.

His smile was wide as a rainbow, his teeth perfect as baby ivory.

When Tempest stepped out of her grandmother's body, she was as shaken as Nana Salem, who looked as if she had just walked out of a daze. Eyes aglow, Salem shook her curly as a poodle's hair and eyed Tempest strangely.

"Child," in a voice filled with awe. A beat fluttered on her temple. "The oddest thing happened . . ." Words faded on a wistful note. Her gaze wavered, as if accepting that old heads did hallucinate.

• • •

Months.

Tempest took courage to execute the stepping upon Tonk. He was sprawled on a damask armchair, reading a newspaper, when she entered. A burst of hostile light raced from the shadows, halted just before a lane whose mouth held a white arrow on a wooden post. Words on the sign read: *The Way*. She pondered it, wondered whether to continue down the path, or turn back. For what if there was no coming back out of Tonk, into the real world?

Before she could decide, she felt the promise of rain in the air. A sweep of wind carried and deepened that scent, before something jungle, a thing animal, invaded her senses. She was almost out of that godawful place when the excited pant of a creature about to eat her touched her neck. She swerved and caught a close-up of the ash man's face. He was only a face, nothing else, and coasted inches from her face.

"Why do you run?" His voice was hard as a gravestone.

"Who are you?"

He laughed loud, so loud that night fled and dawn arrived.

A chase of rain escorted Tempest's bolt, as the man laughed laughed laughed.

Down a valley she shot like a cannon and dived out of Tonk. She found herself quietly sat next to him, a novel fallen from her lap. A sandy filled head and a cardboard mouth made her wonder if it were a dream.

Inside the cool head and handsome face of Nana Margo, Vida's mother, Tempest found birds the color of blueberries. Here, the ashy stranger wore pigmentation. His lips bore the hue and texture of rubies. As her fear of him faded, as she more and more questioned him about his identity, his lips took a playful softness when he smiled. But it was the world inside Ken Stuart, her grandpa, a man always full of amusement with life, that created something special. The ashy stranger that dwelt in him carried a song on his lips, poetry in his eyes. Things in this world came in shadow, rainbow and gold. The stranger crept as though he held diamonds in his toes, and Tempest chased after him. She brushed aside bushes with her fingers, found herself headed toward a moon in full plumage. But as she neared, night folded and light changed. A shift of wind, and the man turned. He watched her approach. His smile was wide, almost wild. His eyes connected with her soul, and she almost ran into him.

"Who are you?" she said.

"You know," he said.

But how could he? Be . . .

"T-Mo is dead," she said.

"Is he now?"

His eyes became stars full of shadows, deep endless shadows. He smiled, waved and walked into a harsh blast of winter.

A crease promised to break into a smile on Ken's face when she stepped out of him. She wondered if he knew, what he knew, and if that was why he was smiling. He coughed into his hands and indicated with a nod toward the kitchen. Sounds of Margo scolding the cat flitted out the doorway.

"It's not funny," said Nana Margo. She walked briskly toward Ken and whipped a baseball cap off his head. His smile vanished, but a twinkle still burnt in his eyes.

• • •

Tempest thought long and hard about her parents, about Myra's mystery and distance, about Vida's tallness and simplicity, and their love for each other. Theirs was an affection that sometimes shut her off.

One day, unable to resist, she did it. They were quietly sat in the reading room, side by side, Vida's eyes not lifting from the screen of a mobi-tech on his lap, Myra reading *Twenty-One Ways*, a book he had written. Each was rapt, as though nothing could break their concentration, but their toes mindlessly slid toward, brushed and climbed each other. Watching them, Vida's handsome face, pale complexion and burgundy hair, and Myra's blue hair splashed with light, Tempest felt a pulse of wonderment, mostly at her mother. Vida, she understood completely. He was uncomplicated and sensible, straight as a pin. She loved him too much to invade his inner space.

But much as she esteemed her mother, Tempest's curiosity overwhelmed her. So she stepped . . .

Myra jumped back, startled. She cast her book aside and black eyes glittered. Slap! "Don't. You. Ever! Try that again."

But Tempest did try it on others. The sensation it roused was of a different nature. She understood that the stepping was something that could mushroom out of control, yet she could not stop it. She saw and heard things, people, creatures. She began to understand the folk like Salem and Tonk and Margo and Ken whose thoughts she reached, whose sight, whose memories she shared. She saw things they had witnessed only moments before. It became an addictive game, one that captured people's fears, affections, imaginings. The experience carried her on a giddy slide more powerful than the tumble of waves in the waterfall she had made years ago on 180C.

But only in her family did she see T-Mo. She sought him and his river-wide smile. He morphed inside Nana Salem, Margo, Ken and Tonk, looked, acted and spoke different inside each one of them.

• • •

Tempest stepped into Balmoral.

That dawn, before the stepping, unable to shake sleeplessness, she slipped out of the house in Middle Creek. She bounded in an exhilaration of wind toward the river. A mile away, she saw light through the trees and sensed . . . tragedy?

She hid in shadows, saw males with lasers drag shackled exiles from Camp Zero. Her heart fell out to them, the prisoners. The live tail in her belly awoke. Swish, swish. Adrenaline gushed. Swish, swish. About to step out into light and dash to the giant ship on a rescue mission, she saw a big flash of radiance. Myra—Vida enveloped in her arms—flapped in from the night. She swooped from the air, onyx eyes alight, and gently released Vida, who fell by Tempest's feet.

Myra had just about time to slap with a bare hand a deadly laser beam aimed her way, when her feet set running before they touched ground. She flashed toward the firing Shiva guards, blocking with her palm blasts of the humming lasers.

Swish. Swish. An undead tail. Tempest straightened to full height. She raised a fist to unhinge something seismic, but Vida tackled her to the ground.

"No baby, don't. Get help. Now."

Plenty must have happened in her absence. By the time Tempest returned to the giant spaceship by the river, a chase of Middle Creek ranger sirens close behind, the situation had changed. Her eyes scanned, sought information and found a bedraggled Mayor Jenkins acting with the incompetence of a complete idiot.

"He can't grill people like hot dogs," a person complained. "Judging by the questions he's asking, he has no clue what happened here."

"Cursing, more than grilling, I'd say," another one said.

"I'd curse too if I were plucked from my bed at the sleeve of dawn."

"A worthwhile plucking if it will trim the swell of that girth from our sweat, that's government for you, and he dares complain."

Half the Shiva guards lay on the ground. Tempest noted their lack of weaponry and took in the picture of Myra, legs akimbo, admiring her work. Her blue as blue hair flew, a single topaz sheet in a leeward float. The lip of Vida's laser gun swallowed any escape ideas the remaining Shiva guards might have fostered.

• • •

It was later as Vida, in pajamas still, sought the wounded among prisoners and Myra talked to Mayor Jenkins, as Tempest wandered aimless, no longer needed, that she saw Balmoral.

He sat among a dulled crowd of rescued prisoners somewhere on the ground, away from the action. He hugged his knees, de-souled eyes pinned toward a space in the horizon. She walked toward him and, just like that, wordless, stepped into him. She saw his terror, his torture, his desolation. And before she stepped out of him, her heart staggered. A dark puddle grew beneath a little girl thick-haired, flat faced, a child shaking, shaking under a straw bed in Camp Zero.

Tempest found the girl inside the log cabin, rocking the head of her brutally ravaged sister. Lake deep albino eyes studied her. When Tempest stepped into them, the world opened like a water lily into a giant emptiness. A pale white sun hovered in the horizon . . . Tempest had difficulty holding her heart down. To her surprise, inside this strange child, she caught the familiar sight of T-Mo. He came toward her, giant feet bounding on air. He wore his river smile.

"You don't belong here," Tempest said. "This girl is not family."

"She is more."

"Than what?"

"More than you know."

"You are an intelligent illusion. I do not believe in you anymore."

"Look."

She looked at tall, gnarled trees and rebel flowers of black gold. She isolated deeper shadows from plainer ones inside the stars in T-Mo's eyes, felt a circular effect of wind on her neck. She found the silence of moving things, the sound of the unmoving. The ground sighed, and then whistled. Tragedy, destiny, and then something vibrant.

The road back was spread-out, deep.

Tempest stepped out of the exile to a wild dog howl in the distance.

The little girl was exactly where she had been, cradling her dead sister. Small knees pulled up, tiny hands, not balled into fists, stroked Jacadi's braids. The eyes like peanuts sunk deep, spread apart, were calm, appraising. There was nothing in the line of beauty to recommend the girl. The absence of emotion confounded Tempest. It was fruitless to attempt.

"But that's stupid," the girl said. Peanut eyes spoke loud, studied Tempest as though they understood her secret.

"What's so stupid?"

"I *know*." This voice scratched.

Something snatched the ground from Tempest's feet. She sank knees up beside the plain girl with bony legs, feet like maitake mushrooms, a girl whose best or worst praise, insult or affection possibly bordered on one word: stupid.

"What's your name?"

"Amber."

"What is it you know?"

"*Fedele crai brook?*"

Tempest returned her gaze, startled. Not because she understood the strange tongue but because Amber did, in fact, really know.

"His name is T-Mo."

"*Fye fi crem put?*"

"He knows death."

"*Clova fo rick max?*"

"His world changes, inside people. In yours, there was wind and song, and the yawn of something empty. *Vosco ani prom. Tat row doman rout.*" Tempest slipped with ease into that new language, a tongue that was not of Middle Creek, nor Hybrid, nor Exile. She kicked off her shoes, curled her feet. "*Mag dir a ti vae.*" Her voice was within a voice. She did not recognize it.

They spoke of things past and present, of places cool as a mountain breeze, of water fresh as lemon mint. They talked of fragments of longing, of rich, clasping terror that was hard to break. And they spoke of wind that struggled, and failed to escape, of amity between brand new strangers. Of an ashy man whose pale, colorless skin was fragrant as honey and sage.

Until they lost time.

AMBER

· 39 ·

Myra steers in and out of a storm cloud. A white streak of lightning inscribes the red sky ahead. The shuttle rolls. It judders through eddies of air, swirls of draft that push it up and down the firmament. Myra aligns the vessel. She reduces speed and moves the throttle. She lowers the flaps, stabilizes speed and noses for landing. She lines up against the planet, brakes at touchdown.

The land's pulse is perceptible even in the vessel. Myra looks back at her passengers. Vida is a little green but recovers sufficiently to smile at Amber and Tempest seated behind him, nonchalantly so.

It is Myra's position as president of the Arbitration Assembly that allows such ease of intergalactic transportation for the family. She could just have easily enveloped all three, transmitted them in a swoop and flash to the remote galaxy. Instead, she chose to borrow a repatriation shuttle not on live commission to the planets. Naturally, government commanded she fund her own fuel. Not a problematic task on dual income, with Vida's thriving professorship in Cosmos Medicine at Techno Institute. His stellar decoding of the navigation map is reason for their early arrival.

Novic is not expecting them—should it matter?

Myra worries. She has not been to Grovea since childhood, not since T-Mo, her bona fide bloodline. Later, when Tonk was wed to her mother, his human status limited the privilege of intergalactic tours, though his prosperity would have permitted it. But Tonk was not a man of the voyaging ilk. The arrogance that curled his lips when he said it made "voyaging" sound like prostituting.

Vida unhitches the girls from the vessel's capsules.

Myra takes his hand. "Your arm to navigate my waist," she smiles. "Our way is this."

Aloft there is nothing of the storm that endangered landing but for Myra's airborne aptitude. Rather than darkness is a jeweled sky pregnant with diamonds, stars each blinking an intimate eye as personal as it is seducing. Out yonder is emergent coral on a volcanic beach. Black pebbles run along Turtle Cove.

Amber and Tempest bob and chatter toward the cove.

"Careful now," calls Vida. "Or you'll be deported for too much happiness."

They arrive at mangroves at the far shore. The coast veers into Rocky Point. Here, amethyst sand falls from waves of the great reef. Far left, a foot trail climbs to the main esplanade of the inner city, Bruthen, the capital of Grovea.

Up on the boulevard, the girls go crazy like freed animals. They tumble straight and in circles, zig-zag and in forward bursts, arms spread like birds, chaotic hair adrift. Now they are doing a waltz, now a foxtrot.

Myra eyes them. "Good seeing Amber like this," she says.

The earthy girl shimmying carefree in the sand is far different from the thick-haired, flat faced child who stepped into their kitchen back home, a little girl wearing peanut eyes and unforgivable clothes, clutching in her hands a bundle of everything she owned.

• • •

It was the morning of the Shiva raid, the day Myra's attack on an alien space-ship full of Shiva guards restored tranquility to Middle Creek. It was the day Mayor Jenkins said to Myra: "The key to the city is yours."

Myra savored the moment, the neat salutes from Middle Creek rangers, a thunder of clapping from rescue teams . . . She sought and discovered adulation in Vida's eyes but found nothing of Tempest who had vanished.

The child emerged several hours later at home in the kitchen with a little girl who smelt a bit rough, whose hair was locked in two thick braids.

Myra looked up, half-frowning and then astonished. "Why, Tempest," she said. "Who's your friend?"

Vida took one look at the girl accompanying their daughter and pointed without a word toward Tempest's bedroom.

The new girl climbed but hovered at the landing. Her arms still nestled her sack. Downstairs Tempest lingered. Her eyes searched Vida's.

"Can we? Can we, can we Pappy?"

She squealed with glee at the tilt of his chin toward the stairs. The two girls scooted all the way up to the bedroom.

"I am exasperated that Tempest never seeks instruction or affirmation from me," said Myra.

"Yet she obeys my chin," agreed Vida. "It is what it is. I am glad to also notice that you don't say *Mum's good* anymore when she insists on calling you Migsy." He smoothed the curl of her brow with a finger.

"Why didn't you suggest a bath?" said Myra. "That little girl she tugged along—"

"That little girl's alright."

Myra closed her eyes. "We don't know a thing . . ."

"In time."

Didn't take long to link the new girl to Balmoral, the broken man rescued from the alien ship. Once you put together what the child had witnessed . . . you couldn't fault Vida tilting his chin up the stairs for the girls.

Despite a fair distance in build between them, not much stood in age between the girls, Myra was sure. She couldn't help but notice vulnerability in the new girl's jaw, something that piled years to her appearance. She was attractive. Sort of—one had to look for it first. The symmetry of one eye to the other, the distance from the bridge of her nose to the flute, the height of her cheekbone from her jaw, all called up a defining beauty. But when she spoke . . . the scratch!

"Amber," said the sand in the girl's throat when Vida asked her name.

Myra stood straight-backed, arms crossed. Something about Amber brought Myra unease. While the girl appeared relaxed with Tempest and Vida, with Myra she stayed remote. Albino eyes looked at Myra as though they knew her secrets, but which?

The girl's father was as good as dead. Last Myra saw him, back in his house in Camp Zero, he was curled in a corner, baring teeth at anything that came close.

Mayor Jenkins agreed without question that medical confinement was the solution, the *only* solution. "If you and Vida wish to adopt Amber . . ." he suggested. Vida was already nodding.

"Does Amber wish it?" snapped Myra.

And frankly, did Myra?

Since the girl joined their household, Myra felt alone, felt she was losing Vida, losing Tempest . . . Even then, despite Tempest and Amber's bond—the girls were close as a thumb and a nail—they had their fights. Spiteful fights that took joint effort, Vida's and Myra's, to snatch apart the girls who were vicious as mastiffs. How the fights started was anyone's guess. One minute, the girls were burrowed in their secret language. Next, Tempest had roared across the room. Or one moment Tempest was stepping inside a hula hoop, bringing its edges to her waist, spinning . . . The next Amber had crept, snagged a foot with a heel, sent Tempest sprawling face down, limbs open. And then a fight.

Sometimes the minds behind the tiffs were rash, foolish. Often they were calculated. Lethal. What Amber lacked in strength she made up with agility. Now a head grip, an elbow combination, reverse swap, then suddenly Amber was on top. Flip, and Amber was pinned. Hook, dodge, kick, block, upper cut. Now Amber had wriggled to offset Tempest, then both girls had tumbled.

Even as Myra and Vida snatched them apart, used monumental effort, there was no anchoring peace. The girls lunged, pressed forward, threw hands and legs. Myra determined that one day she would arm them with gloves, bolt them in a room and let them finish whatever the thing, the one that set them off.

"We need a vacation," said Vida, releasing his seize on Amber after one such wrestling bout.

"And I know just about where," panted Myra, freeing a writhing Tempest.

The look Amber gave Myra was poison.

· 40 ·

Grovea. Myra listens to the fading notes of Amber's song along the boulevard, not understanding a word of it: *"Mah ran en at qu flate vene mondu . . ."*

"Pro al fit set Nov," joins Tempest in sweet chorus. *"Fo ri zett ob!"*

The girls have a code between them, a secret language that is wonderful and carefree. They call it *pa tabe dome.* Now their feet jump so with happiness. Looking at the skip of their happy feet, heads dipping up and down in the distance until they are out of sight, Myra remembers a star dance she once saw in Otis. It held a pattern of blinking that spread from one diamond to another, until the whole sky was a symphony of light.

The children are once more in sight. Tempest is holding Amber by the arm and leg, giving her an airplane spin. Amber goes high, higher, squeal squealing as she flies. Their play spreads. It touches other creatures in Bruthen. Fireflies hover. Cicadas awaken and begin their chant. A Vulcan eagle moves its wings to a slow beat, and then boasts spectacular loops.

Myra and Vida catch up to the girls who are bouncing in topped-up excitement. The girls have discovered a burbling brook whose waters surge against and slap into the coast. Water-sprayed strands of hair streak across Tempest's face. Amber's hair is locked up in braids. The two of them now are nothing like the girls who at other times roared and pulled out claws, who leapt to tear at each other's faces. It's not like they laid in wait for a fight or angled to make it happen. There was no scornful planning behind it. A fight just happened in an instant: one mouth twitched, an eyelid fluttered, and—as if by unspoken pact—the girls flew at each other, and someone clasped ten fingers around someone else's throat.

Now spent from water play, Amber and Tempest are on the ground,

Grovean moonshine in their eyes. "In three days," says Myra, "when the season dips into summer, the moon becomes bloodred, and the sun that rises afterward is a simmering emerald."

Before they reach the tall doors of the Temple of Saneyth, Myra points at a flight of steps leading to a bell-tower. "Wait here," she tells her clan.

She notices Vida's look about him. He is disconcerted, she knows.

The girls are no longer skipping. They are as quiet as Vida, their eyes drawn toward a throng of late night worshippers. Near the temple's entrance, robed men, women in leather sandals and pleated tunics, and a handful of naked children appraise their approach.

Myra finds Novic in the incense room.

"Y-yes?" he says without recognition.

The shadows in his eyes halt her approach. He is much as she remembers him, leathered skin furrowed into itself with age, clinging to bone. His eyes are as old as Jacob. His face looks like death. But his hair! A black magical mane falls to his waist. So black, it shines like metal. So soft, the tresses of it bounce with her words.

"It's me, Myra."

His expression does not change. With a lift of palm, he commands the door shut. The room falls into darkness. She feels rather than sees his approach.

"Are you not afraid, child?" The roll of rocks carrying echoes in his voice is more than she remembers.

"I should be."

"But you are not." His robe carries a reedy scent. The touch of his hand on her chin is coarse. "It is you," he says. "And you bring something new." He takes her hand. "Take me to your people."

• • •

Tempest gasps at the sight of him, at his magical hair long and flowing like a spell. Novic crouches beside her, sits her on his knee.

"Dear child, don't look so stupefied. We have never met."

"But—" begins Tempest.

"I understand how you can be mistaken. Child—" he lifts her chin so her tiger eyes meet the fog in his. "I am not T-Mo."

He puts her down, pulls something from his robe. It is a mouth harp. He plays music, a welcome hymn, Myra explains. His song tells of a pristine beach and falling rocks; of wet tropics and flowing rivers; of chrysanthemum leaves and budding coral.

"This," he says, "is the song of Grovea." He pockets the harp. "Come. I will take you to my clan."

· 41 ·

Novic guides them through tropical palms. Sugar beets line the tableland. They travel up and down rolling hills. A cascade of natural water runs all around. They cross a floodway and find simple cottages, almost country. Past a whistling wind, up a rugged mountain like a camel's back, down a mammoth hill . . . Alas! Mirage Lagoon.

Here, streets curl like a smile. Everything is rounded and smooth, or half-rounded and perfect. Time moves in trickles. Water in the lake does not rock or rollick. It glides. Women walk like queens; men like emperors. Sometimes, it seems, time stalls to merge past and future. Things happen that Myra is not quite sure which timeline they belong to. It seems like she has met village folk long before she actually meets them. Each introduction is like a re-introduction. Like the meeting of Novic's wife, Yaris, now number one after Silhouette left Novic. Looking at the child, Cassius, nestled in her arms, his large, gold coin eyes and mutiny of amethyst hair, Myra knows she has seen this image before.

Or like when wife number two, Vara, her eyes carrying benevolence, unrestricted welcome in them, gushes over the ruby in Tempest's hair, the tiger in her eyes . . . Or like when Xinnia, number three, skin like honey, rests cool fingers on Myra's skin . . . Or like when Clarin, number four, speaks with a plum in her mouth and an accent from France . . . That sense of déjà vu for all these women . . . But the last time Myra saw Novic was as a child. How could she have met these same wives and children?

She seeks Novic.

"Speak." His arms fold around his chest. "Why are you here? Really here?"

She tells him about Amber and Tempest, how they whisper and slip into a secret language when they are not half-killing each other.

His eyes make shadows in the room.

"I know fear," he says quietly. "And you wear it."

"But—"

"You are frightened for Tempest." His tone changes. "I tell you this: if you smother her, she will leave."

"She sees things," says Myra. "Autumn, spring, winter in people's eyes. She knows things I would rather she didn't."

"This is where you go wrong. Tempest does not *see* things; she *is* those things. She is autumn and spring and winter. She is all that and more. You cannot strangle nature."

"And Amber?"

"She tames the beast."

"The beast?"

"The undead thing with a tail that goes swish swish inside your child."

"How do you know of the undead thing?"

"How do you know to sleep or to wake? Is it by the rise and set of the sun or by the inner sense of your body? How do you know to be with a man like Vida? Does your head dictate your heart or does the heart dictate the head? I know what I know, and Tempest's power is not a legend. She is a legend."

"But how—"

"*How* is not the right question. *Where* is what you need. Where there is Amber there is a tamable undead thing. Amber has closeness to you, more closeness than you can begin to understand. She is more than what you know."

"But legend . . . Tempest . . . Legend is good, right?"

"In her inexperience, Tempest does not understand the fullness of her strength." He turns away from her.

"How can I stop it?"

He swirls. "Stop it? But you can't."

"How can I train it?"

He pulls out his harp, puts it to his mouth and plays. His music carries her to a world that is alive, that is hers.

• 42 •

Silhouette...

He laughed himself to death.

Balmoral. B, B, a voiced sound. You feel a vibration in your throat. Lips together, you trap the sound in your mouth, a surge of pressure and the sound explodes. Ba-Ba-Balmoral. I like this sound. Rosellumus, the papers said. That was his surname. Rosellumus, like the bird of Tafou that goes Gwa! Gwa! Gwa! The one that got baby Peaches seated in his crib, pulling himself to a stand, walking holding the rails toward the sound to imitate: Ga! Ga! Ga! Rosellumus. You open your mouth and curl the tip of your tongue without touching the roof of your mouth. R. R. Like a pirate.

Balmoral Rosellumus.

What-am-a-hear? No, it is what-am-a-see. Seven years he had lain in his bed at Cool Oasis, a medical center for crazies. Often he was silent, sometimes he managed a cracked voice, rarely he hummed rhymes from the land of Xhaust where he was born.

One day, he looked at the doctors who treated him, at the nurses who forced medicine into him (when they were not injecting him with drips or changing his diapers), at fellow patients who screamed at him, then at other inmates who picked up wails of the screamers and themselves howled at him like maudlin wolves . . . and he saw dead clowns. A single, happy clown lay on the head of each and every person except himself, and Balmoral shook his head in wonderment.

One day, the toe of a clown on someone's head twitched, and a small smile accompanied Balmoral's shake of head. Another day a dead clown moved a body part and Balmoral grinned. The day a clown's eyelid fluttered, its grin twitched, a finger jerked and a knee kicked, Balmoral could not hold back the chuckle that slipped out of his smile.

After three days of smiling and chuckling, he saw something of the clowns that changed him. Perhaps it was how they sat up and began to dance on people's heads. Or how they gouged out eyes from their own smiley faces and played eyeball with each other. Or how porridges of blood dripped from the gouged eye sockets down merry cheeks to soak the medics' coats.

Balmoral threw his head back and laughed laughed laughed until he died.

· 43 ·

The outside world fell in a rush of wind. Vida drove through rows of pines swarmed with creepers. Once, twice he cast a glance at Myra. She sat silent in the hired hearse. She rolled down her window, brooded. It was still drizzling. Water washed her face sidewise.

Light rain chased the car miles before petering under rays of white sun. The hearse paused outside black gates of a Gothic building. Gates groaned, swung inward. The car nosed into a lawn hosting medics and the body of Balmoral, Amber's father.

Collapsed left atrial valve, the medical certificate said.

• • •

The body was first at a nearby morgue before they moved it the following morning, one that promised a sunny and calm day, to Le Piste funeral home.

Amber stood ashen outside the porch.

Myra pondered how, since Amber joined her household, the child's affections had fiercely navigated toward Tempest and Vida, and how with Myra she continued to remain aloof. She thought of the girls' code between them, their secret language that was wonderful and carefree but how today even that was of no use to assuage Amber's grief. Most of all, Myra recalled what Novic said in Grovea: "Where there is Amber there is a tamable undead thing. Amber . . . is more than you know."

Myra wondered how much Novic had *not* told her.

Perhaps for wanting to find a way into Amber's affections, this child who tamed the undead thing, or perhaps for a tugging in her heart at the sight of a child's unspoken grief this day of Balmoral's burial, Myra's chest popped. Her mind was made up in a heartbeat. She spread her arms, folded one knee and launched herself. She soared up the skies until thousands of miles opened up from Earth. Her hair flapped all the way to Xhaust.

There, she swooped down, straight into the Justice Library. Xhaust was renowned for documentation. Every citizen, every event was carefully charted into the books of history. Myra was determined to find record of Balmoral's crime. What thing had brought him trial and condemnation, a sentence of life exile in Shiva had the prison shuttle not spiraled from the skies to crash into Middle Creek? What terrible thing had he done to warrant such punishment for him and his family? That was the thing Myra sought.

She was uneasy about what she might uncover but try finding it she would. Perhaps if she unearthed it, Amber might see. As right now, the girl couldn't hold sense for grief. If her father was better dead than alive, soon Amber would know. Myra would see to it that Amber knew.

• • •

The documentation Myra found of Balmoral's crime was not that of the guilt she sought. The papers said a man had died. He was thrown from a roof he was repairing, and slowly choked until he died, strangled by a hoisting rope that looped around his neck. The man's name was Setius Rosellumus. He was Balmoral's rich uncle. And his sole heir? Balmoral.

Myra flipped the page. Palatio, the first wife of Setius, raised the accusation. By and by, witnesses came forward. They attested to catching glimpse of Balmoral in the vicinity of the crime about the time of the uncle's death. But it was a time nobody exactly could pinpoint, one only ascertained by the depth of rope-cut in his neck, by the degree of rigor mortis in his fingers . . .

Balmoral was tried. The jury that convicted him did so by a single deciding vote. He escaped execution, a punishment the weight of his crime deserved, and was sentenced to exile with his family in Shiva.

However, oh however!

Five moons later evidence emerged of Palatio's hand in her husband's death, having carefully staged it with the help of a lover, a hit man named Spoon—named so for he was dumb as a spoon on all matters except murder. Spoon had made this murder look like an accident. The law caught up with Palatio. Spoon confessed his participation in order to escape execution. He brought to court receipts of transaction between him and Palatio, payment for the hit. Spoon was exiled to Shiva. Palatio was convicted for the murder of Setius Rosellumus and was executed by disintegration.

If so, wondered Myra, why was Balmoral not exonerated? Why was he not allowed return to Xhaust from his temporary refuge in Camp Zero, before all those terrible things happened to his wife Nickel and teenage daughter Jacadi in the hands of Shiva guards?

Balmoral's framing and subsequent familial persecution encouraged Myra to wonder how many people and their families in Xhaust had suffered wrong persecution. She contemplated how she could drum up interest in the case.

She sought audience with the chief magistrate, dubbed as a prominent personage in Xhaust, the very whisper in the Premier's ear.

A servant, solemn at the main door, observed the topaz in Myra's hair, the pulse beating in her neck, and ushered her in. More servants popped in and out of the waiting room before the chief magistrate himself breezed in. He had eyes that not only bulged; they were dichromatic too. They changed hue from tsavolite green to opaque. Despite his nasal voice that was exasperating to listen to, Myra understood he was a temperate man of good listening.

But he would not delve into her serious matter until she was watered and fed. He talked about his country, about many other things, about anything in fact that popped into his head, but steered clear of politics.

"Wife," he introduced an equally bug-eyed and nasal-voiced creature, but how beautiful! "Is name Astrid."

Astrid wore a lemon kimono sprigged with olive and gold petals. Her robe swept the floor, and Myra could not catch glimpse of her feet. She glided, not walked. Her hands were laden with gilded trays. Her first serve was finely garnished in little tents. Myra lifted a tent and found what looked like a stalk of fried asparagus that turned out to be a roasted worm. The snail caviar, sickly sweetened, Myra tried, but her stomach turned at skewers of frog legs.

At last Astrid glided away with the last of food trays, and true conversation was possible.

"This business you bring," the chief magistrate encouraged, his tsavolite green eyes going opaque.

Myra cleared her throat. "I've had many years as President of the Arbitration Council of Refugees."

He nodded.

"I have bustled in and out of worlds in nanoseconds to mediate for refugees."

He nodded.

"My husband encrypts and decodes intergalactic signals and has a professorship in cosmic sciences. Often he has helped me in search of homes for the displaced in strange worlds. Often we have succeeded."

He nodded.

"The one time I failed and my refugees landed in a harem, I flew right back to save them. All this and more I have done for no gain to myself or to my family."

He nodded. "I am clear in my mind this thing you are speaking," he said.

"By coming to you today," said Myra, "I am staking my career because I have signed an oath of neutrality. But I cannot stay neutral on this matter. In fact, I am very biased. You see, I come to speak of one Balmoral Rosellumus, an exile whose child I have raised in my house as my daughter. For her, mostly, I seek justice." She leaned forward and handed him documentation from the Justice Library.

"Now, Your Honor," she continued when he lifted his eyes from the evidence, "despite my lack of neutrality, I have no real gain now in the righting of an injustice. It would be much easier for the child to think of her father as a murderer, as a lunatic, and not as a saint. That way, she might forget him and his passing."

"I am clear in my mind," the chief magistrate said.

"Now," said Myra. "Did you know there are many kinds of madness? To simply say that one is mad is like saying today is winter. What kind of winter? Gray fog winter? High wind winter? Rain bucketing winter? Is it slush snow winter? Hailstorm winter? Ice pellets like big golf balls falling from the sky winter? It is like saying I like food. What kind of food? Sweet? Savory? Boiled? Fried? Is it plant food or meat food? Is it chewable or drunk?"

"I am clear why you is Arbitrate President of Refugee Council," the chief magistrate said.

"Now, your Honor, so it is that there are many kinds of madness. There is madness that brings something wild and evil to the eye of an individual. This type of madness makes one carry out things of such atrocity that people shake their heads and refuse to remember. There is a type of madness that makes one mistake his fingers for someone else's and cut them off. This type of madness makes people shudder about it for generations to come. There is a type of madness that reduces a full grown man to a baby, enough for him to say, "Are you my mummy?" to men, mice and marigolds. This type of madness walks like feet and makes someone strap tins to their ankles and they roam the world.

"The atrocity against Balmoral and his family brought a different kind of madness. This one made a husk of a man whose memories returned to surrender to a river in his head, a river that drowned those same memories. That water one day brought along laughter, tear-drawing, shoulder-clapping laughter, that finally killed Balmoral."

The chief magistrate spat on the ground. "This Balmoral," he said, "may the gods of rapture walk by his rib."

"Why was he not exonerated when Spoon and Palatio were convicted?"

The chief magistrate's bulging eyes changed hue. "I hear tell of Shiva corruption, buy slave labor in Xhaust but I no take serious. Me take serious now that innocent Balmoral still sentence to Shiva when Palatio is true crime. Palatio she executed, why Balmoral not exonerate? I investigate who responsible for take money."

"And, your Honor, I would like you to remember that his entire family was also punished . . ."

"I investigate. Premier take action! This corrupt of worst kind!" When he had calmed, he said, "I deal with important matter first."

Turned out that not only was he the chief magistrate, he was also chairman of Xhaust's treasury. Together with a certificate of posthumous pardon, he handed Myra a bag of gold. "For Balmoral child," he said.

The recompense, he said, was nothing compared to the ill done.

"One last I ask question," he said. Myra paused at the door. "Now dead one child: maybe she grow, she marry well?"

"Yes," said Myra. "Yes," with conviction. "I will see to her future."

• • •

Le Piste Funerals coordinated the service. There were pies, cupcakes and sandwiches that were too pretty to eat, lemonade and cider too sweet for the somberness of the event, an evening reception where a local band played jazzed up numbers to the congregation until Tempest changed the beat.

When Myra returned with Balmoral's pardon, Amber's face found something softer, something that sometimes permitted a hug. As for Tempest . . . Protecting Amber became a vocation. Her agitation was instant when anyone pointed out Amber with a chin or a nod or a finger.

The night of the vigil, Myra headed out the door to the balcony where Amber stood alone but Vida's mother, Margo, beat her to it. So Myra joined Margo's husband, Ken, who stood by a bookshelf rubbing his chin. Together they observed Middle Creek townsfolk. Salem carried around trays stacked tall with biscuits, sandwiches and champagne.

In remembrance of Balmoral's life and his unassuming spirit, Tempest changed the music's tempo and the band played *When You Were Young*. To everyone's wonderment, Amber sought and found Myra, took her hand and together they danced.

· 44 ·

The keeper at the gate in the land of Shiva was a man named G2 from the tag on his breast. Another guard, 0141, refused to meet Myra's gaze.

G2 was hairless. His eyes were close-knit and his skin wore a coating of lime. Myra scrawled her details into the visitor's book and took from G2 the chained pass embossed with her name.

Shiva was expecting her.

"I am take you to Commander Deimos," G2 said. He stepped out of the glassed hut. "Follow," he said, and took her bag. Myra cast one more look inside the hut. 0141 paused scribbling, crisply nodded. She felt his eyes on her back as G2 guided her into the steel fortress whose walls were spiked with a battalion of more metal.

Along the way she encountered, to her shock, not another guard but a scruff-faced tot, naked, who peered from a white-lit alley between two steel blocks. G2 turned his head and the child retreated.

"Malinger no good. Be already late," G2 said. "Is good hurry or Deimos be angry."

"This Deimos . . ." began Myra, but G2 widened his stride.

They approached another hut. This one stood small on the hyperarid ground, triangular shaped like the glassed one at the gate, except it was all metal and no window. A guard with a laser gun stood sentry against its door and from inside its walls came a burst of screaming that ended in sobbing. G2 did not break the pattern of his stride. "Follow," he said when Myra's curiosity lingered.

They came to another gate where, it seemed, a new batch of prisoners had just arrived and was being processed. Rows and rows of males and females stood at attention in a chain gang. A hover hangar with more guards, more weapons, monitored the ground from the sky. Beams from a tower blinked on the prisoners at intervals.

Myra noticed the prisoners' leanness, their muscle tone and prominent cheekbones, their thick-set brows that sent a spasm to her heart because they all reminded her of Amber. Guard D1394 doodled over paperwork at the head of the parade, verifying aloud people's names and their crimes and places of origin, and then assigning them a number: "Lani Surrimon, robber, Xhaust, prisoner number X6531. Tallefiele Velano, tax evader, Xhaust, prisoner number X10105."

G2 led Myra from the parade and down a set of thin steps and inside a building whose maze of corridors, overhead monitors and locked doors overwhelmed.

Her mind returned to Balmoral's framing and how Amber and the rest of her family dearly paid. Shiva had been their fate but what they had endured was worse.

The chief magistrate of Xhaust, long after Myra had sought his audience for Balmoral's posthumous pardon, had come back with figures: 129 families wrongly persecuted in the year of Balmoral's tragic fate alone. While the Premier of Xhaust exonerated every single one of them, a reprieve that secured the families' rightful place back to Xhaust from the barbed fencing of Shiva slave camps, Myra could not help but wonder. If history had proven that Xhaust might succumb to shoddy procedures like failing to exonerate innocent people, how many more innocents still languished in these camps?

Her mission to Shiva in the pretext of officiating the opening of new housing for exiles was ostensibly to undertake a secret audit of the settlement.

"I not clear in my mind," Chief Magistrate had said, "the fair hand of Commander Deimos on Shiva prisoners. Be my eye, report mission."

Commander Deimos, when at last Myra met him, was an ageless man with scorched almond eyes, cold. Busy eyebrows part silver. Body straight from Apollo, the god. He looked like someone she should know. "Be here at last," he said.

"There was a blizzard," she said.

"Government nosy to bring you," he said.

"Can't mind it's business, can it?"

"No." He appraised her. "I expect big, tall president of Arbitration Assembly. You small. Beautiful." He spread his hands. "I am delight to be your host. I entertain."

"As you will appreciate, Commander, my visit is not for pleasure. If you may, I would like to inspect the new quarters."

"Beautiful woman, thorn mouth." He clapped his hands, an action that summoned G2, dutifully stood outside the door. "Take president, she refresh. One hour, bring back. We tour." He gestured toward the exit. "President, please."

Myra followed G2 down a corridor. There were so many of them, these corridors. She was annoyed with herself for making plain her dislike. For her ostensible mission to bring success, it was best not to raise suspicion.

Her resting chambers were spartan, as was everything about the settlement. Things sat solid, nothing collapsible except the prisoners.

"A window," she said in wonderment. G2 turned, perplexed. "And it opens."

He shrugged, closed the door behind him. The sound of his heels clipped away through the walls, the sound getting small, smaller. Myra threw open the window, leaned her head outside. She surveyed a barren field in the vastness of arid land.

Back in the commander's office, he was smoking. An overhead fan revolved without pace, spread the white curls until they vanished.

"Cigarette, President?" he loosened one from the pack.

"No thank you, Commander. I don't smoke."

"Deimos." Horns of smoke out of his nostrils. "For you, President, is Deimos."

"Then I must insist you call me Myra."

He stamped out the cigarette. "Pretty name, it roll in my mouth. What you suggest is good bargain. Deimos. Myra. We shake on it?"

Myra stretched her hand. "We shake."

• • •

There were no windows. Everything was butternut gray with no windows.

Myra faced Deimos. "These? The new quarters?"

"Fully furnished. Each unit be family house. We make near to natural habitat."

"This?" She looked at the iron walls.

His face closed. "You not like?"

"I expected . . ." She bit her lip. "A simple miscalculation of the eye, mine. You are doing the best you can in the circumstances."

He dropped the cigarette, crushed it with a foot. "Best we can, yes. For integrity of settlement. Xhaust give no funding. Prisoner work in mines:

make money. More mine, more money. Who hurt? Prisoner." His arms folded. "We do best we can."

Gate seven led to the sick room, block fifty-three. Here was a place, Myra understood, where inmates no longer useful found their end. Quarantined to die alongside other dying, prisoners were reduced to pus and bones. Eyes on skeletons looked back at her. Some of the inmates muttered, some lay silent, others whimpered.

"Water," someone begged from a corner.

A guard passed round with a bucket and a ladle, scooped and poured muddied liquid into open mouths. Myra snatched the bucket, hurdled over bodies but by the time she reached the one who had begged, knelt by him, ladle in hand, he was motionless on the cold, gray floor.

• • •

She couldn't sleep. She stood by the window, gazed outside. A dazzle of lights melted the night. She wondered how anyone could sleep in this miserable world, but eventually she did.

She woke up to a sound of boots, and then distant droning that grew louder. She peered out the window, saw two guards with weapons by the open doors of a chopper. Explosions rattled the compound. Pause, and then she saw a prisoner running. Bursts of fire tore through the blackness. A volley of lasers, then a scream. More lasers, one flash after another. The running man dodged, whirled, the chopper on chase. A second chopper appeared and a fresh volley of fire ended the chase.

Shaken, Myra wondered if this was a bad dream. All was once more silent. But the dream had a real body on the ground below. The slain runner was not moving.

Somewhere out there, someone, perhaps a guard, laughed. The dream was reality. Only a guard would laugh in this forsaken world.

Two prisoners entered the field at a trot, yanked the body out of sight by its feet. An owl *whooed!* Myra looked out to the cold, starless night and covered her face. She would never again fall asleep in this place, she swore.

But sleep she did. Matter of fact, she slept so well, she dreamt of pressing against a window, one that gave and collapsed to a million little pieces.

She woke up to the sound of boots, prisoners on a dawn run.

· 45 ·

Silhouette...

We must be satisfied that we might never find answers for Amber, or the citizens of Xhaust. Keera's words when I told her of Balmoral.

• 4b •

Summer came, radiant as a bride. Her smile fluttered like meteor dust. She caressed flowers that swayed carefree in merry wind. These flowers, already painted and peppered wide along the landscape by spring, transformed the parks of Middle Creek into highlights akin to the canvas landscapes of Master Oschin Palomar, an artist way before his time. He portrayed water that held fragrance, painted mountains that flew, and penciled moonlight that throbbed against the horizon.

Wind shared hearty whispers with the carefree gardens, sometimes called upon her own laughter to make merry with the natural world and her myriad talk. That same summer, as the river pounded surf along the shores, a little man named Fuller Goodwill, four feet nine, tattooed to the lips, stepped from a private yacht into Middle Creek. Accompanying him was a colorful entourage of a butler, a houseboy and a maid named Fifi.

Chap turned out to be a vet and a bachelor, but what he largely vetted were not dogs or horses. Fuller was promiscuous and diverse in his pickings. Perhaps it was the shorts and knee-highs he loved to wear, how he showed off chubby legs, bottle-shaped like a woman's. Or was it those tattooed lips? Women loved him. Or perhaps they loved his scent, the scent of a woman—a variation of ylang-ylang, marjoram, sandalwood and some complex floral nectar. Whatever it was Fuller's charm spread. The mayor's wife, a woman who was noble, intelligent and hitherto loyal, was the first to betray her husband. And then it was Dallas Lonsdale, the postmaster's wife, a young woman, a spring chicken, really, with shoulder-length hair. She too joined Fuller's harem. Discarded for a little man, the postmaster, who was six feet five, was as baffled as he was desolate.

That summer of the town's colorful gossip on the wiliness of Fuller Good-will on hitherto virtuous housewives of Middle Creek was the same one that Myra took it upon herself to ship her family to 180C.

The terraformed planet boasted her conversion over years from rugged rock to a new populace of botanical mermaids and knights, even a few rebels and odd pirates—such as the *impuritan* blooms with folded ears and unusual patches on their faces.

As for Lake Oorong . . . she was one thousand times more alive, more beautiful, arching her back to send turquoise tongues of thermal waters to lick the shores. The sleeves of the shoreline possessed as much corsetry as the ample breath that flourished bird of paradise flowers, far-spreading gladiolas, Peruvian lilies, cream magnolias, poinsettias, hybrid hellebores and anemones. Even the lilysanthums deepened their blush and cast an ardent waft of fennel and clove.

It amplified the heady mood that had touched Amber and Tempest, both nearly nine—well, possibly. Nobody quite knew Amber's age, especially when she smiled that blue rose smile, organic. The one Myra first saw the day the band played *When You Were Young* and Amber asked Myra for a dance.

Nothing remarkable had happened over the years with reference to the beast in Tempest's belly or the storm in her fist, until that wild summer of Fuller and his entourage. Same summer Tempest disabled with a ball of lightning a purse thief at Central, in the middle of a bus zone, right opposite Chinta Ria (the women's shop, not the restaurant). She stunned the teenager enough for him to forget about suing but it earned her more punishment than Vida's thinking chair. First, she peeled potatoes and onions one week straight for the boy's grandmother who had raised him, and with whom he lived after being orphaned young.

Grandma Helga was a woman simple enough to not know about prosecuting but shrewd enough to keep Tempest on her toes with added chores: the baking of bread after bread, the mopping of floor after floor, the weeding of garden after garden . . . But Myra was quick to notice when Tempest's malevolent silence at the dinner table after Grandma Helga's chores transformed to animated chitchat surrounding the quarters of her penance. Not only had Tempest long made friends with old woman Helga, the prepubescent girl was being swept off her feet by the thieving teenager, Flavel.

Tempest's infatuation with Flavel—a lad who blinked asphalt eyes with innocence moments before his hand slipped for the wallet at the back of your pocket—created distance with Amber: fewer secrets, more scrapping. Amber fought silently. She used stealth and speed, creeping before an attack, her heels just barely touching the ground as she stepped lightly, moments before she rolled, leapt, tumbled without a sound and bowled Tempest over. Tempest had a sound. When her muscles twitched, or her pupils dilated, she growled or hissed before she roared . . . Amber stayed silent.

Finally it was all too much, enough to convince Myra that the craftiness, the maudlin air Fuller Goodwill had brought to Middle Creek, was no fake. That gave another reason for a getaway, an excursion to 180C.

At the remote planet, Amber and Tempest were enchanted as usual. They raised besotted eyes to shooting stars spiraling in the sky like gems in broad daylight. They lowered those same eyes to an effervescence of lively, lime-green springs at their feet; to the crash of waterfall against giant rocks down south; to the mushroom carpets alive with bees east of the lake. It was a wonder, Vida later said to Myra, that the girls had managed to mislay the newfound ladylike poise that often accompanied the novelty of menstrual rags. Amber's bony legs presented a more bottle shape. Budding breasts pushed out her chest. And though Tempest stood twice as tall as her adoptive sister and was thrice as curvy, the girls stayed as like as twins in countable ways.

As Myra took photos, Vida warned the girls: "Your mother is going to frame you."

T-Mo

· 47 ·

Silhouette . . .

He was kindred with evil, or my name is not Silhouette.

The day he stood on a crag by the river, shaded by fog, cloaked by night, his eye focused westward. He sought and found an upstairs room somewhere in Middle Creek where titian locks of a nine-year-old spread wide on a white, white pillow.

· 48 ·

Myra's topaz hair was also spread on her pillow but her night was awake. She struggled to find sleep. Beside her, Vida stirred in his dreams. He was her world but not in the same way as it had been between T-Mo and Salem, because for Salem, T-Mo was it and a bit; no wonder his leaving broke her. Unlike them, Vida and Myra were partners, there was equality in their togetherness. In their freedom. No one's leaving would break the other, but their bonds were no less strong.

Myra was in the heart of thinking, of pondering how she understood Vida, knew the volume of his body to the weight of it; was contemplating the tenderness of his fingertips when the bedroom door burst open.

It was Amber.

She rushed in and bounded on their bed, startling Vida. He sat, unfocused for a moment. Remembered he was naked and clutched a sheet. Myra was never sure the foster child liked her. But here she was on their bed. The girl's eyes held a plea.

"What is it?" said Myra.

"It's Tempest."

"What about Tempest?"

"She's gone."

"Gone . . . Where?" asked Myra.

The child shook her head.

"What do you know?" asked Myra.

A shrug.

Myra gripped Amber by the shoulders. "Where did Tempest go?"

The girl shook her head again.

Tempest was not in her room. But the bed had been slept in.

"Perhaps to Nana Salem's?" Myra's question was to nobody in particular.

"At this time of the night?" said Vida.

Still they phoned. Got Tonk who practically yelled: "At this time of the night!"

Myra circled the backyard, front yard, out the gate, called at the top of her voice. "Tempest? Tempest!" Ran down the streets that bordered the house. Footloose and eyes roaming, she searched further out. Vida stayed home with Amber; someone had to mind the child and Myra wasn't a stay-at-home person. Her voice grew hoarse with roaring. "Tem-pest!"

She found her on the weather coast opposite the crag where the river shouldered the forest of Solemn.

"Tem-pest . . ."

The child was swallowed in a wave. Her flame head bobbed in and out of tide. While she was a dominant swimmer, the water's malevolence was potent.

Myra plunged. She got no further than three meters before a giant wind pushed her back. She charged back the same time that a monster wave first spat, then gobbled Tempest. Its lips opened for Myra. She got no closer than three meters.

"I command you!" she yelled at the gobbling waves. "Let my daughter go!" Without thinking, without knowing why, perhaps a pure act of instinct, she cried, "T-Mo!"

A wash of water spat Tempest ashore.

• • •

Water no longer arches and thrusts her back. She is tranquil, close to slumber. She is replete, her hunger gone.

Myra allows Tempest to gather herself. When the child speaks, she tells of sleep and dreams, of waking and walking, of hearing a call. She found herself at the river's edge. The rest Myra knew.

On the way now home, to where Amber and Vida would be at the gate or a window policing their return, Myra speaks.

"I know you see things," she says.

"Yes?"

"I know about the stepping. How you step inside people."

"Do you know about T-Mo?"

"What about him?"

"When I step, he is inside."

"Inside what?"

"Who. Inside people I step into."

"Like?"

"Nana Salem and Nana Margo and Pappy and Ken."

Myra goes on her knees so they are facing. "I have thought about this, argued with it." Her eyes are shining. "The events of tonight have brought me to a decision." She lifts Tempest's chin so the child looks into her eyes. "No one but Salem knows T-Mo better than I. He is, after all, my father. Step into me."

"But you slapped–"

"Now."

"But–"

"I said now."

• • •

It is like walking into a mirror and it gives. The moment Tempest steps in, Myra sees what the child sees. There is the fading shadow of an ashy man. He is walking in giant treads toward the Forest of Solemn by the river. Tempest trails him. He leads her miles, miles away from the river into the woods. He casts a huge shadow on the ground, thunder feet going *boom! boom! boom!*

They arrive at a grave lane at whose mouth a stilted post reads: *Immortality*. Myra transforms into an eagle. She follows in a soar the soft footfalls of Tempest's tread below until they come to a shout of wind. Tempest pauses. She eyes a vortex.

"Wait!" cries Myra.

But Tempest has already dived into the jaws of the eddy. "Weeee-e!" fading sounds of her glee inside the black jaws.

Myra, now a water mole, plunges into a slap of cold. Things come undone in her head as she tumbles, fingered by darkness. Now she is crawling—or is she slithering? She is not sure any more which part of her body is which, what belongs here, belongs there. She reaches with a finger or a knee—or is that a neck? By the time she sweeps to the bottom of the tunnel, claws out of its toe into a kelp-filled trail, acres and acres of kelp, there is no Tempest. No sign anywhere, just ungovernable silence. Then: "This way . . . way," a woman's voice, ancient as dusk. Myra looks about, no one there. "This way . . . way." A whisper of feet, laughter in fragments inside the wind. Myra follows the sound.

A weave of corona ivy, the kind with tails and sunspots, runs along a wrought iron balustrade. Myra follows its climb up a spiral of outdoor stairs. It leads to a door whose handle turns easy. She steps into a dim room filled with the scent of dried poppy. The house, upon entering, is a tomb—stillness, darkness everywhere. Then . . . movement, kitchen sounds in an adjacent room. Water runs. A spoon tinkles on glass, the peal of a whistling kettle . . .

Myra shape-shifts into a gecko, pushes past swaying beads, glass beads of many colors forming drapes. A man coughs. He is on a bed, his eyes full of space. It is the ashy man, the one of the woods. His skin is ancient, a work of art. His hair is frayed, aged hemp. It's T-Mo. Not as she remembers him from when she was little. Then he was strong, held honest shoulders before he became sick.

To Myra's surprise, Tempest enters the room bearing a tray. It holds a steaming bowl and a goblet full of berries. She rests it on a side table. Myra's heart staggers. She replays a scene of many years ago, the one that happened when Myra was four. T-Mo was in a sickbed moments before he vanished. But the scene is now, and the child not herself but Tempest, the one with a bowl. If he dares! If he dares harm her daughter, what would she do? Bite him to pieces with gecko teeth?

"Why did you drown me?" Tempest asks him.

"It's complex."

"You didn't have to half-kill me."

"And if I said it wasn't me?" His voice is silk, his eyes not quite so fogged.

"Who then?"

"Like I said. It's complex." His voice is rasped. More coughing, deep chest coughs that want to call up bile.

"You alright?" asks Tempest.

"Burns."

She lifts the bowl to his lips. "Drink."

He tilts his head, sips a little, pushes away the bowl.

"Ah, better." He closes his eyes. Now he's coughing again.

Myra understands she cannot interrupt. Neither seems aware of her presence, her place as a bystander in the past, present, future.

• • •

Myra's mind returns to her childhood, where she feels rather than sees T-Mo. The strength in his arms, in his adoration . . . She remembers those wilderness jaunts when he tucked her in an embrace or aloft on his back, her hands spread as wings and, together, they wandered the universe. She remembers their descent through the skies just after sunrise.

She remembers that terrible night in Grovea when T-Mo turned into a stranger, days before he vanished . . . Before that, when they first arrived at Grovea, before the many wives cooked a feast, Novic was cold. He received them outside the Temple of Saneyth. Stood at its tall doors and said: "What?" His eyes gleamed glass.

"That the best welcome you got?" T-Mo.

"You done roaming?"

"Thought you'd thaw on seeing my lot."

"Your *lot*?"

"My wife Salem, and this . . ."

"Vanished for eons. Now you show with a human."

"The child, look at the child. Tell me how human she is."

"What'd her daddy say, your human, when you sought her hand?"

"Welcome home, son."

"Right."

"What do you expect? Told me to piss off."

"Sounds more right. Piss off?"

"Best way a pastor can say it."

It took one of the wives to mellow Novic. Perhaps it was Xinnia: number three—or was it Clarin: number four, with an accent from France? She rested a hand on Novic's arm and said, "Be okay." And Novic's eyes of glass warmed. He shifted the weight on his foot and let Salem, Myra and T-Mo in.

• • •

Same way she was a bystander to those events in Grovea (what had happened between Novic and T-Mo?), Myra is a bystander to events now.

· 49 ·

"T-Mo," he speaks from the bed. "Know . . . how I came about . . . that name?"

"How?" says Tempest.

"Could have been Transfix."

"Transfix?"

"Or Trap or Tell." A cough swallows his smile. "T-Mo. Sounds like a T-Missile."

"Yes," says Tempest. "Like war."

"Havoc in all directions. Guaranteed." This time his smile stays. "But I wasn't the trouble. Miss Lill . . . used to say *Little Poetry come to visit, bless those eyes.* Gave me fish licorice."

"Fish?"

"Best licorice ever. Taste like honey and vegetable and fish."

"I don't like any of those." Then: "Who's Miss Lill?"

"The one who found I wasn't the trouble." He is somber now. "Wasn't trouble when I met Salem. She looked like a queen dressed as a nun . . . Worked at a local IGA." He smiles. "They sold milk." He chuckles. Pause. "Salem. So . . . naive. Her youth, her innocence, filled me with something . . . I had known women of glamour, of knowledge, of power. But Salem . . . my Salem. She was the one."

"But you left," says Tempest. "Migsy said."

"Migsy? That what you call Salem?"

"Migsy's my mum. She doesn't like it when I call her that."

"Then why do it?"

"Just. How come you died?"

"Only way they stayed safe. He'd never leave them if I hadn't."

"He?"

"Kwa. Lik. Cain."

"*Who?*"

"Idi. Göring. Bokassa. Pol Pot. He was all those, he was worse. Nagasaki, Kosovo, Rwanda, Chechnya . . . Some things are left silent." He closes his eyes, his breaths rugged.

Tempest holds his head tenderly at the crook of her arm, presses a chalice to his lips. He drinks a little water. She rests his back to the bed, tucks him, softens his pillow.

His eyes are slits.

She sits at the edge, strokes his hair. "Tell me about your mother."

"*Mine?* What about her?"

"What she look like?"

"Silhouette."

"Is that a shape or a color?"

"It's a name. Silhouette."

. . . Later, much later, Myra stands invisible by his bedside.

"Why do you hold a candle at me?" he asks without speaking.

The candlelight flickers. Its light plays patterns on the walls. She answers him the same way, without speaking. "You left."

"I am disgusted with myself."

"Disgust is what I knew," says Myra.

"Disgust about death?"

"That you were never dead. You watched her bury an empty coffin."

"Least I could do."

"Was it me? Did you hate me so much?"

"*Hate?* Never my love."

"Yet you left me."

"My heart stayed."

"I was a child!"

"Your eyes were ancient, young'un."

"Sometimes. T-Mo. Maybe sometimes I miss you too."

• • •

Tempest looks happier, more mature. She carries herself differently. There is a knowing about her. Fingers clasped, no questions asked. She and Myra bounce in a homebound skip. What Myra feels is . . . sweet as amity.

Now she must focus on things that matter.

Vida and Amber glance down the window, they too are holding hands. Their eyes light up. The front door snaps open, nearly off its hinge. Amber whistles out. Her legs—how skinny—peddle at dazzling speed. Tears shimmer in her eyes. She is laughing and whooping, running and crying. Her garble is the distant cousin of "Thank you, oh thank you." She races across the yard, laughing and garbling, and casts herself upon . . .

Myra.

ODYSSEUS

· 50 ·

Silhouette . . .

He climbed sopping wet from the river. His mind was filled with prospect. He stood on a crag, stared further out, away from the shore. Of the fresh seaweed clumped in his hair, some he pulled with his fingers and let slip into white waves that coiled with breeze.

The water's lashes were soft yet bold. They fluttered at the indifferent coast.

He turned his head west and, unlike T-Mo—the one of the stepping who stood still and beckoned—this one nudged himself inland. And although he could bend time and space to teleport through space, extend across alleys, glide through walls, he walked. Only things he changed before he walked were his clothes. And the webs in his feet.

· 51 ·

"That's not him," said Tempest. She pointed at a man sitting at their porch on a brisk April afternoon. He calmly chew chewed a strand of grass, gazed at the family. "Uh-uh. Not him. He is wearing . . . tennis shoes."

"Sure?" said Vida.

"They are white tennis shoes, look." She ran up to the stranger. "You are not T-Mo," she said.

"Miss . . ." Grass in his mouth still. His voice was the same silk as T-Mo's. "Tell me your name. Something pretty I'm sure. Pearl? Petal?" He ruffled her curls. "Ruby?"

"Tempest."

"Aren't you the picture?"

He stood then, took his time rising to full height, placed a hand on her head.

Myra understood he was someone she knew, someone she didn't. He'd shown up with sunnies and a saxophone. Yes, about that . . . indeed. He wasn't T-Mo.

He still chew chewed the grass. If Myra hadn't known better, she would have mistook him. But there were differences. Like dress. T-Mo wore cheesy things like that t-shirt carrying bold white words on its breast, words that said: *Hearts & Beds*. Wore it in front of a prospective father-in-law, Salem had said. T-Mo's eyes gazed at you in a personal way, measured you and determined a fact about you. And he didn't wear hats even though nobody could remember the color of his hair. All they saw was the gator skin, intricately patterned, so creased it looked worse than an ailment before its weaves and crossings morphed into art under their stares. So the man standing there in a moleskin jacket (turn-up cuffs) and a cowboy hat . . .

with sunnies and a saxophone . . . with flat eyes and something smooth, something shifty . . . He wasn't T-Mo.

He dropped the grass, lifted the hat. Tucked one hand in his pocket and approached. Something else too—he had lapis lazuli hair, blue as blue—much intensity in its color. A speckle of ash and gold along his temples.

He stood tall, head almost touching the eaves.

"My name is Odysseus. T-Mo . . . has not told you about me?"

"He hasn't," said Myra. "And I don't care."

This man with his shimmering blue hair looked danger, brought danger, was dressed like a punk and smelt like a forest. She'd had enough inside the stepping and was not willing for any more of these people inside her real world.

He stayed quiet, waiting. For what? An invitation? When it was not forthcoming, he wasn't getting it from Myra, he claimed it. "Dusk soon. This far. Nowhere else."

"There's an inn—" started Myra.

Vida cut her short. "I never turned a person from my door, and I'm not starting now." To Odysseus: "Forgive my wife. Come in, do."

"Should he?" said Myra.

"Will he?"

In that awful silence between them, the first in their lifetime, Odysseus never cast his eyes off Myra's face. "I will come in," he said to Vida, shook his hand. "Someone has manners," across his shoulder to Myra. "I choose you," to Amber. His finger poked her chest. "I trust nobody else but you to stay close to this baby."

Amber took from him the contoured saxophone case.

• • •

Before the visit, they'd been to the fair. Always planned to go, always postponed, something always happened. The one day they managed to go, *one day*, look what they found waiting at the door.

"Ride, ride all day!" the jolly clown on the carousel had cried. Up and down, up, down. Happy thighs rode the ponies. High spirits from the carousel never left Tempest and Amber. They forked out notes like adults to buy head-sized fairy floss from Serious Sweets. Then they ate O'Ghee spiced-ups, drank Tropicana Fresh chillers, Soda Lake pops . . . The fair spoiled them for choice: eat-in munchies, take-away munchies, invitations-only munchies, stall-to-stall munchies. They were breathless, excitable, their merry feet doing whirligigs all the way to noble park rides, ghost train rides, dinosaur hunt rides, shoot the freak rides . . .

Myra, sprawled on the curl of a de-leafed tree, watched the world below go by.

People loved roller coasters for the light-headedness they produced. For the spinning sensation that followed an upside-down loop loop loop. For the seat-pushing-on-the-back feeling, for the feeling of muscles roping and body organs dropping . . . They did it over and over, some straight after vomiting, simply to experience yet again riding with your whole body.

But Myra was different.

She didn't need amusement park thrill coasters to fly high, to feel weightless. She was capable on her own of sky-active performance. Without propelling structures, her body could freely accelerate airborne in twists and spins and free-fall plummet. She understood the full-body sensation, every part of her body individually pushed by gravity. She'd experienced this feeling over and over as orbits rocketed past. So she didn't participate but observed thrill seekers, fire eaters, burger eaters, money eaters.

Vida, who was skipping like a boy around dressed trees, vanished into some haunted ride. Tempest and Amber were tossing coins, twigs and songs into a penny pond filled with snow white swans . . . Everything was perfect, until Tempest pointed.

"Look," she said. "There's a man at our door."

"Look like you, Momma," Amber said.

And he did too, pixel by pixel, a manly pixelation.

Myra shook her head. "Uh-uh," she said. The man poised wide-legged on their porch, sun melting in his face as he chew chewed that ridiculous grass, wasn't family. "Can't be," she said.

• • •

He chatted with Amber as she carried the sax to his room: "My word. You don't look like an Amber."

She flushed. "What do I look like?"

"Don't know. Maybe a Ballard? Or a Bianca? An Olivia. Something pretty."

Her flush deepened.

Vida showed him the guest room but it was Myra who ambushed Odysseus, alone in the room, before he could unpack.

"They're just girls."

"What are you on about?"

"*A Ballard? Or a Bianca? Aren't you the picture?*"

"I see. *That.*"

"Pearl? Petal?"

"I get it."

"Something pretty?"

He shrugged. "Will you keep going? I said I get it."

"Tell me why you are here," said Myra.

"Bored."

"Bored?"

"Came to see. We all need excitement. At some stage."

"To see who?"

"To see what he made." His gesture enveloped the room. "All . . . this. You."

"Why see what he made?" She understood he meant T-Mo.

"Curious, I guess."

"Why curious now?"

"Time is not relevant."

"It is if you are curious about us now. What happened to before?"

"About *you*? It was never you. It's him, really."

"Explain."

He took his time. "Always wondered what he really was."

"What T-Mo *was*? Surely."

"He played Gabriel, acted God. Stood there all holy, eyes watching watching."

"Over what?"

"Cherubim. Serpent."

"So you're a snake."

"I am not the villain if that's your question. Novic is the one you want."

"What's Novic got to do with this?"

"Everything." His eyes burnt.

"How?" said Myra.

He shrugged.

"I said how?" said Myra.

"You always this annoying or is it just for me?" Silence. Then: "All I wanted was to be the same as T-Mo. Like how children lit up when they saw him. Me they eyed and puckered. Grownups saw Lucifer. Even plants wilted, don't know what they saw. Imagine growing up with that."

"Saying you're a victim?"

"Same as he. You. Salem. Silhouette. Novic makes everyone a victim."

• • •

Dinner was strained. Vida's efforts at conversation, at finding history, met walls. Neither Myra nor Odysseus would indulge a different mood between the two of them. Tempest stayed in some daze. Amber was busy, too busy being coy. And Odysseus switched on the charm for her especially. He pulled out her chair at the start of dinner, sat after she sat. Amber reciprocated his interest. She was first to lift his empty plate to the kitchen and, as she did so, Myra noticed a touching of fingers that led to Amber's giddy laugh.

She cornered the girl in the kitchen, where Amber was lustily humming and filling a kettle. Her singing was louder than Red's, and she sang in the secret language she shared with Tempest: *"Al pet rom ned. Carr esli cap orst!"*

"Different buzz, huh?" said Myra.

Amber's hand at the tap shook but her gaze stayed steady. "Don't know what this is about."

"You and me both."

Next morning, Vida was in the kitchen when Odysseus appeared.

"Sleep well?" said Vida.

Odysseus nodded.

"Kettle going," said Vida. "How do you like your tea?"

"Wet," said Odysseus.

By the time the kettle was boiled, Odysseus and the sax were gone.

He was back on the clock for dinner, but Myra stood at the doorway, blocked entry. Behind her, Vida ran a nervous hand at the back of his neck and was relieved when Myra stood aside for Odysseus and his sax.

"Guess one more night won't kill," said Myra. "Don't mean you stay tomorrow."

Odysseus gave no thanks, no protest, not even rejection of her proposal.

But at the dinner table he lost his walls. Regaled them with tales of otherworldly lands, worlds whose wind smelt of baby fennel, whose sun was the color of blood orange, whose phantoms soared without restraint when gods doused the night. His voice remained full of silk, his presence paramount, even Myra could not ignore it.

He spoke loud and he whispered. Mesmeric words like ballads. He spoke with persistence and with slowness. He told of the Temple of Ide, of the mountains of Saturn, of an Atlas of Huygens embossed on a moon in Gaia. The flow and gravity in his eyes shifted with each new place.

Tempest's eyes were content, her smile big, her laughter free and tinkling, soft like a gentle scatter of beads, and ending on big notes. Amber was . . . entranced.

That night it rained, buckets and buckets of it, almost a perfect storm. Amber and Tempest fought their most fitful fights yet. In a pause between the mountains of Saturn and a toilet break, Myra didn't see whose eye went sharp first. All she heard was a growl, then saw a leap. Amber was small as she was fast. She tackled Tempest who found herself knees to the ground before she could throw a fist. Amber's bony palms pressed the girl's shoulders. Tempest, who carried a blaster in her hand, one that called up lightning or a storm, who also executed the stepping, entered memories of other people and saw things, did not summon her powers. She just skirted the table, lunged and fought like a spiteful girl. Her kick knocked Amber to the floor. They wrestled, breathed in rapid snatches. One guided a fist away, another back-pedaled, spun at the nth minute to knock the other into a wall. Currently, no one was winning.

No one saw Odysseus until he lunged his fingers through their hair, snatched Amber and Tempest apart by their scalps. He clutched them under his armpits. When he released his hold, the girls were too numb with shock or embarrassment to resume battle. Mumbled their goodnights when Odysseus bade them. Tempest's face was soft. Amber's was softer.

"Well . . .!" said Vida, after Odysseus himself retired. "Our way is this!"

"That's decisive."

"*He's* decisive. He's staying then?"

"I guess," said Myra.

By dawn again he had vanished, returned by dusk.

Vida lit the fireplace, more for aesthetics than need.

Myra leaned, arms folded, against a bookshelf. Odysseus declined the chair Vida offered, stood one hand in pocket in the living room, sipped wild berry cider that Vida had also offered. The girls were nowhere.

So Myra spoke freely. "Finished your genocides?"

Odysseus laughed. "The worst," he said.

"Beg your pardon?

"You'd like to think the worst of me."

Myra remembered what T-Mo had said: *Idi. Göring. Bokassa. Pol Pot . . . Nagasaki, Kosovo, Rwanda and Chechnya . . .*

"Where was it today?" she asked. "Yemen?"

"Not going to do it . . . I'm afraid."

"Do . . . what?"

"Bite your bait," he said. "Soon you'll blame me for *all* of Earth's pandemics."

Later, in their bedroom, Myra explained it to Vida. "You have no idea what he is capable of."

"Nor have you."

"You are defending him?"

"You are conjuring more than he is."

His ultra-charm. She couldn't believe how well it worked. She set it aside and forgot. Until Amber changed her hair.

· 52 ·

It sifted in quietly, fine as baby dust. Myra noticed it quite by chance. At first it was the way the girl held herself when she anticipated his presence: her soft waist and new face too. Then it was the angle of her neck when he stepped into the room. The way her eyes fluttered and then shone when they fell upon him. The way her eyes dropped to her feet when he looked at her closely. The way she trembled when he took her hand. The secret smile that crossed her face when he turned his face to some other thing . . . Then, only then, when his focus was some other place, did she look, devour him with a dreamy sadness, the tender kind of one who yearned. Hers was a bottomless kind of dreaming.

When he walked in the garden, Amber stood at the window. She pressed her nose against the glass, cupped with her palms her love-struck face. She looked as if he was oxygen, and she bottled—gazing at him from an airtight jar. When he threw his head, laughed over a private or shared joke, she too smiled. She was at ease this way, looking at him unnoticed, listening to the silk in his throat. Sometimes her lips moved, silent words to herself. Knowing eyes made their own laughter. At times, thinking she was alone, she would shut her eyes, tilt her neck, open it to an invisible feather along her nape. Her shoulders went loose, then occasionally, once or twice, she touched her nape, caressed the skin inside thick, roped hair.

Suddenly, hair she had always locked in braids opened up. It fell tenderly to one shoulder or both. As it had always been locked up, Myra was astonished to find the true color of it when the hair came loose. It was reddish-brown, the color of brandy. Seeing it now, feeling it, how lustrous its strands, Myra noticed how silvery red sometimes changed to silvery russet with angle of light. She fingered Amber's hair as they stood at the terrace, watching Odysseus strolling out the front yard. Tempest was by his side. She slipped her arm into his, her face glistened with more than bliss.

Myra nuzzled her chin against Amber's rust-red head, spoke against it. "You love him," she said.

• • •

Myra wondered about him even more now. *What* was he? What did she know? What if he was the kind who courted prepubescent girls, the kind who sketchily or carefully found invigoration in youth? In the innocence of unmade faces, the vulnerability of young cheeks, the boldness of coning breasts, the half-formation of hips that had known nothing of birthing. Was he looking for short term gain; instant gratification? It was without doubt he was living large and irresponsible . . . how he explored a sense of trespass that was nectar to Amber and Tempest.

The knock began from inside, specifically in Myra's heart. It slapped into her belly, weakened her knees. By the time it turned into a wild hammer that preferred her head, her mind was made.

He sat on the low branch of a ghost gum at the edge of the garden. Tempest was dancing around its trunk. She was singing, ducking clumps of olive leaves that hung from the branch upon which he sat. Amber was nowhere to be seen.

He looked steadily at Myra, as if waiting for her mind. He nodded calmly, as if understanding already, wondering how she would say it. Something present in his eyes devoured with interest her intention, dared her: do it, do it, do it . . .

How would she say it. . .?

Who do you think you are?

We need to talk?

Won't have you messing with their hearts?

How would she respond if he said, *Amber is adopted, how is that incest?*

In that blink of silence as they stared at each other and he stared her down, she knew. She knew with conviction that she wouldn't, couldn't, ask him to leave. Because, honestly, she didn't know how.

Until the first death.

· 53 ·

Before the deaths, sometimes Myra would sit with Odysseus on the patio. They were each enshrouded in a world, buying time, catching up with time, not talking about things, or things that came with time. They clawed at normality. But nothing taunted them, not any more. Their silence was easy, more so for their lack of endearment.

One day, she tried. "I don't know how to do this," she said.

"Do what?"

"This, this . . . kindred thing."

Odysseus looked up. Then he smiled. "It's not a *thing*."

"Where do I start?" she said.

"*This* is a start."

Myra had no reasoning to argue with the strength of her heart, her fondness for someone about whom everything was not right. He had a habit of creeping in unannounced. A shadow would touch her, and she would look up from a book, a pruning of roses, a wide ajar fridge door . . . And there he was, standing there, ultramarine hair blinking with radiance. Only when she actually saw him did she catch his forest scent, a fruit forest smell that sometimes overwhelmed.

• • •

They found Fuller Goodwill face down in the Forest of Solemn. His skull was caved in, but his face stayed calm. It was as if he was unaware of danger when it happened. Middle Creek rangers, keen as chili, cordoned what they could—perhaps a clue would lead to his assailant. After nine days of hunting, of fanning out and tearing that region of the forest, of sifting through terrain like archaeologists, it became clear they had nothing. Rumors didn't help. Townsfolk whispered of Mayor Jenkins, vengeance for his adulterous wife. Just like that, the slaughter was bagged.

A second man vanished. He was an able man, a first-rate wrestler. He was also a family man with no reason to vanish. The missing man was as strong as Samson, his strength perhaps born of defiance to his name. Syke Putnam. He was known in the ring as Artveneta, a mythical god of power; and his agent as the Tandoor, a result of shrewd business sense. The Tandoor secured Artveneta prime fights, all won. Now Artveneta, that infallible man, had vanished. This crime carried no motive for Mayor Jenkins. Nor did the third killing—a Camp Zero woman this time.

By the third crime, the nervousness of the inhabitants of Middle Creek had turned to fear, then horror. Not knowing what pattern or frequency the killing might take, horror begot panic. As reporters swarmed to Middle Creek, Myra's eyes moved to Odysseus. That began the crack in their relationship.

They were alone in the kitchen. Myra rinsed glasses, Odysseus dried them.

"I will ask," she said.

"Is that a question?"

"Did you?"

"No."

"Why these . . . such games?"

"Games are for children." His eyes were flat. "And the one you're proposing is unwinnable. I don't wish to fight with you, Myra."

"What makes you deadly is you do not present as evil."

"Those are words of a hot-head."

"I can put it in a different way if you like."

The crack stretched into a ravine.

Thoughts of his guilt came at dusk to haunt her. In the heart of a dream he would take the shape of a beast. She would wake up cotton-mouthed and miserable, only again to wonder about his guilt. Or innocence.

Someone walking a dog found Artveneta face-down and melted into grass at the sleeve of the forest that ran away from the river. He too had a caved skull. When Middle Creek rangers flipped him, they found his face was gone. But his flaxen-haired wife said it was him. The clothing was Artveneta's, she said. She touched him and naked skin came loose in her hands. No character is left when you take away a person's face. But she said it was her husband.

The length of his hands, the curl of his toes, it was him and she was taking him home to bury him.

Middle Creek folk conjured tales of the forest to paralyze wandering children or wayward husbands. Solemn became a place where the macabre happened, where the wind barked and trees changed shape to phantoms. In this place, in its inmost space where it bordered different worlds, where wilderness came alive to stalk wandering feet, to poke or grab hold of a person, the earth was said to shift and pull a man out of his skin.

· 54 ·

Weeks, months passed. No more killings, or answers to them.

If Odysseus knew what Myra was thinking, he did not say it loud. She scoured her mind, his background. She pondered his reasons for silence, asked herself if they were as sound as her craving to press him for a confession. The desire to know was one thing; tolerating the knowing was another. If she asked right, eventually he might tell. But what if, after the telling, she felt no disenchantment, no revulsion of him? What, *what*, would that make her? If he were, in fact, monstrous, she had allowed him in the presence of her children. One girl was in hapless adulation of him, the other weakened to tears by a sleepless longing that ran feathers on her nape, that opened up hair. What mother was she?

As the finger of doubt reseeded itself, and the unsafe question hovered on Myra's lips, the crack that had stretched into a ravine became a tiered gorge. As if biding time, Odysseus took to shining shoes. He was slow and careful, nourishing and gentle. His precision was almost military as he polished, polished . . . to mirror finish. He took Myra's pull-ons unasked, her knee highs, zip ups, cold weathers . . . and polished them. He took Vida's wellies, his mudguards, four-eyeds, twelve-eyeds, even thongs . . . polished them. By the time he reached the girls' rain and shines, everyone was too agreeably surprised to protest any more.

After the shoes, he picked through jewelry. Time went. He repaired the pin stem in Vida's broken watch. Soldered a wrecked chain Myra had not worn since her twenty-first. Cleaned a rhinestone bracelet Salem had gifted Myra last Christmas. Pulled apart and restrung a choker of pearls. When he offered to mount anew the stones of her bracelet charm, Myra said no. He did it anyway. Soon they were absentmindedly asking him to do things and he threw himself to do them.

Until the day Myra read out loud from the *Evening Times* of a suspect who had confessed to all three killings in Middle Creek. Didn't anyone care—Myra asked, again aloud—that the article also reported how the alleged suspect was said to be bipolar, prone to aberrations of the mind and delusions of grandeur? Why was everyone keen to accept his confession, if not for the quietude from terror such acceptance allowed?

· 55 ·

That night she found him knelt on the floor at the back of his room. She watched as he clipped open chromed latches on the hard-shell case, as he lifted the curved sax from its plush lining and placed it on foam cushions. He disassembled it. He took a brush, dipped it in alcohol, cleaned the mouthpiece.

"*Germs* kill," he said.

Silence.

He used a swab, then a cloth cleaner, for inside the sax. He cleaned it bell to neck. "Saliva is decomposing to the instrument," he said.

He rubbed the rods, the keys, was more careful around the springs. He caressed the bronzed body, took time to polish, polish, polish the sax until it shone. He assembled the crook, placed it in its compartment. He used his fingers to straighten the padded interior. He assembled the rest, gingerly laid the sax back into its lining. He clipped the latches, arranged the carrying strap.

Myra watched as he did all this. Now she looked at a crack on the ceiling above his head. "Owe you an apology," she said.

His eyes filled with shadows. He raised the cowboy hat from a doornail, thumbed its inside layer. He arranged the hat on his head, removed it, laid it next to the sunnies on the mirrored dresser. He spoke through the mirror's glimmer.

"Better make tracks," he said. "Crack of day."

It dawned upon Myra as she lay in bed next to Vida's dreamful stirring that she had never heard Odysseus play the saxophone. Not once. What was his truth? The finger of doubt regenerated, and once again the unsafe question.

· 5b ·

Silhouette . . .

"Whoop! Whoop!
A Ballard? A Bianca? An Olivia.
Something pretty. He took.
Gone, gone.
Forever in a day.

Whoop! Whoop!
Her heart in a swelling for a Ballard.
Something pretty. He took.
She's gone.
Forever in a day."

The plant's dirge at first light shook up the house. Red sang in a frenzied way that dawn. It wailed. It squawked: Whoop! Whoop!

Indeed Odysseus was gone, and so was Amber.

Amber!

She is more than what you know—Novic and T-Mo both said it. With Novic it was trickery, his play with our minds. With T-Mo, why did he say it? Who planted the seed in Odysseus to snatch the girl?

Odysseus!

That was the truth of him, the truth Myra sought. He snatched away things from people who loved them. He destroyed. "What makes you deadly is you do not present as evil," Myra had said. Didn't know how close she was. Didn't Odysseus take a fistful *of heart with bare hands from that tail-wagger at Miss Lill's? Took four men—four!—to pry him from savagery, and he was just four and foaming in the mouth.*

So what if he healed the girls from continually squabbling, from fights increasingly bitter, to united obsession? What if he let them flirt with him a little, jump his lap and all? That's a what! Leaps out, don't you think? Then he did worse: skulked away with one, Amber, left a smitten one behind. Tempest.

"Whoop! Whoop!"

Once the plant roused the house, it was the beast in her belly, the undead thing, that sent Tempest roaring into the Forest of Solemn where she lunged into trees. She flattened with bare fists century-old trunks, ancient trees that had stood on their own for millennia. Trees that had grown fifty meters and then some toward the sky. She stormed to the river where her screams formed a half-moon gorge, and big water arced and fell. It took Myra and rangers with rifles in their hands, plus a doctor with tranquilizer enough for an elephant, into the buttock with a dart rifle, to contain the girl.

Myra was beside herself.

Didn't take long to find the stolen chile. Found her trembling, dress torn, all alone at the heel of the forest.

"Did he. Hurt you?" asked Myra.

Amber shook her head.

What-am-a-tell? He wanted to, started to, but something happened before he could harm the poor chile.

Poor chile—how to explain to her momma a T-Mo/Odysseus conundrum? For what Amber saw was the strangest thing. One moment he wanted to hurt her, next he was fisting himself, banging himself, like . . . like . . . he was warring with his self. When she ran and collapsed at the mouth of the forest, she had run from roulette. For who knows which one, T-Mo or Odysseus, might have emerged?

Tempest was swift to forgive the abandoning—Amber's betrayal. The girls locked themselves in their room and spoke in pa tabe dome, *that secret language that allowed them to speak of unspeakable things, past and present:*

"Gen ba cool fi esk ung mes loc est way che bran . . ."

"Cor ank wod tem zi bo set que . . ."

It coded the language of wind, of rain, of death, the harmony of wilderness, until they lost time.

A wonder then that Myra didn't kill him when Odysseus hauled himself limping to her door. Completely tousled, he was a mess. His lapis-lazuli hair was a mess. The sax and sunnies were gone. But so were the flat eyes, the smooth and shifty in them.

"Why are you here?" she said.

"Just so you know, I love her."

"Amber?"

"Amber?" He was surprised. That's how she knew it was T-Mo.

"Why return now?"

"To see."

"See what?"

"See who, not what."

"Who, what, why, does it matter?"

"She matters. Take me to Salem."

"Why?"

"It's a story you think you know. But you don't know it."

"You took her from the IGA; that part I know."

"Good."

"What I don't know is the rest of it, after the coffin."

"That part you don't need to know."

"Give me the truth."

"Truth is the same."

"With you it isn't. I don't trust you."

"That's no good. Take me to Salem."

"You let her go."

"Had to . . . told you already."

"What will you say when you see her?"

"Enough."

"You are not to tell me when I am finished—"

"I will say to her just enough. I'm not here to break her. Now will you take me or do I have to find her myself?"

He wouldn't listen to rage or reason, Myra's or Vida's. Refused suggestion to see Salem at the manor, the one full of balustrades, the one that bore Tonk's name. So they agreed to meet at dusk, when shadows were long, at a clearing ringed in webs in the Forest of Solemn.

· 57 ·

Salem wore a gown with a skirt that ballooned like a little girl's. Myra was surprised to see this unthwarted self. Wasn't the T-Mo who wanted to see Salem now the same one who years ago had abandoned them both? Myra had never thought she would ever put Salem and T-Mo in the same sentence. Clearly, for the effort Salem was putting, something was yet unextinguished.

Salem also wore fragrance. She had always loved scents. Sometimes she would break a sprig of rosemary from her garden, sniff it, and say it helped her remember. What didn't she want to forget? She never said.

"I'd f-forget my head if it wasn't s-screwed on."

Her scent now was something sweet. It was sultry and intense.

"A bit rich," said Myra, as they walked.

Salem did not reply. Perhaps this was a wiser version of Salem who understood something that Myra was yet to grasp.

She insisted on walking, Salem, said she didn't want any "s-scaling of trees or c-climbing of air". Flights in people's arms weren't really her thing.

Tonk, who thrived in his own civil war, had shaken his head at the audacity of the proposed meeting. "Imbecile. Martian! He would want her? Now?" Slammed the door of his study to Myra's face, locked out the ridiculousness and impossibility of such a concept: The insinuation that Salem was still desirable, and T-Mo might want her back.

Vida stayed home with the girls.

Myra and Salem walked in silence down the hill to the fork of the road. One path led to the Middle Creek Community School and further away into the suburbs of Seal Rock and Passings Lane, the other past Little River to the fold of a valley surrounded by shrubbery and trees.

Myra remembered this pocket of land: years ago it used to host the night market.

• • •

She stumbled upon it at the edge of Middle Creek in one of her dusk jaunts. It was the second or third year of moving into Tonk's manor, and he had already put Salem in a fishtail gown for the altar, having already wooed her with a diamond necklace and a ring whose dazzle made your eyes flicker.

The night market ran every third Saturday of the month. It stayed open past midnight. Tonk's lip curled when Myra suggested a family excursion to peruse the fair, because it really was more than a market. Despite its temporary constructs, stalls sprung up to last a single night (there were cardboard shacks, wooden huts, mobile carts and portable panels), an array of amusement for all ages rendered the nocturnal market good as a carnival.

"Fire eaters," said Myra. "They do nothing like you've seen before."

"Peddlers," said Tonk. "They have fleas like you'd never wish for."

"And there are artists," said Myra. "They play accordions and bagpipes and harps and banjos."

She liked best the tom-tom drummer with his cymbals, roped hair to his knees, and beats that shifted from something straight to layered loops and jams. Costumed dancers arrived at intervals. They were skimpy clad or wrapped in color—colors that hopped, stepped and wriggled to melody.

Nothing Myra said impressed Tonk and his curled lip.

"Such terrible peril," he said. "Everything I've got and you insist on malingering with ruffians."

"There are fresh fruits and vegetables," said Myra. "Straight from gardens."

"Hang out in stalls like wet washing," said Tonk. "Straight for a stomach ache. Or worse."

Salem, who appeared to feel average about Tonk's goading, still needed persuading. She was not contemptuous but was hesitant. It took coaxing to nudge her any time out of the door and into the world. So a night market was a big deal.

Myra took her hand, and led her.

"Leave the parasites out the door when you get back," said Tonk. "And don't hesitate to fumigate yourselves."

It was then that Myra knew she wouldn't pee on him if his entire body was on fire.

Salem brightened at the sight of oil lamps and lanterns that lit the market. Stalls competed with lights: paper lanterns, hanging lanterns, battery charged lanterns, light-in-a-box lanterns . . . Some attractions were more popular than others, like the man on stilts who was swallowing knives. Toward him banjos got louder, crowds rippled like tidal waves. There were bodies every which way, a slow churn of performers and watchers. Trick entertainers bamboozled gullible folk like Salem, but never Myra who nevertheless allowed herself to be impressed by their efforts.

Coming their way was a throng of dancers, a shimmer of glitter on their bodies, a sway of plumes on their heads. A young woman in tights took Salem's hand, pulled her to join the gyrating. Salem's resisting feet found motion. Her body sway swayed to the banjo and drumbeat. She switched, swaggered and stepped. She was light on her feet, at ease with the infectious throb of music. She was still laughing when Myra tugged her sleeve, dragged her from whirling bodies, from reviving melody to a calming of cool air.

By then Salem had opened up enough to sample smoked sizzles on a stick, to nibble offerings of mushroom and partridge burger that Myra otherwise wolfed. Salem's opinion, timidly offered, of the sweet corn and saffron ice cream was favorable. But it was Myra who stuffed her face with the ice cream, then peach pudding and banana hotcakes. The market offered an itinerant feast of all kinds: leafed food, sizzled food, scooped food, poured food, balled food, fried food . . .

At the oil stall, Salem really loved the wild rose, even bought a cosmetic jar for herself. But massages were too big an ask, and she stepped away from the girl with a box haircut, big shorts and athletic legs that ended in boots, when she offered cheaper rates than announced on her placard.

Myra did not volunteer advice that the seaweed soap and gum soap that Salem handpicked for Tonk were both a waste of effort, as were the sandalwood scented candles. She and Salem spent a good chunk of time in the homeware stall, where Salem fingered cooking pots, ladles, dinnerware, cushions, rugs, linen and throws but bought none. Nor did she take away any of the bark, wood, cloth and glass ornaments or animal figurines from the arts and crafts stall. Somewhat to Myra's surprise, her mother *did* choose invitation cards, brushes, gold foil, bags and ribbons that were just right for hosting activities when Tonk invited townsfolk to his manor. Salem, dear shy Salem, *did* care about the hosting.

When Myra's eye caught an array of glassed islands (real plants and soil inside blown glass) Salem let her pick. The pottery stall did not inspire

Salem's interest but the jewelry one pulled out a giggle. She ran fingers over necklaces, pendants, earrings, rings, bracelets and watches made of shell, coral, gold and amethyst.

It was the fruit and vegetable stall that won hands down. Salem came alive and haggled with the short man and his scowl for the best pearl onions, teardrop aubergines, butternut squashes, plums, elderberries and quinoa. She judged quality by the gloss on a fruit or a vegetable's skin, and the item's hardness or sponginess to a gentle press of fingers. She tapped the butternut squash and sniffed it, and settled for the right shade of yellow.

Naturally, Myra carried the whole lot.

Back home, Tonk's brow rose at the new bracelet on Myra's arm.

"Beads only a troll would wear," he said.

Salem showed him her glass jewelry box with a mirror on the inner lid.

"It has compartmented shelves c-cushioned with v-velvet," she said.

Tonk rolled his eyes and said, "You can't patch foolish. The both of you are dumber than a box of hammers. Can't see jack shit through this nonsense. I'm going to look for a bridge and hurl myself from it."

And he stomped out of the house, slammed the door.

Myra harbored rude thoughts of what she'd like to do with Tonk's food before he ate it.

Tonk had nothing to worry about in relation to frequent visits to the market. Where initially stalls could only sell iced tea, spiced milk, lemonade and cola, they were soon allowed drink licenses and began to serve mulled wine and hot cider. It was the alcohol that attracted the ruffians Tonk had predicted. The louts' pattern was to stun the crowd and slip away with something, and their presence made the market unsafe. Benign pickpocketing graduated to malignant muggings where perpetrators brandished weapons albeit crude: clubs, handhelds festooned with nails, slingshots. Beneath the softness of dusk inside shadows of bordering stalls, someone managed to stun a mother enough to let go her child's hand, and thugs slipped away with the child. The mother was never the same, and the tot never recovered. Inside a month, the music, bubble and itinerant feasts were gone. Government shut down the market.

• • •

Past the pocket of land, Salem, who had started off withdrawn, came out of her shell enough to casually say, "Is this a f-forever trail?"

She was lighter on her feet, but slowed and went cautious once they entered the forest. Perhaps it was the brush of arm-high grass that bordered the new trail just before grass went knee-high. The trail was one some creature had made. Salem pulled up her skirt, clutched it in a fist.

They stepped over fallen bark on hardened soil. Tussocks of grass struggled to climb between rocks. They went past an ant nest. Trees around were so old they had developed hollows but still had leaves that wore a glint of moonlight.

Salem picked a gnarled wildflower that curled into itself.

"L-like a fetus," she said.

They came to a place where trees stood tall and thin, where light filtered in shivers through leaves, and currants shone under the stars. Myra halted with an elbow grip Salem's slip over a fallen branch.

Finally, they came to a clearing that was picnic ground before the killings, unused after the killings. A memory of death haunted it. The wind carried a howl of fear. Ground trees broken to logs had served as benches and tables. Here, people had once sat to eat sandwiches on good weather days. Not anymore. No one else visited the Forest of Solemn. A bird screamed. Another creature cawed, or laughed. Somewhere behind, the sound of water falling. It was smoggy out yonder, but here was moonshine.

They found him leaning against an undead tree under a low cloud. A dusting of leaves coated its hardened trunk. Salem's curly as a poodle's hair shook as they neared, even though she had needed no convincing to come. Soon as she heard T-Mo would be here, would be waiting, she did not ask how or why. Simply agreed on a pickup time. When Myra returned for the fetching, Salem took Myra's hand and they walked to the forest.

T-Mo cleared his throat at their approach. He lifted a finger, whirled it in the air. A twirl of leaves rose off the ground in a cloud.

"Care for a spin?" he said. His tone was tender, conciliatory.

Myra didn't think those were rightful words with which to start a conversation after all those years. She said nothing. She glanced at Salem whose neck was flushed, who fidgeted: wrung her hands, dug her toes. There was tension in her shoulders. Her chest rose and fell fast.

Myra laid a hand at the small of her mother's back. "Don't have to do this, you know."

It was as if she hadn't spoken.

"Such a s-special effort," Salem said to T-Mo.

"Say jeepers creepers still?"

She nodded. "Holy moly too."

She looked less afraid. She glanced at Myra. "B-be alright."

Myra walked away from the clearing, but stood where she could watch them. Sometimes Salem stood with crossed arms, made little or no eye contact. Sometimes T-Mo made progress. Myra couldn't hear what he was saying but now Salem raised an eyebrow, glanced at him. Now she was nodding, understood something. T-Mo spoke in earnest. Salem answered, opened her hand to explain her own thing. T-Mo replied. Now Salem was relaxed, smiling.

She had seasoned with years. T-Mo didn't look a moment older than Myra's memory from when she was four, when he disappeared. The T-Mo inside the stepping was again different.

T-Mo moved forward, now he was too close. He said or whispered something. Salem nodded, then laughed.

The heck, worried Myra.

She thought she saw a woman gliding in the air. She was riding a flamingo. Behind them, a flying squirrel stayed close. And just overhead was another woman perched on a tree. She had one vivid eye and another one bold. The telescopic eye filtered, turned inward and came back at Myra without translation. The bold one blazed blind.

The woman on the tree pressed a finger to her lips. *Not yet*, she said. *Not now*...floated her memento. *Not yet*...adrift in the wind. *Not now*...She also said a word: *Silhouette*...*Silhouette*...And Myra remembered a conversation:

"Is that a shape or a color?"

"It is a name. Silhouette."

Myra chided herself to stop hallucinating, particularly now when T-Mo's nearness to Salem had gotten dangerous. His touch was intimate, palms on Salem's elbows.

"The hell?" Myra wanted to yell. "You're right on top of her."

Now Salem and T-Mo's hands were entwined. Their foreheads touched. They stayed like this, minds and hearts connected—how long? At first, Salem resisted the kiss. She was yielding when, just then, a blast went.

It was the woman with the telescopic eye.

· 58 ·

Silhouette . . .

Salem was responding to the kiss when Odysseus emerged. His hands reached for her neck. My magic hurled a missile that caught him on the head. He staggered, recovered. He grabbed Salem, used her as a shield.

Myra, impulsive thing, her feet had already set running before the blast settled. Onyx eyes alight, she broke Salem away from Odysseus. She ran wide from him as another fireball rocked him.

He lunged, swerved, dodged. He rose in his sprint as he rushed at me.

"Oo-mmea paralyso!" I cried. "Di Blasta!

The blast seared his chest, opened it. Odysseus fell. His expression was one of disbelief. Unlike Achilles, whose strength and weakness was in his heel, or Samson, whose stayed in his hair, Odysseus had put his in a common place: his heart. Hate had strengthened it, the more of it he stored, the stronger his heart became. Now he put his hand in the hole, hunting the heart, its strength and the weakness I had destroyed.

He stretched a hand. "Mother."

My heart kicked. "Sorry. Son," I spoke gently. "I was never your mother."

He started to rise, got to his knees, collapsed.

The sound that came was not Myra's.

This time it was Salem's face that went all wrong. Her sound, like the one Myra made years ago in Grovea, was animal. She wrenched from Myra's grip with unnatural strength. Ran, fell to her knees, cradled his head the same way she had done those many years back in Grovea.

"My love," over and over she said.

She pressed his head to her breast. Her head was tilted, her eyes fixed to a distant place. Time stood. Stood as the blast that had put a hole in his chest began to spread *and disfigure the skin on his neck. It rose to his face, burnt his skin to crisp, separated it from his frame. He disintegrated, thickened to a porridge that slimed through Salem's fingers.*

She stared at her hands. Even as she stared the porridge flattened, became cloudy and then clear before it evaporated into smoke. It drifted in the air away, away . . . and was gone.

Salem looked lost. Myra came to remove her from it, all that awfulness, but Salem again screamed that terrible sound. It was finished. Odysseus, T-Mo . . . was gone.

In the love for our children, for each other, we three—Salem, Myra and I—had in our own ways ousted darkness. On this day, we won. Yet in winning, we had lost a precious being. Tragedy blackened this victory.

• • •

But wait . . .

Crystals—molecular things with corners—crystals with faces were forming on the ground. They stacked, interlocked into aggregate forms that scattered light, the dazzle of moonlight. Red fire radiated from the crystalline mass. The crystals softened into granular flakes that started molding into a shape.

He lay once more in her hands, his skin smooth as a baby's heel. The gator skin, all its lattices and weavings, was fully gone. Salem ripped her skirt, only the petticoat left, and covered his nakedness.

He opened his eyes.

"T-Mo?" whispered Salem. "Is it r-really you?"

"Yes," he whispered.

"Is Odysseus. G-gone?"

"I think, yes." He studied her face. "You do," he said in wonderment.

"D-do what?"

"Love me still."

"C-could I stop?"

She was after all the one for all of him. Even death could not keep him away.

As for Tonk—whatever would happen to him? How would he account for the impossibility happening and live with himself?

I saw a flutter in the air. There was Miss Potty, all this time in the horizon. She was riding a companion. A flying squirrel trailed them. The length of Miss Potty's face exactly the same all these years; the brooding still in her mouth. There it was, the bring-the-hut-down laughter. She was wearing a batik gown full of flakes that became starbursts.

I waved. "I found—"

"The color of language," she finished my lines, same as she always had.

"My soul—"

"Is now learnt. No more isolation."

"Yes! Yes! The key—"

"Is balance. Allow yourself to receive as much as you give."

"I'll be true—"

"To you always," called out Miss Potty, flying onward with her companions. "You must think of yourself too!"

Myra saw all this, heard all this, and was astonished. Perhaps she made a sound. Salem, who had seen, heard, none of it, looked up and saw me.

"Y-you?" she said.

What-am-a-say? She remembered me from the bus stop.

T-Mo turned, saw me. He smiled.

I remembered how it had taken three whole nights for him to emerge that day in Grovea when he was four and Odysseus had done that terrible deed. How when he surfaced, his twinkle for me was back, his eyes full of poems. Same smile was on his face now when he rose from the ground. He took Salem's and Myra's hands, held them in light clasps, and tossed important words over his shoulder: "Walk with us, Mamma, let's walk."

In time he will forge his own connections with Tempest and Amber, walk with them too. When they are healed, from Odysseus.

T-Mo. Now I can claim him, my son. Can't wait to bring him home to Keera. K, K, K, my tongue stops air at the back of my throat. The sound is voiceless—K. I smile, long for her scent of a tree—oaky yet soft. Long for her smile—a mirror full of flowers. Long for . . . such beauty on an elbow. Mine . . . enchantress.

T-Mo and Peaches should get along just fine. Peaches with his white as white eyes full of snow. He is grown, one and a half size my length. No more plays monsters: "Rawr!" But still a bird whisperer: "Koo-wee-oo! Koo-wee-oo! Gwa! Gwa! Gwa!" Same big laughter, one that finishes with squeals and a hiccup. One time he left his mother's house, came back with a girl from Sic'defi. As Moth used to say, "Far more than Earth is and sun is and wide cloud is." She has freckles on all her skin, baby-soft hair that catches light.

Acknowledgments

To Associate Professor Dominique Hecq, my PhD supervisor and mentor who guided my journey, and who stays close as we continue engendering knowledge while creating art. To my generous reviewers who studied my work seriously with an open mind. To my wonderful publisher Meerkat Press—how so privileged that I met you! To you dear reader, I entrust you with a personal experiment gone public. Riding shotgun on this road trip with the characters of my novel, smell their rawness, taste their normality in the otherworldly, touch the rise and fall of their chests . . . magnified by language.

About the Author

Eugen Bacon is a computer scientist mentally re-engineered into creative writing. She has published over one hundred short stories and articles, together with anthologies. Her stories have won, been shortlisted and commended in international awards, including the Bridport Prize, L. Ron Hubbard Writers of the Future Contest, Copyright Agency Prize and Fellowship of Australian Writers National Literary Awards. Her creative work has appeared in literary and speculative fiction publications worldwide, including *Award Winning Australian Writing, AntipodeanSF*, Andromeda, *Aurealis, Bards and Sages Quarterly*, and *New Writing* (Routledge). Eugen's latest books: *Writing Speculative Fiction: Creative and Critical Approaches* from Macmillan International, May 2019, and her debut novel, *Claiming T-Mo*, from Meerkat Press, August 2019.